TWIST OF FATE

SALLY RIGBY

Storm

This is a work of fiction. Names, characters, businesses, places, events and incidents are either the products of the author's imagination or used in a fictitious manner. Any resemblance to actual persons, living or dead, or actual events is purely coincidental.

Ebook ISBN: 978-1-80508-921-6
Paperback ISBN: 978-1-80508-922-3

Cover design: Tash Webber
Cover images: Shutterstock, Unsplash

Published by Storm Publishing.
For further information, visit:
www.stormpublishing.co

ALSO BY SALLY RIGBY

Detective Sebastian Clifford Series

Web of Lies

Speak No Evil

Never Too Late

Hidden From Sight

Fear the Truth

Wake the Past

Question of Guilt

Cavendish & Walker Series

Deadly Games

Fatal Justice

Death Track

Lethal Secret

Last Breath

Final Verdict

Ritual Demise

Mortal Remains

Silent Graves

Kill Shot

Dark Secrets

Broken Screams

Death's Shadow

A Cornwall Murder Mystery

The Lost Girls of Penzance

The Hidden Graves of St Ives

Murder at Land's End

The Camborne Killings

Death at Porthcurno Cove

Detective Sebastian Clifford Series

Web of Lies

Speak No Evil

Never Too Late

Hidden From Sight

Fear the Truth

Wake the Past

Question of Guilt

ONE

Tuesday, 23 June

Sebastian Clifford slammed his foot down on the brake as a tractor pulled out in front of the car. It was five years since he'd moved to East Farndon, and the slower pace of life could still take him by surprise. The question was, did he *want* to get used to it? He continued the slow crawl behind the farm vehicle as his cousin Sarah's offer for him to buy Rendall Hall circled his mind.

He'd need to decide soon. It wasn't fair to keep her hanging on.

'You know, I swear that farmer was waiting for us to appear. He did the same thing to me yesterday and the day before.' His partner Birdie, aka Lucinda Bird – but woe betide anyone who called her by her first name – tapped her fingers against the passenger seat. 'I mean, look. There's no one else on the road, so why did he turn out in front of us instead of waiting two more seconds? It's got to be on purpose, hasn't it?'

'It's always a possibility,' Seb agreed, biting back a smile. His business partner might be from the area, but she had little patience, especially with tractors. 'Though I suspect with harvest coming up, he might be pre-occupied thinking about what needs to be done.'

'Thank you, Dr Reasonable. I prefer my own theory,' Birdie

retorted as the surrounding fields of wheat swayed in the early summer breeze. 'Anyway, what's going on with you? You didn't even complain when I opened the window and all that dust flew over your pristine upholstery. That means you're distracted.'

Seb winced. When he'd first asked Birdie to join Clifford Investigation Services, he'd done so because she was an excellent detective, and they worked well together. Unfortunately, she was also well-versed in reading him. Still, it was only fair they discussed what was on his mind, since the decision would affect them both.

'I spoke to Sarah this morning,' he said.

After the death of his cousin's husband, and with her twins at university, Sarah had decided to take an extended travelling break and asked Seb to look after her manor house until she returned, which was what he'd been doing for the last five years.

Except now her plans had changed.

'How are the Rocky Mountains? Has she defrosted yet? There's no way I could cope with two feet of snow outside my front door.' Birdie shuddered, despite the mild June weather.

'Slight exaggeration, but nevertheless I don't think that's put her off,' Seb responded, taking a quick glance at her.

Birdie chuckled. 'Does that mean it's going *well* with the new boyfriend?' She made some air quotes with her fingers.

'You could say that. He's proposed and Sarah's accepted. She's planning to live permanently in Canada and has asked if I'd like to buy Rendall Hall, providing it would always be home for the boys, if they want it.'

'Wow. I didn't expect that. I'm happy for her. She deserves it.' Birdie stopped tapping her fingers and twisted to face him. It wasn't the first time they'd had the conversation about the future of the agency once Sarah returned, but this news had given it a different perspective. 'What did you tell her?'

'That I need to think about it,' Seb replied.

Tractors aside, he'd started to feel at home in this part of the country, and their business was thriving. But there was still his flat in London and the cost of maintaining a large house to consider.

'Yeah, but it's not outside the realm of possibility, right? It's a much better area for Keira to live, even if she's away at uni much of the time.'

Seb nodded. It was true that ever since discovering he had a daughter, three years ago when she was seventeen, he'd felt that his London flat wasn't an ideal base for her.

'You're right, but I'll need to discuss it with her first. If I do buy the hall, there'll be no point in keeping my London flat.'

'Except it's useful for when we work down there,' Birdie reminded him.

'That's true.' Seb kept his voice mild. He was lucky that he could afford to buy Sarah's home without having to sell the flat.

The tractor turned into a farm and Seb sped up, heading towards the nearby town of Market Harborough. He'd planned on spending the morning going through the accounts, but Birdie's old boss, Sergeant Jack Weston, had requested they go to the police station.

'About time. I thought we were going to be stuck behind him all the way into town.' Birdie glared at the receding taillights of the farm vehicle, before leaning back in the car seat. 'I wonder what Sarge wants. Do you think he needs us to go undercover for him?'

'I've no idea, although it's strange that he couldn't explain over the phone?'

'Maybe it's because he likes being mysterious?' Birdie suggested.

Seb smiled. The old-school sergeant was the least mysterious man he'd met. They'd worked together several times in the past, but Seb couldn't remember the man behaving like this before. Which, ironically, did make the unexpected summons come across as mysterious.

Birdie must have read his expression and gave a snort of laughter. 'Ha. So, you agree with me.'

'I agree it's out of character, but not that he's going to offer us an undercover job,' Seb admitted as his phone pinged with a text message and the notification flashed up on the car's screen.

'It's from Keira. Want me to read it?' Birdie asked, already reaching for his phone.

'Yes, please. She had her last exam yesterday.' Seb slowed as they came to the outskirts of Market Harborough. 'I've been waiting to hear from her all morning.'

'She's probably hungover,' Birdie retorted. 'Huh. That's weird.'

'*What's* weird?' Seb tightened his grip on the steering wheel. 'Is everything okay?'

'Sorry. I didn't mean to freak you out. Yes, it's fine. Keira's on her way home from uni and should be back early afternoon. Oh, and can you get her favourite ice cream if you're near the supermarket.'

'Tell her I got two tubs in last week.' Seb released his grip on the steering wheel and let out a breath. From the moment he'd met Keira, everything in his life had changed. Especially when it came to worrying. His mother assured him it was entirely natural to fret about children and that it never went away, no matter how old they got. All Seb could liken it to was stepping onto a rollercoaster that never ended. Yet he wouldn't have it any other way.

'Will do.' Birdie tapped the phone screen but let out a sigh.

'Is there something wrong?'

'Not exactly. It's just... There are no emojis... or exclamation marks. That girl lives for them.'

Seb wasn't a fan of emojis, but Birdie was right. Keira peppered all her texts and emails with tiny faces and pictures and used more exclamation marks than was reasonable.

'Do you think she's worried about her exam?' He swallowed.

Birdie shook her head, sending her red curls bouncing. 'Can't see it. Her last exam was theory and thanks to inheriting that super brain of yours she remembers everything she reads.'

'Oh, yes. I forgot about that,' he retorted.

'Haha. You're so funny,' Birdie said but her frown didn't lessen. 'She's just replied, "Thanks" about the ice cream. Again, no emojis. Something's *definitely* up. Do you mind if I scroll up and look at the messages between you yesterday?'

'Be my guest.'

'See... These are normal. You wished her good luck, and she had more emojis than words in her reply. I wonder if it's to do with Hamish?'

'Do you think he's hurt her?' Seb growled. Despite his reservations about Keira being in a serious relationship at such a young age, he liked the young man.

Although he was more than prepared to change his verdict at a moment's notice.

'For his sake, I hope not. You look fierce.' Birdie put the phone down as Seb turned into Market Harborough police station.

It was a typical building from the nineteen-sixties with a grey facade and no hint of personality. It was also Birdie's old workplace before she joined Seb's business. After jumping out of the car, she strode across the car park at her usual speed. Seb pocketed the keys and joined her.

They stepped inside to where Detective Constable Neil Branch, a middle-aged officer, was staring directly at them, his brown hair unruly, as if he'd been running his fingers through it.

'Twiggy.' Birdie threw her arms around her old partner.

'Alright there, Birdie. No need for the dramatics,' Twiggy grumbled, pulling himself from the hug. He gave Seb a brief nod. 'Clifford, hope you're not going to maul me as well.'

'Most definitely not.' Seb held out a hand and the two men shook. They hadn't always been friendly, but for Birdie's sake, they'd reached an impasse and remained civil towards one another.

'Thank goodness for small mercies,' Twiggy responded, folding his arms. 'What took you so long? Sarge has been pacing around like a caged tiger, waiting for you to arrive.'

'Then he should have given us a set time,' Birdie bristled. 'If he thinks he can have a go at me for being late, then he has another think coming. I'm a reformed character.'

'Keep your hair on. He's just anxious – so don't shoot the messenger.' Twiggy held up his hands.

'Sorry.' Birdie gave him a rueful smile. 'Must be muscle

memory from all the times Sarge got onto me about my timekeeping. Talk about a dog with a bone. So, what's this about? He wouldn't tell me anything over the phone.'

'Who says I know?' Twiggy protested.

'Because I know you. You make it your business to know,' Birdie instantly retorted. 'Come on, spill the beans.'

'And have Sarge put me on desk duty for a month? No thanks.'

'Come on, Twig. At least give us a hint,' Birdie persisted.

The man let out a long-suffering sigh. 'Look, it's not my place to say. Although be prepared for the unexpected.'

'What the hell does that mean?' Birdie rolled her eyes and Seb bit back his amusement as the pair of them fell into their familiar cycle of banter.

'It means exactly that. Now, I'm taking the lift, and I'll see you up there. I'm guessing you still prefer the stairs.'

'Correct,' Birdie agreed. Twiggy disappeared into the lift and she turned to Seb. 'So much for my excellent interrogation skills.'

'Don't take it personally. Sergeant Weston probably put the fear of God into him.'

'Sarge does have a knack for doing that. I suppose we'd better go up before he comes looking for us.'

Seb let out a sigh. Twiggy liked to gossip, and the fact Birdie couldn't wheedle the truth out of him didn't bode well. Still, the sooner they went up to the sergeant's office, the sooner they'd find out what was required of them.

TWO

Tuesday, 23 June

'About time.' Sarge gruffly gestured them through into his office. It was as messy as ever, but Birdie was used to that. What she wasn't used to was Sarge's own ruffled appearance. His pale blue eyes were clouded and his skin was pale, as if he hadn't stepped outside in a long time. She wondered if it had anything to do with the empty desks out in the main office.

'Good to see you, too,' she replied not nearly as scared of his fierce persona as she'd once been. She sat down in one of the chairs that flanked the paper-strewn desk, and Seb sat next to her. 'Come on then, what's this about?'

'Straight to the point, as ever. Still, at least you don't bore me with small talk.' Sarge raised an eyebrow in Twiggy's direction then crossed back to the other side of the desk and picked up a folder. 'I have a case for you.'

'A case?' Birdie sat up straight. They'd worked together several times in the past, but it was usually when she and Seb needed help. This was the first time the tables had turned. For good reason. Police budgets were notoriously tight and hiring private detectives wasn't approved of. 'What's going on and why can't your team handle it?'

'Unless it's escaped your notice, I'm somewhat short-staffed right now. The officer I brought in to replace Sparkle is off for at least six weeks. And don't get me started on what happens when I train up raw recruits and turn them into vaguely useful officers only to have them snatched up from under my nose.' This time he raised an eyebrow at Seb, despite the fact it had been Birdie's decision to leave the force.

'I do have a mind of my own, you know,' she said. 'It's not my fault you didn't replace me.'

'Relax. The shit's hit the fan now Tiny's on paternity leave, leaving just a few of us,' Twiggy muttered and Birdie widened her eyes. Ouch. No wonder Sarge was so grumpy.

'If I want a commentary, I'll ask for one.' Sarge glared at Twiggy.

'What's the case?' Seb broke through the tension with the same calm voice he always used. Birdie stared directly at Sarge, also curious what would be so important as to call in private investigators.

'There's been a spate of burglaries in the area.'

'You've got to be kidding me. Surely you don't want us to try and find home computers and bikes?' Birdie's brows pushed together. It was almost impossible to track down stolen goods, and while burglaries were a step above surveillance of wayward spouses when it came to bread-and-butter jobs, it wasn't by much.

'This isn't a case of opportunists stealing someone's shopping money. These burglars have hit three times and taken over three million pounds' worth of art and valuable artefacts from high-profile people.'

'Three million?' Birdie whistled, suddenly understanding why Sarge looked so anxious, and why he'd called them in. She'd grown up in a regular family, but Seb's upbringing was very different. His father was Viscount Worthington, who owned two fancy homes plus thousands of acres of land. Seb never traded on his name but there was no hiding that he'd gone to a very posh school and knew his way around the top end of society.

'Was one of them Nigel Kaye?' Seb asked.

Sarge nodded. 'You heard about it?'

'It was in the local paper. Kaye's a well-known artist and he has some pieces in the Tate Modern. I've been to several of his exhibitions. The article didn't mention other burglaries, though.'

'That's because we're keeping it quiet. The other two victims are Cynthia Thornton, who was CEO of a tech company before retiring, and Susannah Limbrick, who runs some kind of vegan food delivery company.' Sarge handed over the folder.

'Green Meadows,' Birdie cried, unable to hide her surprise. She might not have heard of the artist, but she knew all about Susannah Limbrick. Or, at least about her recipes. 'Her company makes those vegan food boxes that get delivered to your door. It has all the ingredients and instructions and somehow makes vegetables taste delicious. Picture me converted.'

'Well, that's a first. I remember a time when you refused to eat a single lettuce leaf.' Twiggy smirked and Birdie swatted him.

'I could say the same about you,' she said before Sarge gave them both a sharp glare. 'Sorry, Sarge. Who's Cynthia Thornton and what kind of tech company did she run?'

'Something to do with payroll software,' Sarge said. 'They invented a thing that does a thing that does another thing, that made them a lot of money.'

'No wonder I've never heard of her.' Birdie bit back a grin. Sarge never pretended to be a fan of technology and while he could operate a computer well enough, he wasn't one to spend his eyes glued to his phone. 'Do you know of her, Seb?'

He gave a slow nod. 'I've never spoken to her, but she's been at several charity events I've attended.'

'That's useful to know.' Birdie made a mental note to follow up on it. Seb disliked pomp and ceremony but he'd attended several events on behalf of Sarah, and occasionally for his brother, Hubert. 'What kind of security systems did they all have? Is there a link?'

'Each security system's different and installed by separate contractors. Yet the burglars managed to bypass them. No alarms were triggered.'

'Which means whoever's behind it must have had some way of switching them off,' Twiggy, who'd been silent, suddenly announced.

'It's possible.' Seb rubbed his chin. 'But it's also possible that the system itself was hacked and disabled. It wouldn't be the first time.'

'Or someone on the inside helped. Or they were bribed to give the code away?' Birdie suggested as they fell into their regular brainstorming pattern.

'It's also possible that the retailers of the security systems were involved. They could be working together.' Sarge folded his arms. 'This is why I've called you in. There are too many avenues to go down for my limited staff. Plus I have them upstairs breathing down my neck to get these burglaries solved.'

Birdie wasn't surprised. Three million pounds' worth of stolen goods wasn't something that could be kept from the media forever.

'What exactly was stolen?' Seb asked. 'You mentioned art and artefacts – what about jewellery, money or electronics?'

'This is the part I don't like.' Sarge nodded towards the folder in Birdie's lap. 'Everything's listed in the case notes. But they didn't try to open the safes or wreck the places looking for other valuables. The owners were adamant that only a certain number of items were taken from each property.'

'It makes no sense. Some of the pieces they left behind were far more valuable than what they took,' Twiggy added. 'Seems daft to me.'

'It depends on who the buyer is,' Seb responded. 'If they're stealing for a collector who wants to add something specific to their collection, the burglars wouldn't waste time on other items. Or.. if they're speculating on how much money they can make, they might purposely be avoiding anything that's easily traceable, or difficult to fence. History's rife with ambitious thefts that no one dared sell for fear of alerting the authorities.'

'If we can identify who's in the market for the items, we might get to the bottom of it,' Birdie said with a nod.

'It's one possibility,' Seb agreed before fixing Sarge with a flat stare. 'What are the insurance companies doing about it?'

'Nothing yet, but it won't be long before they come in making a mess of my evidence and giving me headaches I don't need.'

'In other words, you're getting pressure from everyone,' Birdie said.

'And you're too smart by half,' Sarge mumbled in a gruff voice. 'I need this thing solving like yesterday, before it gets messy. Will you help?'

Would they?

Birdie's skin prickled and her fingers tightened on the folder in her lap. They had just wrapped up a missing will investigation and had several client meetings lined up, but nothing pressing. And certainly nothing this interesting.

In the past she'd have answered without thinking, but she'd learnt to be less impulsive. Instead, she turned to Seb, whose mouth was pressed together. This meant he was already running through the logistics of the investigation, and how many work hours and resources it might involve. He was more considered, which meant that when it came to quoting, she trusted his judgement. Especially now she had a mortgage of her own to pay.

He rolled his shoulders and gave her an affirmative nod.

It was a yes.

Birdie grinned and turned back to Sarge. 'We're interested. But... has DI Curtis okayed you bringing in outside help?'

Sarge's mouth twitched at the mention of the detective inspector, who split his time between the Market Harborough and Wigston stations. 'You leave me to worry about that. If you need help, I can let you have Twiggy.'

Birdie raised a questioning eyebrow at her friend but he

smiled. Clearly Sarge had already discussed it with him. She stole a glance at Seb, who didn't appear bothered by this.

Sarge's desk phone rang and he gave them an exasperated look. They were being dismissed. Birdie got to her feet and they trailed out to the main office. It was empty but she glanced over to a messy desk with several coffee cups and a small giraffe statue lying across a notepad.

'Glad to see Rambo's still here,' she said, recognising the signs of her old colleague.

'No show without Punch.' Twiggy crossed the room to his own desk. 'He got landed with an argument between two neighbours about overhanging fruit so is bound to be out most of the morning.'

'Wow... And to think I could've been a part of this, if it wasn't for joining Seb. I'm beginning to regret my decision.' She threw a grin in Seb's direction, who shook his head.

'Ha ha... Very funny,' Twiggy said. 'Now, where do you want to start?'

'We need to read the case notes and do some research before speaking to the victims. We'll do that today and then interview them tomorrow?' Birdie opened the case file for the first time. 'Let's see where the three properties are. That will give us an order and save us zigzagging back and forth for half the day.'

Seb leant over her shoulder and scanned the addresses. 'Cynthia Thornton's house is closest. Then Nigel Kaye, and finally Susannah Limbrick.'

'Sounds good to me. Twig, can you make the arrangements? I'm assuming it won't be an issue.' Birdie closed the file.

'I'm yours to command.' Twiggy gave a theatrical bow, which made her smile. After he'd been diagnosed with frontotemporal dementia, she'd been hypervigilant around him. He'd faced numerous challenges, including sticking to a diet for the first time in his life. These days Birdie was grateful that he was still able to work and live like he used to... relatively speaking.

They said a quick goodbye and made their way back to the car.

'Thoughts?' she demanded as soon as they were out of earshot.

'It's not uncommon for private investigators to be brought in to assist the police,' Seb said, his expression turning serious. 'I suspect that whoever's behind the thefts has a strong network and has put a good deal of thought into the robberies.'

'All the more reason to get back to the office and start researching. And I swear if that farmer's waiting for us with his tractor, I'll scream.'

'I pity the person who gets between you and a new case,' Seb said, pulling out of the car park and heading in the direction of East Farndon.

'I'm a busy woman, and if you're right about this case, the sooner we start the better,' she retorted, flicking open the folder Sarge had given them. Time to get to work.

THREE

Tuesday, 23 June

Rendall Hall was bathed in midday sun as they drove up the long driveway and came to a halt. Birdie was used to working in such lovely surroundings, but she'd always thought of it as temporary. Now, it might be Seb's permanent home. Although she knew he was independently wealthy, it was still a big commitment. Especially considering the ongoing maintenance the place would require.

It was something she could more fully appreciate now she was the proud owner of a two-bedroom flat in Market Harborough. Even though it was only five years old, she forever seemed to be calling the plumber or electrician about one thing or another.

No wonder Seb needed to think carefully about Sarah's offer before accepting it.

A familiar car was parked in the driveway and a tall, willowy figure was dragging a large pink suitcase over to the door. Birdie smiled at the sight.

At twenty, Seb's daughter, Keira, looked more like a supermodel than ever, with her dark hair hanging loosely over her shoulders.

Hearing the engine, Keira straightened and looked over to them, but her usual smile was gone, and her eyes appeared pensive.

'You were right. Something's wrong,' Seb said, bringing the car to a halt with unnecessary force.

Birdie swallowed, recalling the text messages she'd read. There had definitely been something off in them, and Keira's slumped shoulders seemed to prove it.

Should she have kept her observations to herself? Next to her, Seb's knuckles had whitened on the steering wheel. It was clear he'd been worrying about the text message the whole way home, thanks to her opening her mouth.

'Don't give her the third degree.' Birdie put a restraining hand on his arm, knowing how protective he could be. 'If something's wrong, she'll tell you in her own time.'

Seb's jaw clenched as he turned off the engine. 'But suppose it's serious? Isn't it best to find out straight away?'

'Sure. Because there's nothing better than having your dad demanding a heart-to-heart two seconds after walking in the door,' Birdie retorted. 'Giving Keira some breathing space doesn't make you a bad parent.'

Seb was silent before letting out a long breath. 'You're right. Shall I pretend everything's okay?'

'Just be yourself, but sans too many questions. I'm sure she'll tell us what's going on once she's settled,' Birdie assured him as she climbed out of the car.

'Right. Be myself. I can do that,' Seb said more to himself than Birdie.

Seb strode over to Keira. He wasn't overly demonstrative but Birdie smiled as he took the suitcase from Keira's hands and hugged his daughter. Then he took possession of two smaller bags, which he hooked over each shoulder before marching towards the house.

He paused on the threshold to pat Elsa, his fourteen-year-old beloved yellow labrador, who was stretched out by the front door, bathing in the warm sunlight, her favourite toy, a cream-coloured llama named Larry, next to her. At his touch, Elsa stiffly got to her feet, hampered by the arthritis in her joints. It had been slowing her down considerably over the last few months, but she wagged her tail, picked up Larry llama, and ambled into the house behind him.

If Keira had noticed that Elsa had less energy than she once did, it didn't show, and Birdie frowned. This wasn't right.

'Hey, how was your trip?' Birdie asked in a bright voice, remembering to take her own advice about letting Keira settle in. 'Any tractors?'

Some of the dullness left Keira's dark eyes and she raised an amused eyebrow. 'Don't tell me that farmer's still tormenting you?'

'Like you wouldn't believe. He was at it again today.' Birdie peered around in search of more luggage. 'Do you have anything else that needs to go inside?'

'No.' Keira closed the car's boot and walked towards the house. 'My very own pony express took everything. What's up with him? He's acting weird.'

Birdie sighed and hurried to catch up with Keira's long stride. Maybe she should've let Seb follow his instincts.

'Sorry, that was my fault. I stupidly mentioned that your last text message didn't have any emojis, and now he's worried.'

Keira let out a long groan and headed for the kitchen. 'I should have known I couldn't get anything past the pair of you. Maybe in my next life my dad will be an absent-minded inventor or something.'

'Sounds risky. What if he blows up the house? Or worse, manages to singe your eyelashes while doing an experiment?' Birdie retorted before steering Keira in the direction of the wooden farmhouse table. 'Let me stick on the kettle and find the biscuits your dad bought the other day. He hid them so I wouldn't eat them all before you got back. But I know exactly where they are.'

'The tin marked rice,' Keira said, dropping into a chair and letting her long legs sprawl out. A bunch of furniture catalogues were sitting in a pile because Birdie had been trying to decide on a new sofa. Keira picked up one and began fiddling with it.

'You've got it.' Birdie retrieved the packet and made two steaming mugs of tea before carrying them over to the table. She exchanged the mug for the now mangled catalogue and sat down. 'How did the exams go?'

'Fine.' Keira reached for another catalogue and twisted the edges, as if trying to shake off an excess of energy. 'No surprises, which I suppose is a good thing.'

'Better than failing,' Birdie agreed, reaching for the second catalogue. 'We don't need to talk if you don't want but at least let me select my furniture before you continue on this path of destruction.'

'Sorry, I didn't mean to come home in such a bad mood.' A flush crept up Keira's neck and she slumped back in the chair, like a puppet whose strings had been cut. 'I'm just so mad.'

'Don't apologise, it's your house. You can be in whatever mood you want.' Birdie put down her own mug. 'If you want to talk, I'm always here. So's your dad.'

Keira took a biscuit from the packet but didn't eat it. 'Why are men so annoying?' she suddenly blurted out.

Birdie bit back her smile. So, it *was* about Hamish. 'As someone who has dated both men and women, I hate to tell you that *all* relationships can be tricky.'

'Yeah, but I bet Melinda would never ruin your summer plans at the last minute,' Keira retorted, referring to Birdie's current girlfriend. Birdie was forced to agree, but Melinda was also ten years older than Hamish, and in a different phase of her life.

None of which would be of any comfort to Keira. Especially when she'd spent the last six months carefully planning a backpacking trip around Europe, that included several music festivals.

'Did you have a fight?' she cautiously asked.

'No, nothing like that.' Keira sighed, tears glistening on her long lashes. 'We haven't broken up, but at the last minute he was offered the chance to go to Ethiopia with Amnesty International and he'll be away for six months.'

'Six months?' Birdie put down her tea and frowned. She knew that Hamish had just finished his law degree and was focused on international human rights but hadn't realised he wanted to live overseas.

'I know. It's going to feel like forever.' Keira sighed, brushing away the tears. 'I didn't tell him I was upset because this is such a great opportunity, and I'm really proud of him for getting accepted.'

'Is it something people apply for?' Birdie asked.

Keira went into a detailed explanation of the application process and the many interviews that Hamish had gone through before getting the placement. As Keira spoke, her mood seemed to improve and pride shone from her eyes.

Once she was finished, she gave Birdie a grateful smile. 'Thanks for hearing me out. You must think I sound like a right spoilt brat.'

'Not at all. It's never nice to have your plans changed at the last minute,' Birdie assured her as Seb appeared in the doorway, his eyes full of concern, while Elsa pushed past him and nudged at Keira's leg.

'Hello, girl.' Keira bent down and kissed the dog on the head. She then looked over to where Seb was hovering. 'Hey, Dad. Thanks for taking my bags upstairs. I was just telling Birdie about Hamish going to Ethiopia. Which means you're going to be stuck with me all summer.'

'He got accepted?' Seb's frown cleared and the worry lines around his mouth disappeared.

Birdie glanced from father to daughter. How come she didn't know about this? Then again, Seb wasn't great at sharing. He probably hadn't thought to mention it. Still, the main thing was that Keira's distress wasn't over something seriously bad.

'Yeah. Which is great... For him,' Keira said. She went through all the details for a second time, and what it meant for her summer plans.

'Maybe you can backpack next year,' Seb said in consolation, once she'd finished. 'In the meantime, if you want something to take your mind off it, we've been offered a new case and could use your assistance, if you're interested.'

'By Sarge, no less,' Birdie added.

For the first time since she arrived home, Keira's eyes sparkled with interest. 'I always knew he was an old softy. What's the case? I hope it's something juicy.'

'We've got three burglaries and, in each instance, they targeted valuable artworks. We have no idea how they breached the security systems,' Seb explained. 'We're waiting to hear back from Twiggy about when we can conduct interviews, so there's plenty of research to be done. We'll go through to the office now if you're up to it.'

'Sounds right up my alley.' Keira gave Elsa another kiss on the top of her head and followed her dad and Birdie into the large study that was currently their workspace. Birdie and Seb headed to their desks and Keira walked past the armchair over to the slim desk that Seb had set up for her the last time she was home. 'Send me the names of the three victims and I'll start going through their social media accounts. That will help us build an informal profile.'

'Excellent. I'm going to work through the case notes Sarge gave us and put together a timeline,' Birdie said.

'I'll investigate their finances to ascertain if there were any cash flow issues,' Seb said, turning on his computer.

'You think they might have faked the thefts for insurance? All three of them?' Keira's head snapped back up.

It appeared that her thoughts of Hamish were, at least momentarily, pushed to one side. Birdie pressed her lips together, fighting the urge to smile. Like Keira, she'd always found the best way of dealing with life's ups and downs was throwing herself into work, which meant the timing of the case couldn't be better.

'It's always a possibility. It wouldn't be the first time it's been done,' Seb said, also sounding a lot more like his usual self. 'Birdie, once you've gone through the case file, I'll use it to put together a list of what was taken.'

'The more theories we have the better. It'll stop us from jumping to conclusions,' Birdie agreed as her phone rang and Twiggy's name flashed up on the screen. 'Hey, Twig. How did you get on with Cynthia Thornton?'

'She's expecting us at ten tomorrow morning. She's in Little Oxendon, up the road from you. Then we've got an eleven o'clock with Nigel Kaye, before heading over to see Susannah Limbrick.'

'Nice work to get them all on the same day. Do you want us to collect you on the way?'

'No, I'll meet you there. Sarge has me running around like a hyperactive eight-year-old right now so it will be easier if I have my own car.'

'You, hyperactive? That I'd like to see,' Birdie said with a giggle.

'Rude,' he muttered from down the other end of the phone.

'You know that teasing's my secret sauce.' She laughed. 'See you tomorrow. We're doing some research to see what we can shake loose.'

'I hope you have more luck than we did,' Twiggy grumbled, before finishing the call.

Birdie sucked in a breath and returned to the case notes. So did she. And it wasn't just for the money. She was still eager to show her old boss that leaving the force and working with Seb was a good decision.

She didn't want to mess this up.

FOUR

Wednesday, 24 June

'Wow... what a place,' Birdie said the following morning, a low appreciative whistle escaping her lips, as Seb pulled up outside the three-storey Georgian mansion less than a mile from Rendall Hall. 'Then again, considering how much Cynthia Thornton's worth, it's hardly surprising.'

'It's also very private,' Seb added, taking in the perfectly maintained grey slate tiles and yellow limestone of the building that sat in the middle of sprawling, well-kept grounds. 'Not ideal considering there's little chance the neighbours would have noticed anything untoward occurring.'

He turned off the engine as his mind catalogued what they knew. As well as running a highly successful company, Cynthia had married Nathaniel Easton, who was wealthy in his own right. Their art collection alone had been valued at over five million pounds, which was the puzzling part. Instead of taking everything, the burglars only stole three paintings by lesser-known British artists and a haul of antique coins, including several dating back to the fourteenth century.

'I know. It's so far back from the Oxendon Road, that I had no idea it was here, despite driving this way most days.' Birdie climbed out of the car and peered around. 'No wonder they have so many security cameras. Do you think they can be turned on and off with a clap of the hands?' She clapped her hands in the air and looked around, shrugging. 'Okay, perhaps that wouldn't work because anyone could do it. What about a retinal scanner?'

'Considering the size of the collection, it makes sense to have state-of-the-art security,' Seb said, stifling a grin at Birdie's humour, and instead focusing on the fence line, which was dotted with cameras. There were more nestled under the eaves, their red eyes blinking to confirm they were active and working. He noted the placements, then let his gaze sweep the area for above-ground power lines, wondering if there was a way to shut off the power by cutting them.

Wishful thinking. Sergeant Weston might be short-staffed, but he ran a tight team, and Seb couldn't imagine something as obvious as a cut power line would slip through the initial investigation.

They'd gone through the case notes the previous evening and there had been no clues as to how the security system was circumnavigated. Sighing, Seb turned back to Birdie just as the crunch of tyres alerted them to Twiggy's arrival.

The man had lost weight in the last few years but still managed to look like a scruffy schoolboy stuck in the body of a fifty-year-old man.

'Morning, you two. Hope you haven't been waiting long.' Twiggy smoothed down his crumpled tie.

'Only a few moments,' Seb said. 'Birdie was pointing out all the security cameras. There weren't notes in the case files about their positions.'

'Sorry about that. The file you took from Sarge wasn't complete.' Twiggy waved a folder in the air. 'All of the missing stuff's in here. Despite CCTV cameras, no one was caught on film. After getting onto the property, the thieves disabled the house alarm system and entered from a door at the rear leading into the boot room. Once you've chatted with Cynthia, we'll do a walk-through.'

'Good. Do you know if the door automatically unlocked when they disabled security?' Seb asked as they walked towards the front door of the stone mansion.

'It had a deadbolt, but they prised it open easily enough,' Twiggy said.

'So much for my idea of retinal scans.' Birdie sighed, sounding disappointed. 'To think they simply broke the lock and helped themselves to all that valuable stuff. It's hard to get my head around. What I want to know is how can a bunch of old coins be worth so much?'

'The coins are part of our British heritage and some of them are incredibly rare, which makes them of historical significance and value,' Seb explained.

During his time at the Met, he'd worked on several cases involving antiquities and wasn't so much surprised at the value, but more at why this particular collection hadn't been housed in a vault... or better still... a museum.

'If only the ten-pound note in my purse was considered rare. I could pay off my mortgage.' Birdie took the folder from Twiggy's hands. 'I'll take a quick look at this. Is there a list of staff in here? Because there wasn't in the other one.'

'We're not *complete* amateurs.' Twiggy scowled at his old partner. 'The staff is listed and we have their statements. Even though Mrs Thornton's retired, she still has a personal assistant to help with her charity work and other admin. She's on a few boards and does the occasional bit of consulting. There's also a housekeeper and gardener.'

Seb nodded. He imagined there'd also be a list of tradespeople to help with the ongoing maintenance of the property, too.

'What about family?' Birdie asked.

'Her husband's dead and she has four kids, but none of them live in the area. She's loaded, as you'll know from the research, and the art collection's well known,' Twiggy explained. 'Come on, let's go and meet her.'

When they reached the front door, Birdie pressed the gleaming brass doorbell and the door was opened by a woman in her mid-fifties. She had a pleasant smile, and was neatly dressed in a grey skirt and loose white blouse.

'DC Branch, it's nice to see you again. You must be Sebastian Clifford and Birdie,' the woman said. 'Mrs Thornton's expecting you.'

They followed her past a wide reception area into a large, square drawing room. Despite the recent thefts, there was a stunning array of art on the walls, almost giving the impression that nothing had been disturbed.

The housekeeper announced their names and a petite woman stood up from behind an elegant writing desk by the window.

Cynthia Thornton had silver hair and a pair of blue eyes that matched the dress she was wearing.

'Good morning, Mrs Thornton. Thank you for agreeing to see us at such short notice.' Seb crossed the room and held out his hand.

'Please call me Cynthia. It's been very challenging. People often think of art in terms of its monetary value... but it's so much more. The pieces that were stolen had been curated by me and my late husband. It's been like losing him all over again.' Cynthia dabbed her eyes with a handkerchief before inviting them to sit down.

Seb and Birdie settled on a long, dark blue sofa before Cynthia lowered herself into an armchair, leaving Twiggy to perch on an upright walnut chair.

'We're sorry for the loss of your husband,' Seb said, as Birdie flipped up her notebook and poised her pen.

Despite not needing the notes because of Seb's ability to remember everything, writing assisted Birdie in seeing patterns that might otherwise be lost to them.

'Thank you. It happened eleven months ago but still seems so recent. They say the first year is the worst, and considering what's happened, it's hard to disagree.' Cynthia swallowed. 'Please excuse me, it's been a trying few weeks. DC Branch said that you're private investigators. Is it usual for the police to call you in?'

'It's not uncommon for the police to call on outside help when necessary,' Birdie assured her. 'We were both police officers in the past.'

This appeared to relax her, and Seb took the opportunity to move on with the interview. 'I'd like to ask about your staff. Do you have anyone new working for you?'

'No. They've all been with me for many years.'

Birdie glanced up from her notebook. 'Do they all have access to your security system codes?'

'Yes, because they need to come and go whenever necessary. I'm not always around. But I trust them completely,' Cynthia quickly added.

'Do they live here in the house with you?' Birdie continued.

'No. They're all local to the area. Right now, I'm here on my own. It's too big for me, really, and I'm considering selling. But there's no rush. To be honest, I'm not in the right headspace yet.'

The housekeeper walked in, carrying a tea tray, and they were silent as the drinks were poured.

'How often do you change the security codes?' Seb asked once the housekeeper had left the room.

For the first time Cynthia gave a soft smile. 'It's something I'm vigilant about. They're changed monthly. I suppose it's a hangover from working in the software industry for such a long time.'

'Excellent,' Seb said, with a nod. 'It states in the police report that it was you who discovered the burglary. Please could you talk us through what happened?'

'That's the most upsetting part. I'd been on a cruise, and on returning I found the back door had been tampered with. Then I noticed the paintings and coins weren't there.' Sighing, Cynthia rose to her feet and gestured for them to follow her to an old mahogany display cabinet. It was lined with a pale blue fabric, and while the indents suggested there had once been at least fifty coins in there, the cabinet was currently empty.

Seb leant in closer to inspect the cabinet. There was an old-fashioned lock, but even as a child, he could have opened it with a small knife.

He rubbed his chin. 'Why did you have such a valuable collection in the house?'

'It was Nathaniel who loved coins, not me, and he always liked to have them on display, saying that the risk was worth it for the enjoyment he received. I suppose I just carried on, not wanting to admit he was no longer with me.' Cynthia's shoulders sagged.

'What did you do after discovering them missing?' Birdie gently asked, clearly noticing the woman's distress.

'I called the police and DC Branch came out to see me.'

'Crime scenes officers went through all the rooms but there were no fingerprints,' Twiggy confirmed. 'We also checked the security footage but again there was nothing.'

'According to the police report, the paintings were kept in separate rooms,' Seb said.

'Yes, it was like they knew exactly where to look because nothing else was disturbed,' Cynthia replied, as she led them back to the seating area.

Seb exchanged a knowing glance with Birdie. Twiggy and Sergeant Weston had suggested that the burglaries had specifically targeted certain items and this confirmed it.

'Although you were on a cruise, didn't your staff notice that the security system had been disabled?' Seb asked.

Cynthia shook her head. 'I gave them the week off. My daughter wanted me to get a house sitter, but I thought it unnecessary, considering the security I have in place. Unfortunately, she was right.'

'Have you had any dinner parties or social events recently, where you've employed additional staff?' Seb asked, his brows pressed together.

'No, I don't entertain right now.' Cynthia shook her head before stiffening. 'Well, apart from the fundraiser last month.'

'What fundraiser?' Twiggy spluttered, almost toppling out of his chair. 'I don't remember you mentioning it.'

'It wasn't in the case file,' Birdie quickly added before turning to Cynthia. 'Was it held here?'

'Yes. I didn't mention it because it was a couple of weeks before my cruise. It was a garden party and held outside on the front lawn. It was to raise money for leukaemia.'

Seb nodded. The same cancer that had taken her husband's life.

'How many people attended?' he asked.

'At least a hundred, including the media and caterers,' Cynthia said, the colour fading from her cheeks. 'Do you think it's relevant?'

'We don't know, but it's important for us to consider everything,' Birdie answered, giving a reassuring smile.

'Were attendees allowed into the main house, or did they stay outside?' Twiggy asked.

'We left the house open so guests could use the loos, and the caterers prepared the food in the kitchen. Oh, dear. Do you really think one of the guests snooped around and was responsible for the thefts?'

'It's possible,' Seb said, keeping his voice low. 'How many people knew about your cruise?'

Cynthia's face tightened and she let out a groan. 'It wasn't a secret... and I mentioned it in my welcoming speech. How could I have been so foolish?'

'Don't blame yourself. Whoever's behind this robbery planned it in great detail,' Birdie said in a brisk voice before extracting a business card. 'Please could you supply us with a list of people at the fundraiser? Including caterers and wait staff.'

'Yes of course. I'll email it to you.'

Seb stood. 'Would you mind if we take a look around on our way out?'

'Please, go ahead.' Cynthia sank back into her chair as the three of them left the room. It didn't take long for Twiggy to show them the rooms from where the paintings had been taken, and the entry point back door.

'A hundred-plus extra suspects to add to our list,' Birdie groaned when they were back in the car and following Twiggy to the next house. 'And we still need to visit two more victims. It's going to be a long day.'

Seb nodded and pressed his foot down on the accelerator. It certainly was.

FIVE

Wednesday, 24 June

Birdie closed her eyes as Seb drove along the narrow road towards the village of Kibworth Harcourt. It was eight and a half miles away, and she needed to get her thoughts in order. It still blew her mind that one person could have so much money that they could afford to buy up a bunch of old coins and leave them lying around the place on full show for whoever went there.

She caught herself. They were being paid to solve the case, not judge the victims, and it wasn't as if Cynthia hadn't taken steps to keep her home secure.

Birdie opened her eyes and scanned the notes she'd written on Nigel Kaye. He was a well-known artist with a large collection of art himself. But the burglars had only taken a single Picasso, worth over a million pounds. She also knew that he was born in the East End of London and had moved to the Leicestershire area five years ago with his second wife.

'Is it weird that Nigel Kaye has his own art collection?'

'Not particularly. For some artists, it's a source of inspiration. Of course, not all of them can afford the kind of collection that Kaye has,' Seb replied, giving her a quick glance.

Seb turned a corner and she caught sight of a large house at the end of the long drive. It was a three-storey property and had been built in a traditional style, as if trying to mimic the kind of house they'd just come from.

'Bloody hell. What happened to starving artists living in poverty?' Birdie shut the folder with a sigh, and watched as the car swept past several fields and a long wood. To the right was a paddock containing several horses and, as they drew closer, she could see the stables. A brick wall flanked the green lawns, forming an extra layer of protection. It was like a fortress.

'Nigel Kaye moved out of poverty some time ago. His paintings regularly sell for seven figures,' Seb explained. 'He's also been nominated for the prestigious Napworth art prize.'

Birdie blinked. 'I knew he seemed like a big deal from my research, but this place is next level. I should have paid more attention to my art teacher, Mrs Hislop.'

'You do draw impressive stick figures.' Seb's mouth twisted into a smile as they pulled up behind Twiggy's car. 'It could be the next big thing.'

'I'll be sure to invite you to my first exhibition,' Birdie retorted, as she jumped out of the car and walked over to where Twiggy stood. 'Hey, why didn't you warn me how fancy these places were?'

'I figured the multi-million pounds' worth of stolen goods might have given it away,' Twiggy responded, giving an eye roll. A man appeared in the doorway, smiling. 'That's Nigel Kaye. He's obviously been waiting for us.'

'Then let's not keep him any longer.' Birdie strode over to where Nigel Kaye stood.

From her research, she knew he was fifty-five, but apart from several streaks of grey in his blond hair, he could have passed for much younger. His clothing was typical *country gent*, but there were smudges of paint on his hands and around his fingernails, suggesting he'd been working.

'Thank you for taking the time to talk with us,' she said.

striding over to him and holding out her hand. 'I'm Birdie, and this is Seb.' She pointed to her partner.

'When Twiggy said you were helping with the investigation, I was relieved. It's hard to sleep well after knowing someone walked into your home and stole your favourite painting... and all without setting off the alarm. Please, come in.'

'This is a lovely place,' Birdie said as Nigel led them down a long wide hall dotted with paintings.

They all looked like a blur of colours, to her, but Seb paused several times to study them. She assumed that he was doing an inventory of the art that hadn't been taken.

'Thanks. My wife Bianca's the one who convinced me to move out of London. She's a horse rider and fell in love with the woodlands. Plus, it's great for the kids to connect with nature. They love the indoor swimming pool, too. It means they can swim every day.'

'I understand your property comprises twenty-eight acres,' Seb said. 'That's a considerable amount to maintain.'

'So I'm discovering. To think that I grew up in a council flat without any green space whatsoever.' Kaye laughed. 'Bianca's the gardener, thank goodness. Otherwise, I'd never have any time to paint. Let's go in here. My daughter's not well and is off school so the kitchen's a bit messy right now.'

'Poor thing. I hope she's okay,' Birdie said as the man pushed open a wood-panelled door and ushered them into what she assumed was a library. Bookcases lined three of the walls and the other was filled with several huge canvases of swirls and shapes in muted tones of browns and pinks. It was hard to tell if the shapes were figures or just blobs. But she recognised them as Kaye's.

Were these all worth seven figures, too?

If so, why hadn't the thieves taken at least one of them? It seemed like a lot of money to leave behind.

Her confusion must have shown on her face and Kaye sighed as they sat down. 'I take it you're wondering why they didn't take more pieces, mine included.'

Birdie nodded. 'According to the police report they only took your Picasso. It seems like going into a sweet store and ignoring everything except a single bar of chocolate. Are you sure nothing else was taken? Sometimes it can take a while to realise something's gone.'

Kaye shook his head. 'Our insurance assessor was very thorough with the original inventory, and we used that to ensure nothing had been overlooked.'

'That's reassuring,' Seb said, with a sharp nod. 'Please will you explain in detail exactly when the robbery took place.'

'It was a Wednesday evening and we were at the school play. Both kids were playing horses, and Bianca had spent hours making their costumes. Bloody fantastic they were.' His eyes sparkled at the memory before dimming again. 'The burglars came in through the sitting room French doors. They literally just walked in. I still can't believe it happened. I mean, what if the kids had been at home and had discovered them.' His face tightened, and suddenly he looked more like a worried father than a famous artist. Not that she could blame him. What was the point of all that money if you couldn't protect your family?

'Are you sure you set the alarm?' Birdie asked, scanning all the motion sensors.

Kaye pulled a phone from his pocket and held it up. 'Yes. I've got a smart home, which means everything's linked up and I can control it remotely. I paid a fortune for the bloody system and trust me that I've had words with the company who sold it to me.'

'We've already followed up with them,' Twiggy added. 'We're waiting for them to pass over their records.'

'It doesn't make sense.' Kaye placed his phone on the coffee table. 'I have cameras all the way up the drive, which are on a separate security system, so how the hell did they manage to bypass two totally different systems?'

How indeed?

'Are both systems controlled by your phone?' Birdie asked.

Kaye shook his head. 'The exterior alarms have a panel that needs to be set. It's not part of the smart home. But it was activated when we left. I remember double checking that, myself. I'm one hundred percent certain.'

'Who knew you'd be at the concert?' Seb asked.

'I mentioned it on social media.' Kaye's face coloured. 'I never show the kids' faces, but Bianca was so proud of the costumes and my publicist is always telling me to post more personal content... so... I've been kicking myself ever since; what if that was what prompted the robbery?'

'There are many other ways for people to find out your location,' Seb told him. 'Other parents would have assumed you'd be attending the concert and might have informed their friends. Your calendar could've been hacked.'

'I see. I also keep a paper copy of it in my study. I suppose someone might have seen that, too.'

Birdie and Seb exchanged a look. Cynthia Thornton had left her house open during the charity event for people to come and go. Had Kaye done something similar?

'Have you had any social events here recently where the public were invited?' Birdie asked.

'No.' Kaye shook his head. 'I'm deep in the middle of producing my new collection so we haven't been doing any entertaining.'

'What about close friends or family?' Birdie asked.

'I'm totally anti-social when working. Can't stand having to break away from the studio unless it's an emergency.' He paused. 'Sorry, that sounded rude. Clearly I don't consider this an interruption.'

'That's okay,' Birdie said. 'There's nothing worse than being disturbed when you're in the middle of something. So to confirm, no one has visited the house recently?'

'What about for the Napworth Prize?' Seb asked. 'We found several interviews and photos of you in your studio after being nominated. When were they conducted?'

Kaye straightened. 'Damn. I'd forgotten about them. You're right. After the shortlist was announced my publicist arranged for a series of interviews. I couldn't take time out to travel to London and I'm not a fan of doing these things online, so we arranged for reporters to come here.'

Birdie nodded in Seb's direction. She never got tired of his attention to detail. Then she turned back to Kaye. 'When did they take place?'

'The week before the burglary,' he admitted, giving Twiggy a sheepish look. 'Sorry, I can't believe I didn't mention that.'

'It's understandable considering what's happened,' Birdie assured him, knowing how difficult it was to recall traumatic events. 'Can you give us a list of everyone who visited? Or arrange for your publicist to send it to us, please?'

'She's on maternity leave right now, but I can get it together for you. It might take a day or two because I don't have a personal assistant.'

'As soon as you can is fine.' Birdie passed him her business card, then peered out the window to the fields and woodland that flanked the long driveway. 'You said that you have twenty-eight acres. I am guessing there must be other ways to enter the property.'

'Yes, our boundaries aren't all fenced, though we do have cameras around the immediate fence line.'

'Could you show us?' Birdie immediately got to her feet. She worked best when she was active.

'It's quite a trek.' Kaye's eyes widened, as if surprised by the question.

'That's okay.' Birdie held out her own boot-clad feet. Despite the warm weather, she always tried to dress for any situation, which meant she had on Doc Martens, jeans and a plain T-shirt. 'There hasn't been much rain lately so hopefully it's not too treacherous.'

'Not unless you include stinging nettles,' Kaye said grimacing, as he stood.

'On the way, please will you also show us where the burglars entered the property?' Seb asked.

Kaye led them into a huge room that was flooded with natural light. There was more art on the walls and huge white sofas that seemed asking for trouble if the kids were anything like Birdie and her brothers had been.

'Here,' Kaye said, unlocking the French doors.

Seb looked around, appearing pensive.

'Forensics couldn't find a thing,' Twiggy said, standing beside Seb.

They stepped outside and crossed the lawn. A gate had been cut into the brick wall and Kaye led them across a paddock and into the woodlands. Several horses grazing nearby watched their progress and Birdie's fingers twitched, longing to pat their velvet noses.

The path was narrow and winding, but there was no sign of the stinging nettles, and the lack of weeds suggested it was well used. The silence was only interrupted by Twiggy slapping at the occasional bug that seemed attracted to his arms. Finally, they reached a narrow lane. It was little more than a dry dirt track.

Dust lifted as Birdie stepped along it, and while she could see the outline of tyre prints, she wasn't sure there would be enough of an imprint for forensics to use. But there was enough trampled-down grass to suggest people had been there recently. To the side, something metallic gleamed in the grass.

Birdie bent down to inspect it. It was a cigarette lighter. She slipped on some disposable gloves, picked it up, and dropped it into an evidence bag.

Seb walked over and began searching the area. 'No cigarette butts here, which makes me wonder if the lighter fell out of someone's pocket.'

'We didn't check this far out,' Twiggy admitted. 'I'll get the team out here.'

'Could this mean something?' Kaye asked.

Birdie pressed her lips together. There'd been no mention of this lane in the case files, and it wasn't her intention to suggest her friend hadn't done a good job. He'd be feeling guilty enough, she suspected.

'It's too early to say,' Birdie admitted cautiously. 'But once we have the list of journalists and photographers, it'll give us more to go on.'

'I'm onto it,' Kaye assured them as he led them back through the woods and to their cars.

They said a quick goodbye to the man and Twiggy called in the forensics team.

Hopefully they'd discover from this area a clue as to how the burglars had managed to bypass the security cameras without being seen.

SIX

Wednesday, 24 June

'Don't say it,' Birdie said as they turned onto the A6. 'The ball was dropped because they didn't check as far out as the lane alongside Kaye's property. Twiggy was clearly gutted. It was written all over his face.'

'These things happen,' Seb replied, not wanting to point the finger.

'Well, I totally get why Sarge needs our help. Whoever's behind these burglaries knew the houses very well and had visited them prior to stealing the items. That can't have been easy to orchestrate.'

'We need to cross-reference Cynthia Thornton's charity event and the authorised press officers who interviewed Nigel Kaye.'

'Although on the surface it seems unlikely there'd be a link,' Birdie said with a sigh.

'We should also consider tradespeople, or anyone else who might have visited both houses,' Seb added, his own mood not improving.

'True. I bet that's where we'll find the link. Hopefully Susannah Limbrick can confirm it,' Birdie said while studying him.

'I can't believe you haven't tried her meal kits. Even my mum's used them.'

'It's because I'm not a vegan,' Seb suggested.

Birdie shook her head, making a tutting noise. 'Neither am I, but haven't you heard of meat-free Monday? I'm surprised Keira hasn't persuaded you to sign up. Mel and I used it at the beginning of the year and will definitely get it again. The spinach and mushroom patties are sublime.'

'I'll take your word for it.'

Seb smiled to himself. Birdie was prone to diving headlong into whatever came along, be it an investigation or when, on a whim, she'd decided to learn Spanish. Vegan food services didn't even make the top ten on the list of impulsive things she'd embarked on. He frowned. Did that mean he was stuck in his ways?

Don't go there.

'And so's the tastes-like-chicken,' Birdie added. 'Or, should I say, tofu?'

'It doesn't quite create the same image. But... maybe I'll subscribe while Keira's home for the summer. A few meat-free meals won't do any harm.'

'Ooohhh. Father/daughter cooking dates. That'll be worth watching,' Birdie teased, which Seb ignored.

Susannah Limbrick's old stone farmhouse came into sight and Seb headed down the drive. It was as well-maintained as the other two properties they'd visited and again security cameras were prevalent around the tall fence that protected the property.

Seb turned off the engine and mentally ran through what they already knew about the victim. The chef was forty-one, married with no children. In addition to her food service, she'd published several best-selling recipe books which, according to their research, had allowed her to buy the property ten years earlier. The burglars had taken two Edward Hopper paintings and a collection of military medals, with a combined value of one million pounds.

It was clearly preplanned. No one looking at the hewed stone farmhouse would ever guess it housed two paintings by one of

America's most lauded realism painters. Seb sucked in a breath. Why *did* someone living in a typically English, old-stone farmhouse in the middle of the countryside have two Hoppers on their wall?

'What is it? Have you figured something out?' Birdie suddenly demanded.

He glanced at his partner. She didn't miss a trick. 'I was wondering *why* Susannah Limbrick would own two Hoppers.'

Birdie frowned. 'Do you think she couldn't have afforded them?'

'No, that's not my rationale. I looked online at her company's financial records and, on the face of it, I'm sure she could. But Hopper's work is very American-centric. They seem out of place here.'

'Wow... it's not like you to be so stereotypical.'

'That wasn't my intention,' Seb clarified

'Maybe she inherited them. According to Twiggy's report, the medals came from her husband's family.'

'Good point,' Seb conceded as Twiggy pulled up next to them.

Once they were out of the car, the farmhouse door opened and two tiny Chihuahuas raced across the gravelled driveway.

'Come back here.' A man strode out behind them, his face red from the exertion. 'Loretta. Lewis. That's enough.'

The two dogs came to an abrupt halt, turned, and returned to the man, affectionally nudging his leg. He scooped them up in his arms and joined the investigators.

'DC Branch, it's good to see you again.'

'Thanks for agreeing to see us at short notice,' Twiggy said. 'Seb and Birdie, this is Susannah's husband and business partner, William Limbrick.'

'Nice to meet you.' The man held up both dogs as the reason he couldn't shake their hands. 'I hope you have some good news for us. Or at least an update.' There was a tightness to his voice and Seb wondered if it had been the Limbricks who'd put pressure on Sergeant Weston to solve the case.

'We're coming in as consultants and would like a clearer picture of what occurred,' Birdie said smoothly as they followed William Limbrick and the dogs into the house.

They were joined by Susannah. With long brown hair and warm eyes, she looked exactly as she did in her photos, apart from the dot of flour on her nose and the old apron tied around her waist.

'Honey, do you want to sit in the sunroom, or would you like to be close to the oven?' William asked.

'The sunroom's fine. I'll be through in a minute.' Susannah held up an old-fashioned egg timer and waved it in the air. 'I have thirty minutes before it goes off. Stuffed peppers,' she added as an afterthought.

William led them through to a bright room adjacent to the kitchen. A tea tray had already been laid with a plate of scones. The decor was minimalist and a mid-century sculpture sat in the corner, along with what appeared to be an original Eames chair.

Seb had misjudged their artistic tastes. The two Hoppers wouldn't be out of place in this environment.

'You picked the right day to come. Susannah's been working on several new recipes and these scones are delicious. She's also developed a cashew nut cream that will change your life,' William explained as they sat down. Seb refused the scones on the basis that he'd had a big breakfast, but Birdie and Twiggy both indulged and several minutes of chit-chat went by before Susannah finally joined her husband, and her ever-present smile began to fade.

'What would you like to know?'

'Could you take us through exactly what happened, please?' Birdie suggested. 'I know you're probably sick of going over it, but you might remember something that might not have seemed significant earlier.'

Susannah drew in a long breath and nodded over to a recipe book leaning against the sideboard. 'I've just released my next cookbook and I was in London for the launch on the day of the burglary.'

'Did you both go?' Seb asked. He knew that the house had been empty, but not where the occupants had been.

'Yes. Not only does Will do all the marketing, but he's my support system,' Susannah said before one of the dogs barked from their spot in a basket by the door. 'The dogs came, too. We always travel together.'

'Have you had problems with your security system in the past?' Seb asked, recalling everything he knew about the model they had. Much like the one Nigel Kaye used, it was controlled via a smart phone, and not cheap to buy or install.

'None. We bought the system four years ago and apart from a couple of blips at the beginning, it's been amazing,' Susannah replied. 'Well, maybe not, after this.'

'Do you have any security cameras that aren't linked up to the main system?' Seb craned his neck to study the discreet motion sensors.

'We have a separate camera that's connected to the doorbell at the front of the house,' William said, taking over. 'But the police have already checked that.'

'There was nothing on the footage showing anyone walking up to the door,' Twiggy confirmed.

'We'd like to see where the burglars entered, and where the paintings and medals were kept, please,' Birdie said.

'Of course.' Susannah was instantly on her feet, the two dogs joining her as she led them back through the house, still clutching the timer in her hand. 'They came in through the utility room at the back of the house.'

'We keep a lot of the gardening gear and fresh produce we've picked from the garden in there,' William explained as they headed past the kitchen, the rich scent of garlic and tomatoes filling the air. 'But they left no evidence of coming through there, apart from the door being crowbarred open.'

'It's true,' Twiggy agreed. 'We went over every surface and nothing had been touched.'

'We've since repaired the door and changed the locks,'

Susannah said, leading them from the utility room into a second sitting room. She pointed to an empty wall. 'This is where the two paintings were hung.'

A flash of pain marched across her face, as if losing them was still like a raw wound. Seb peered around and frowned. By the far window was a David Hockney. He raised an eyebrow and Susannah joined him.

'It's hard to fathom that they left the Hockney behind,' Seb said.

'I'm grateful they did,' Susannah replied.

'Were the medals also in this room?' Birdie asked.

'Yes.' William stood in front of a wooden cabinet, and opened the doors. 'They were in here. Unlike the paintings, they were never on display. They're worth a lot of money, although to me the value is in the history of them.'

Seb inspected the space. The other shelves were filled with collectables, and they appeared undisturbed. Clearly the thieves knew exactly what they wanted, and didn't allow themselves any distractions.

Next to him, Birdie shifted from foot to foot, her hand jiggling as if she was balancing a cricket ball. 'Had there been any strangers in the house, during the weeks leading up to the burglary?'

'Prior to the launch, I held several publicity events,' Susannah admitted.

'You didn't mention that,' Twiggy said, a hint of defensiveness lacing his voice.

Susannah flushed. 'I'm sorry, I didn't think it was important.'

'What were the events, and when were they held?' Seb cut in, hoping to get the conversation back on track.

'I can help you with that,' William said, patting his wife's arm. He opened a calendar app on his phone. 'We had a pre-launch party three weeks ago, with a guest list of fifty, including industry professionals and celebrities. Susannah cooked up a storm and gave them a taste of what was to come. Her last book was number one in the charts for over a year and we're hoping for similar results with this new one. Then there was the audiobook production team who came over to discuss the edit. Susannah's been going to London to record it you see. Now... what else do we have—'

'Maybe you could send me a list of everything?' Birdie gently suggested, to which they agreed.

Seb asked a few more questions about the security system and who they'd purchased it from, before they left. Twiggy stayed behind to go over some of the older details of the investigation and arranged to meet them back in Market Harborough for a debrief.

As they left Birdie's mind was in overdrive, calculating the ever-increasing number of people who'd entered the three houses in the weeks leading up to the thefts. They definitely had their work cut out for them, that was for sure.

SEVEN

Wednesday, 24 June

'The forensics team's searching the area on the other side of Nigel Kaye's boundary right now.' Twiggy put down his phone and glared across the café table, where they'd decided to have lunch. His voice took on a belligerent tone. 'For the record, I wasn't in charge of the case so you can't blame me for not thinking of it.'

'No one *is* blaming you,' Birdie retorted. 'There are twenty-eight acres of land and it would have been impossible to go over every inch. So, pull your head in and stop thinking that we're having a go at you, because we're not. Right, Seb?'

Seb opened his mouth but before he could speak, Birdie shot him a telling glare. Sighing, Seb turned to the DC. 'This case has headache written all over it, especially considering the number of people who had access to each property, which is why we need to discuss our next steps.'

The answer seemed to appease both Twiggy and Birdie.

'Well, between you, me and the wall, it *has* been a headache, and I'm sure that's one of the reasons Sarge got you two in,' Twiggy conceded as the waitress brought over their order.

The food seemed to lighten the officer's mood, which was a

relief. It was going to be a hard enough case without having to worry about upsetting Birdie's ex-partner every step of the way.

Once they'd eaten, they discussed what they'd learnt from the three interviews.

It wasn't much, other than confirming that the victims had been specifically targeted, and the burglaries carefully planned, without leaving any noticeable clues. It was time to expand the perimeter of their search.

Seb made eye contact with Twiggy. 'While we're waiting to hear back from forensics, let's check for CCTV footage on the lane behind Kaye's house, and also areas around the other two locations.'

'That's already been done and there aren't any cameras nearby. The closest are at an intersection two miles away,' Twiggy responded as he pushed his empty plate to the side.

'Pity.' Not that Seb was surprised, and it was one of the reasons that so many owners who lived in remote areas had such good security systems. 'Could you arrange for someone to check CCTV footage and look for the same vehicles showing up close to the three properties?'

Twiggy nodded and reached for his phone. 'I'll get Tiny onto it. He's finally back in the office, and I'd hate for him to have too much downtime.'

'Tell him there's a jam doughnut in it for him.' Birdie smirked in a way that Seb assumed was a private joke between the pair of them. He'd met DC Aleki Tuala several times but had no idea where doughnuts fitted into the relationship.

Still, if Tuala could get them a break, it would be worth the cost. But it didn't help solve the more pressing problem of how the thieves bypassed security measures at all three properties.

Once their plates had been cleared, and they'd given their orders for coffee, Seb opened the file that Twiggy had given them earlier with the security layouts for each property. He spread them out on the table.

'Let's go over what we already know about each security system, because there must be something we're missing.'

'Easy,' Birdie said. 'They were made by three different manufacturers, sold by three different companies, and installed by three different technicians.'

'And they all swear that their systems are state of the art and un-hackable,' Twiggy added as Seb used a pen to mark the CCTV cameras and motion sensors he'd seen at each property. Not only had the thieves managed to get into the houses without setting off the alarms, but they'd also managed to avoid all the cameras.

'Everything's hackable,' Birdie corrected. 'Whatever they might say. It could've been someone who worked for one of the companies and had access to the other companies' systems? Did you check all the employees?'

Twiggy nodded. 'Yes. They're all small companies so it wasn't hard. Most of the staff have worked there for a long time, and they do their own police checks before any new hires.'

'Do you have details of the insurance companies? Sergeant Weston mentioned he was holding off speaking to the investigators, but I'd be interested to know who the insurers are,' Seb said.

'Why?' Twiggy frowned.

'Because they'll employ an investigator to go through everything with a fine-tooth comb and look for any reason to void the claim. More importantly, they would have exact details of each collection along with their valuations, property address and layout, and security systems.'

Birdie's eyes went wide. 'You think it was an inside job?'

'Or a data breach,' Seb said. 'I've worked enough cases to know breaches are a matter of *when* not *if*.'

'I doubt it's something the companies would advertise, because it's not good for their reputation,' Twiggy said.

'They wouldn't have a choice, if I remember correctly.' Birdie scrunched up her nose.

Seb nodded. 'That's correct. They need to alert the Information Commissioner's Office if it was a serious breach, and anyone who's affected. However, that doesn't stop organisations from trying to hide it.'

Twiggy nodded and made some notes. 'I'll get Tiny to follow up with the security firms and see what he can find. It's like the thieves took a pill and became invisible.'

'But even if they were invisible, they'd still trigger the motion sensors,' Birdie argued.

It wasn't a good sign when their best theory revolved around an invisibility pill.

'I recall reading an article about sensors,' Seb said. 'There are often dead zones in rooms and if you know the layout you might be able to move around them.'

'Like *Mission: Impossible* when they dropped Tom Cruise in through all the laser beams?' Birdie's eyes danced with excitement, and Seb had the feeling she was wishing she could be lowered down in a harness.

'Yes. I've also heard of people using thermal blankets to conceal body heat and spreading their weight out to avoid triggering any floor sensors.'

'Sounds more like a circus than a criminal activity,' Twiggy muttered.

'But it's a good point.' Birdie frowned and stared at the three maps on the table. 'Let's go through all the theories of how they got in. We didn't see any cut power lines going into the properties and the hardwiring wasn't tampered with.'

Seb nodded and pointed to one of the CCTV cameras on Kaye's property. 'Twiggy, did the team look at *all* the footage? Is it possible the video feed was hacked and they cut out their presence and looped in prerecorded footage to conceal it?'

Twiggy flipped back through his notebook. 'Kaye's security firm checked the footage and confirmed it hadn't been tampered with. We're still waiting to hear back from the companies who work for Cynthia Thornton and Susannah Limbrick. I'll follow up.'

Seb nodded. 'If there was a power outage the owners would

have known about it, because it would have affected their other electronics, so we can rule that out. But there are several other ways they could have bypassed the systems.'

'Like what?' Birdie wanted to know.

'Electromagnetic pulses would disable the system. But, like a power outage, it would also affect other devices. Then there's a system overload, where so many alerts are triggered that the system crashes.'

'Sounds more like a computer hacker.' Twiggy looked up from what he was writing.

'Exactly,' Seb agreed. 'The burglars might have hacked the system, which is why it's important to consider whether there's been a data breach.'

'Anything else?' Birdie tapped her chin, a sure sign she was already playing out different scenarios in her mind.

'In a less sophisticated approach, they could have used signal jammers, which overwhelm the frequency through which the security system communicates,' Seb said.

'Wouldn't the security company know that the signal had been jammed?' Birdie said.

'Not necessarily. They only temporarily disrupt the circuit, which can be set on a timer. They can also allow a periodic check of signals, which make the system appear to be working properly.'

'Sounds easier than dropping someone down from the ceiling.' Birdie reached for her phone and tapped something in. 'It says here that a signal jammer is a small device, not much bigger than a charging plug, and that it needs to be near the main panel. That means it would need to already be in the house and set to a certain time so once it was activated, the thieves could enter.'

'That's correct,' Seb agreed. 'Thanks to the numerous people who had access to each property, we know that it's possible for any one of them to have planted it.'

'Do they take the device with them when they leave?' Birdie asked, putting down her phone and frowning.

'That's an excellent point. They couldn't take it with them, because it would reactivate the alarm before they'd left the property.'

Birdie sat up, almost bouncing in her chair. 'That means the devices could still be there. We need to go back and search for them.'

'The burglars might have gone back and retrieved the devices later,' Twiggy said. 'After all, if they had access to the houses once, they might have been able to get back in a second time.'

'Yes, and that's something we can double check once we get all the names,' Birdie said. 'But it doesn't mean we shouldn't look for the devices. If they look like phone chargers, they won't be large.'

Twiggy sighed and got to his feet. 'Fine. You've convinced me. I'll take a team back and search each of the properties, while you two start going through the lists of people who had access to them. I'll also ask the three victims if they can provide a list of people who have visited since the burglaries.'

'Even more research.'

Birdie stood while Seb folded up the three maps, and they made their way out of the café. Despite Birdie's energy and inability to sit still for long, she was an excellent researcher – so was Keira, thank goodness, because he suspected it was going to take a long time to go through the suspect lists.

EIGHT

Wednesday, 24 June

'You're back already? I wasn't expecting you until later,' Keira said, having darted out of the kitchen as Birdie and Seb walked into the house. Her eyes were bright, and there was a nervous energy to her, which didn't match the mood they'd left her in when she'd been hunched over her cereal bowl, reading the numerous text messages Hamish had sent the previous evening. But now, for some reason, she was all jumpy and excited.

'I sent you a text to say we were on our way back,' Seb said as Birdie took off her jacket and hung it over a coat hook.

'Um... I must have missed it. Sorry. My phone's in the study.' Colour stung Keira's cheeks but she didn't move from her position in front of the kitchen door, effectively blocking them off.

'What's going on?' Birdie demanded as she tried to peer past Keira, into the kitchen. 'Since when do you leave your phone in another room? It's usually glued to your hand. And why aren't you letting us through?'

'Nothing's going on.' Keira quickly shook her head. 'I wasn't expecting you back for another half hour, and... umm... before you go in there... I need to explain what happened. You see—'

Woof.

Birdie's eyes widened as a dog's nose peeked out from the kitchen door.

It belonged to a vaguely familiar fox-red labrador. Its brow was creased in a way that made it look perpetually concerned and its velvet ears drooped softly around its face. There was a quiet sadness about it, as though it understood more than a dog should.

Keira immediately dropped to her knees and put her arm around the quivering dog. 'It's okay, Bonnie. They won't hurt you. This is Birdie, and my dad, Seb. They're both really nice. I promise.'

Woof. The dog barked in reply.

Birdie looked from Keira to Seb. 'Do you know what's going on?'

'I do not.'

Seb lowered himself to the ground and held out a hand as Bonnie tentatively took a step towards him. Birdie followed suit and the dog gingerly sniffed them, before returning to Keira's side and nuzzling her leg.

'See, I told you they were lovely,' Keira crooned before nodding for Birdie and Seb to join her in the kitchen. 'Thanks for not spooking her. Poor darling is so nervous around strangers.'

'She doesn't seem to think *you're* a stranger,' Birdie said, following her through to the kitchen, where Elsa was curled up by the French doors. Bonnie trotted over to the sleeping dog and settled down next to her. 'Or Elsa for that matter. Where has she come from?'

'She belongs to Mr Whitman. You know, the man who lives at the end of the road. Elsa and I often bump into him and Bonnie when we go for walks.'

'Ah. That's why she looks familiar.' Birdie nodded, recalling the elderly man who often walked his dog along the country lanes. 'But why do you have Bonnie? Has something happened to him?'

'That's the thing. His daughter came around not long after you left. Mr Whitman had a fall and it's no longer safe for him to live alone. He's in hospital but when he gets out, he's moving to Brighton to live with her. Unfortunately, there's no room for darling Bonnie.' Keira's words tumbled out in a rush. Then she turned to Seb. 'Mr Whitman mentioned us to his daughter; that's why she came here. I swear I didn't promise anything. But I did say we'd look after her for a few days while they try to rehome her. She's only three years old, and totally adorable.'

'If they can't rehome her, what's the plan?' Seb asked. His tone was serious but there was a smile tugging at his lips.

Keira sucked in a breath. 'It would be so cool if she could stay here with us. Elsa's her friend and she knows the area well so all the smells will be familiar. Poor Mr Whitman has been fretting about what will happen to Bonnie. I know it would help him get better if he knew she was in safe hands. We could even send him videos and photos so he won't miss her too much. What do you think? I'm sure Sarah won't mind.'

There was silence and Birdie caught her breath.

Seb was devoted to Elsa, and while he never talked about the arthritis that was slowing her down, Birdie knew it must worry him. How would he take to the idea of having a second dog in the house? Especially one that was younger and more energetic.

Keira was obviously worried as well, judging by the way she hopped from foot to foot. It was also clear that Seb hadn't discussed Sarah's offer to buy the house with his daughter. Then again, between the new case and Keira's tears over her summer plans, it was understandable.

Seb turned to Bonnie, who was now pressed up against Elsa's side. His face was expressionless. Honestly, the man was impossible to read at times. Finally he gave a quick nod.

'I think it's a good idea. Do you have the daughter's phone number? I'll call and make sure her father's happy for Bonnie to live with us.'

'Thank you, thank you, thank you.' Keira threw herself into Seb's arms while Bonnie let out a little woof of excitement.

The next half hour was spent getting to know the new addition to the family. Finally, Bonnie curled up on one of Elsa's old beds and went to sleep.

'Now we have a second dog to support, I suggest we do some work,' Seb said.

'Oh, yes. How did it go?' Keira asked, trailing after them. 'Sorry, I haven't had a chance to do as much research as I'd planned. But you know... what with Bonnie and everything.'

'That's okay. You can make up for it now,' Birdie said, sitting in her chair.

She filled Keira in on everything they'd discovered, with Seb adding extra details about the jamming devices.

'Yikes. If Cynthia Thornton had a charity event, it would have been well attended,' Keira said. 'Do we have the guest list yet?'

'Yes. Cynthia's assistant sent it through while we were on the way home,' Birdie said.

'William Limbrick also sent through the names and contact details of everyone who visited them,' Seb added.

'Cool. Do you want me to start there? Or, if they had public events, I could comb social media for any mentions and photographs. There's sure to be loads of hashtags and maybe some local articles as well.'

'Rather you than me.' Birdie shuddered.

She always found it tedious trawling through other people's social media posts and was happy to leave it to Keira, who had a real aptitude. Instead, Birdie settled at her computer and opened both guest lists. It didn't take long to merge them together, before programming it to search for duplicates. It was the fastest way to see if there was any crossover.

There wasn't. Still, it had been a long shot.

A soft clack of computer keys filled the room and a surge of energy went through her as the three of them fell into the familiar rhythm of research. Her inbox pinged and an email from Susannah Limbrick appeared.

It was an apology for forgetting to include several people who'd attended the event. Birdie quickly replied and then plugged the names into her spreadsheet and ran her search for duplicates again.

A name appeared. Deanna Church.

Excitement zapped up her spine at the match.

'I've got something,' she said, already going back to the email to check for the name of the company. 'Have you heard of a company called The Curated Feast? They catered Cynthia's event. One of them, a woman called Deanna Church, was also at Susannah's tasting event.'

'She's the owner,' Seb immediately said. 'I've met her at several events over the years. She's a popular choice for catering around here. I believe the company's based in Oadby.'

'I'll call her now and see if she's available,' Birdie said, but before she could, her phone rang and Twiggy's name flashed up on the screen. Grinning, she snatched it up. 'I'm in the office and putting you on speaker. Do you have anything for us?'

'You could say,' Twiggy's voice boomed from the other end of the phone, his excitement almost palpable. 'Tiny and I are at Cynthia Thornton's house and we've found something.'

'Well, don't keep us in suspense. Was it a jammer?'

'Possibly. We're sending it to forensics for analysis.'

'How long will that take?' Birdie frowned.

'How long's a piece of string?' he retorted. 'Don't worry, I might have lost weight but I can still throw it around when necessary. I'll get them to fast-track it. I'll text you a photo of it.'

'Fantastic. Where did you find it?'

'In the hall, plugged in behind a small table,' Twiggy said.

'Twiggy, could you ask Cynthia if she noticed any issues with her phone before she went on the cruise?' Seb asked. 'Maybe there were sudden dead spots in her house where the Wi-Fi wouldn't work, or that she couldn't make or receive calls all of a sudden.'

'Sure. Why do you want to know?' Twiggy demanded.

'Even if the jammer wasn't activated to turn on until a certain time, it might have caused issues. If she suddenly noticed anything, it might give us a better idea of when it was planted,' Seb explained.

'Good idea,' Birdie said as Twiggy went to enquire.

'I have them occasionally,' Seb said with a smile. Birdie grinned but before she could answer, Twiggy came back onto the line.

'Bingo, Clifford. It turns out that she did notice her phone acting a bit strange towards the end of the charity event at her house.'

'That means we can confirm it was placed there at some stage during the event. Ha.' Birdie punched the air.

'Assuming it is a jammer,' Twiggy reminded her. 'We still need to hear back from forensics.'

'Yes, but if you don't find devices in the other two houses then I'll eat my cricket hat.'

'Promises, promises.' Twiggy chuckled. 'We're heading to Nigel Kaye's place right now. I'll let you know how it goes.'

Birdie finished the call and stood up to stretch. 'This is great news. Especially since we now have someone who was in two of the houses—'

'No way.' Keira suddenly yelped and brought over her laptop.

'What's wrong?' Birdie frowned. 'You don't think we should suspect the caterer?'

'Sorry, I didn't mean to break your flow. The caterer's definitely top of the list. But check this out. One of my friends from school has posted photos from Cynthia Thornton's fundraiser. See.'

Keira twisted round the screen and pointed to a photo of a young woman with long blonde hair and a wide smile. She was standing with Cynthia next to a large banner with the name of a well-known cancer charity on it. They were both dressed in floral dresses.

'ZaraH.' Birdie peered at the woman's name then blinked. 'Whoa. She has a lot of followers.'

'I know. It's bizarre. Her real name's Sara Hunt. Last I knew she was going down south to study anthropology but it says here she's a social influencer and climate activist.' Keira scrolled down the profile showing them hundreds of perfectly filmed shots. 'She's a fashion/travel/beauty vlogger.'

'In other words she convinces people to give her clothing, makeup and free trips,' Birdie retorted. 'Then tries to make it all look glamorous.'

Keira rolled her eyes. 'Not all influencers are shallow and fame hungry. Most of them become successful because they have a point of view and build their platform around it.'

Birdie winced. 'Sorry, you're right. Now I feel old and cynical.'

'Relax, you're not over the hill – yet.' Keira grinned. 'But it's pretty convenient that I know someone who was there. Shall I text her?'

'When were you last in contact?' Seb asked, his arms folded. 'It must be a while if you didn't know what she was doing, or that she's changed her name.'

'We haven't spoken since school, but I've still got her number. It's got to be worth a shot.'

'It won't do any harm. But don't text. Give her a call instead. It will be easier to speak to her in person.' Birdie didn't add that the distraction of an old school friend might ease the pain of Hamish being so far away.

Seb must have been thinking the same thing because he suddenly shrugged. Was that why he'd agreed to adopt Bonnie as well?

'What will you say after all this time?' Seb asked.

Keira grinned. 'Easy. I'll tell her the truth. That I saw her photo and realised it was her.'

'As long as you don't mention the burglary, or our involvement in the case,' Seb warned.

'Duh.' Keira leant forward and kissed his cheek just as Bonnie appeared in the doorway. 'Hello, sweetie. Do you and Elsa want to come for a walk? I'll call Sara while I'm in the garden.'

Once she'd left, Birdie turned to Seb. 'A piece of evidence... a lead to interview... and a dog. It's been a busy afternoon.'

'You're not wrong,' Seb agreed and returned to his desk. Birdie followed suit. Now they had more direction, the real work could finally begin.

NINE

Thursday, 25 June

'Nice work, Twig,' Seb heard Birdie say, as he wiped down the worktop from the debris of Keira's breakfast. His daughter had promised to tidy up after walking the dogs, but Seb hated to leave the house in a mess, and they were due to leave to visit Deanna Church in five minutes. Besides, he was happy to cut Keira some slack since she'd been up half the night trying to settle Bonnie.

He loaded the dishwasher as Birdie continued her conversation at the far end of the room. Finally, she pocketed her phone and rejoined him, her mouth set in a tight line.

'Problem?' He raised an eyebrow.

'Nothing major. Twiggy's in court this morning so can't come with us.' She grinned. 'But it turns out I *won't* be eating my cricket hat after all.'

'They found more devices?' Seb straightened to his full height.

'Yes. Still no word from forensics but they appear to be the same design as the one already found.'

'Forensics will ascertain if they've been hand-built,' Seb said, thinking of the photo that Twiggy had sent them yesterday. It was slightly larger than a phone charger, in a ridged black case with a stumpy black antenna at one end. 'What about the CCTV footage? Did police manage to find any vehicles in two or more locations?'

'No. But uniformed officers are questioning Cynthia's neighbours again. Sarge is hopeful we'll find out more from our visit to Deanna.' She reached into the fruit bowl on the kitchen table and took out an apple.

'Let's hope we don't disappoint.' Seb gave the worktop a final wipe and retrieved his car keys before they headed outside.

Streaks of pale sunlight cut through the clouds and, in the far corner of the garden, Keira was smiling as she bent over Elsa, who had a large stick in her mouth. Seb waved at his daughter, pleased to see her happier again. He started the engine and turned on the satnav.

Deanna Church lived in Oadby but her catering business was run from an industrial kitchen in Leicester city centre. They'd decided not to phone ahead, in case she was involved in the burglaries and made a point of not being there.

'To recap – for me obviously because you'll remember,' Birdie said, smirking at him, 'Deanna Church has been running the company for ten years and they do everything from small birthday parties to weddings and large-scale charity events. That explains why you knew who she is. Is it because she has friends in high places that she's in demand so much?'

'It's possible,' Seb agreed, scanning the road ahead, relieved there was no tractor in sight. 'But I suspect it's more the quality of her food. She uses organic, local ingredients.'

'Now I feel hungry. I should have grabbed two apples,' Birdie said.

It wasn't long before they turned into the tree-lined industrial estate, with cars parked on both sides of the road.

The Curated Feast was on the left. Seb spied a visitors' bay in the almost full car park and pulled in.

Voices drifted from a couple of people in chef's whites, who stood at the far end of the car park, plumes of vape smoke floating above them.

'At least we know they're open today,' Birdie said, nodding towards them.

There was a buzzer at the entrance, which Birdie pressed several times.

'Coming,' a female voice called from inside.

The door opened to reveal a petite woman with short grey hair, styled in a messed-up pixie cut.

Deanna Church.

Her sharp gaze scanned them both, before landing on Seb. He was used to his height making him stand out, but she appeared to recognise him. It was confirmed when a smile broke out on her face.

'Sebastian Clifford. This is a nice surprise. I know your parents. How are they?'

'They're well, thank you. This is my business partner, Birdie.'

'Are you here regarding catering an event?' Deanna asked. 'It's unusual for people to visit in person. Most of my enquiries are initially done online.'

'We're here in a professional capacity,' Seb explained.

'Of course. You're a private detective. I remember now. How can I help?' Deanna asked, smiling.

'We're investigating a spate of burglaries in the area. You catered the charity event at Cynthia Thornton's house last month.'

The smile faded from Deanna's mouth. 'Yes, I remember. Cynthia's house was broken into while she was on her cruise. I'd planned on reaching out to her but then life got in the way. Do you believe it's linked to the fundraiser?'

'We're unsure at this stage, but have to investigate all possibilities,' Seb said.

'Isn't this something the police should be doing?'

'It's a complex case and they've asked us to assist.' Birdie stepped forward so that her foot was in the doorway, although Seb didn't for one moment believe the woman would refuse them entry. 'May we come inside to discuss it?'

Deanna's brows knitted together, before she stepped back from the door. 'Of course. Sorry, I didn't mean to be rude.'

She ushered them into a large square office space with concrete floors and white walls lined with photos. Numerous pot plants softened the starkness.

Seb recognised the backdrop from The Curated Feast's social media feed, that Keira had shown them. It was where they'd photographed the various meals they'd created. He assumed it was part of their marketing strategy to attract clients. He glanced at a wall of photos of past events, including one for his parents' close friends. Birdie paused next to him, her gaze taking in the many prestigious events.

Deanna noticed, and her mood improved. 'Over the last ten years we've been lucky enough to cater for some extraordinary events. I find it helps keep the staff motivated if they can be reminded of our fine history.'

'That's a good idea,' Seb said, although he suspected many of the staff were students, more interested in earning money to cover their rent rather than working out of a sense of pride.

'Thank you.' Deanna led them past a light wood desk and through to a sitting area, gesturing for them to be seated. 'What would you like to know?'

'Please will you talk us through the fundraiser at Cynthia Thornton's house,' Seb asked once they were settled. 'Including the times you arrived and how you got there.'

'Hmmmm.' Deanna pulled out her phone and began scrolling. 'Let's see. I had five staff working and we arrived together in two of my vans. We were hired to run the bar as well as provide food. Two of my staff focused on setting up the bar, ensuring they had enough glasses, ice, garnishes, etc. While the other three, under my supervision, looked after the food.'

'Did you use the kitchen?'

'Yes, of course.' Deanna placed her phone on the coffee table.

'Most of our food is prepared here to ensure the quality is consistent. However, some of the dishes required cooking onsite, so they didn't dry out or be overcooked. After the event we cleaned up and left.'

Next to him, Birdie shifted. Deanna, or one of her staff, had ample opportunity to place the jammer in the house as they moved around.

'Did you notice anyone suspicious hanging around?' Birdie asked, casually. 'Or see any of the guests walking around the house, other than using the bathroom?'

Deanna frowned. 'No, I don't think so. But I was working and might not have paid attention. It takes a huge amount of behind the scenes planning to ensure these events appear seamless.'

'It's certainly an artform,' Seb agreed, thinking of the numerous caterers his own parents had hired over the years, and how quietly the best of them would go about their business.

'I like to think so,' Deanna said, her voice warming up. 'Do you really believe the person was at the fundraiser? It's dreadful to think that such a lovely day could be marred by something so dark.'

'The burglary was pre-planned, and it's entirely possible the burglar was at the fundraiser in order to get the lie of the land,' Seb said, deciding it was time to press her about the other houses. 'As were the others we're investigating.'

'There were more?' Deanna's whole posture changed and it was clear she was shocked. But Seb had seen enough good actors not to be swayed.

'That's correct.' Birdie took over. 'Most recently Susannah Limbrick's property was broken into while she was in London. The week before, you were on the guest list for a prelaunch event.'

Deanna's hand flew to her mouth as she gasped. 'I had no idea Susannah was burgled. The poor darling. She never mentioned it.'

'It's been kept out of the media, for the moment,' Seb said in a cool voice. 'What can you tell us about the evening?'

'Nothing, I'm afraid.' Deanna shook her head. 'I was on the

guest list but there was a last-minute problem, so I sent along my head chef instead.'

'Is it common for chefs to go to each other's events?' Birdie asked, frowning.

'Of course. Think of it as professional development. I've known Susannah for years and she's brilliant at what she does. I've been wanting to expand our own menus and offer more vegan dishes. Catering to dietary needs is becoming big business. Isaac Cross, my head chef, is keen as well.'

'Was Isaac working at Cynthia's event?' Birdie asked.

'Well... yes. It was a very important day, so naturally he was there. You surely can't think he has anything to do with it.'

'Is he in the kitchen now?' Seb asked, ignoring the previous question. 'We'd like to speak to him.'

'Sorry, it's his day off.' Deanna let out a sigh. 'This could be disastrous for my reputation. Are you sure he's involved?'

'We're not accusing him,' Seb reminded her. 'We're trying to build up a picture of events. How long has Cross worked for you, and what else can you tell us about him?'

'I poached him eighteen months ago from a top London restaurant. He cooks like a dream but keeps very much to himself so I don't know much about him. Believe it or not, in this line of work, it's most refreshing. He's always professional, on time, and wonderfully creative.'

'We'd like his contact details, please,' Birdie said, making it sound like an order, rather than a request.

Silence filled the room and Seb pressed his mouth together. It would be much easier if Deanna Church gave them the address and phone number rather than having to rely on Twiggy's badge, but if needs be, that's what they'd do.

Thankfully, his worries were unwarranted.

'No problem.' Deanna retrieved her phone and tapped the screen several times before calling out the details, which Birdie wrote down.

Seb peered back at the wall of photos and rubbed his chin. 'Have you ever catered for Nigel Kaye?'

'Unfortunately, I haven't. I've quoted for several events but he and his wife have always gone with my opposition in Market Harborough. Why?'

Before Seb could answer, a red-faced woman in chef's whites appeared in the doorway.

'Sorry to interrupt, Deanna, but we need you in the kitchen.'

'I'll be right through.' Deanna got to her feet. 'Sorry, I have to go.'

Birdie held out a card. 'Thanks for your time. If you think of anything else, please let us know.'

Deanna nodded and walked them to the door before disappearing back inside.

'That's some wall of fame she has,' Birdie said once they'd reached the car. 'I was surprised not to see your parents up there.'

'Probably because they live in the wrong part of the country,' Seb said in a mild voice, not rising to the bait. Birdie knew perfectly well that not every aristocrat in England knew each other. 'Not good for their carbon footprint to hire a caterer who has to travel so far.'

'You're no fun,' Birdie goaded and then grew serious. 'So how come she knew them?'

'I suspect she was exaggerating. She might have come across them in the past.'

'Although she knew you,' Birdie persisted.

'Possibly through Sarah. I believe she catered events for her in the past,' Seb suggested.

'Well, that aside, it seems to me that she's more worried about the reputation of her company than anything else.'

'That was my read as well,' Seb agreed. 'Though I appreciate why. She'd lose business if her clients thought there was a trust issue.'

Birdie climbed into the car and Seb turned on the engine. 'Let's visit Isaac Cross and see what he has to say.'

TEN

Thursday, 25 June

Isaac Cross lived in a pebble-dashed terraced house with pots of geraniums growing by the front door. Music drifted out and Birdie took that as a good sign he was home.

'Do you think Deanna called to warn him we were on the way?' she wondered out loud.

'I doubt it. She wouldn't want to be incriminated in any way, if we uncovered something,' Seb replied, as he pressed the doorbell.

Birdie agreed but before she could discuss this further, the front door opened and a man in his early thirties stood in front of them. He had dark hair cropped close to his scalp and there were bags under his eyes, as if he'd not long woken up.

'Whatever you're selling, I'm not buying,' he said in a London accent.

Birdie smiled. Over the years she'd become used to getting herself across the threshold, and while the police badge would often make it easier, it also had its drawbacks. Now she used a variety of approaches, depending on the situation.

'Isaac Cross?' she asked.

'Yeah.' He automatically nodded, though his posture didn't change. 'And?'

'I'm Birdie and this is my colleague, Sebastian Clifford. We're private investigators looking into a recent burglary at Cynthia Thornton's house. We're working our way through the guest list from the event she held, where you were working, and hoped you could give us insight into what the day was like,' she replied, not wanting him to feel like he was under suspicion. Well, not yet anyway.

There was silence as he considered the request, before he ushered them into a narrow hallway. He guided them through to an open-plan, L-shaped kitchen/dining/lounge area at the back, which had rows of herbs growing along the window. Steam was coming from a saucepan and the fragrant scent of herbs and onions filled the room.

'Sit down. I need to keep an eye on this.' They pulled out chairs from the oval dining table, and after turning down the heat on the saucepan, he joined them. 'How did you get my address?'

'Your employer gave it to us. Is that a problem?' Birdie replied.

'No. Providing she doesn't also give it to my ex-wife.' He drummed his fingers on the table.

'Did you move to Leicester because you'd split up?' Birdie asked, hoping the question would put him more at ease. It seemed to work and he gave a rueful smile.

'It was one of the reasons. I wanted a clean break, and this job was too good to turn down. I've mainly worked in restaurants and the late nights really get to you after a while. At least with catering, I have the occasional weekend off and most of my evenings are free. Plus, unlike some owners I've worked with, Deanna loves food and is open to collaborating on menus. We're both passionate about using local, organic ingredients.'

'What was on the menu for Cynthia Thornton's event?' Birdie asked, wanting to move the conversation along. He nodded and rattled off a mouth-watering selection of food that made her stomach rumble. 'I can imagine that kept you busy. Please could you walk us through how the day went?'

'Busy is an understatement. I didn't even have time to go to the loo. As well as being in the kitchen, supervising the food, I had to keep an eye on the rest of the staff. There's nothing worse than seeing a tray of canapés go to waste because a waiter doesn't watch where they're walking. We were also running the bar, and I had to ensure the champagne and wine flowed.'

'I thought Deanna was there to help,' Birdie replied, with a frown.

'Hmm. Yeah, she was there, but spent all day networking. She always does that which is why I'm in charge of making sure everything runs smoothly.'

Birdie exchanged a glance with Seb. That wasn't the way Deanna had explained it. Was he saying that to appear more important? Or, if it was the truth, it meant Deanna had even more opportunity to plant the jammer.

'Do you mind?' Birdie asked.

'Not at all. It works well.' He shrugged.

'I assume you would've moved between the house, kitchen and garden frequently during the event,' Seb said in his usual calm voice. 'Did you see anyone who looked like they shouldn't be there?'

Cross barked with laughter. 'You mean apart from me and the team? We might've looked smart in our uniforms, but most of us didn't grow up eating caviar and reading wine labels. Everyone who attended was clearly loaded, judging by their posh clothes. Most of the cars parked in the driveway cost way more than I make in a year.'

'That aside, did anything stand out to you?' Birdie asked.

Cross frowned and ran a hand through his short hair. 'Wait... do you think someone nicked the stuff on the day of the fundraiser? I thought it happened after. Wouldn't the police have got in touch if it happened on the day?'

'We're looking at all angles. You're right that the theft took place after the event, but it was a day that a lot of people had access to the house,' Seb explained. 'If you discovered any guests acting suspiciously, that would be useful to know.'

'Oh right. No. I didn't. Sorry. Apart from some of them wandering round looking for the toilets.'

'What about your team?' Birdie asked.

'No way. Our crew's tight and were all too busy running around to go snooping.'

Ding. Ding. Ding. An egg timer rang out and Cross got to his feet and headed to the hob, where he lifted the lid of the saucepan and gave a stir. Then he adjusted the temperature and walked back to the table, his leg skimming a familiar-looking cardboard box with the name *Green Meadows* printed across it.

Birdie looked at Seb, but he was focused on a computer that was on a work desk against the wall in the lounge area.

'I wouldn't have thought a chef would subscribe to Green Meadows,' Birdie said, nodding at the box. 'Aren't they designed to encourage people to cook?'

'You know the saying about the mechanic's car.' Cross laughed, not seeming to take offence at the question. 'Sometimes the last thing you want to do after work is cook for yourself. Besides, I love her food. I used to dismiss vegan food as being a fad, but was wrong. Deanna wants a better vegan selection available so this is tax deductible. It's research.'

'Does that mean you'll be using some of her recipes?' Birdie pushed.

Wasn't that classed as theft?

He flushed but quickly shook his head. 'I'd never take something wholesale, but there's nothing wrong with being inspired by flavour combinations.'

'Is that why you were happy to attend Susannah Limbrick's pre-launch evening in place of your boss?' Birdie asked.

Cross's eyes widened. 'How do you know about that, and why does it matter?'

'Deanna told us. Were you aware that Susannah was burgled not long after Cynthia Thornton?'

'She was?' Genuine surprise crossed his face.

Birdie decided to push him further on it. 'It happened while she was in London with her husband for the book launch. But I suppose anyone at the event would've known they'd be away at the time.'

'Not to mention anyone who reads the trade papers. It was plastered everywhere,' Cross replied with a shrug.

'Did you offer to attend in place of Deanna, or did she suggest it?'

'She did. I'd planned on getting some coding done that evening. Not that I minded.'

'Did you recognise any of the other guests? In particular anyone who'd been at Cynthia Thornton's event?'

'I can't say for sure. At Cynthia's, I was running around like a maniac so didn't notice much.'

'We appreciate that,' Seb said, his eyes once again drifting to the computer desk at the far end of the room. 'That's some set-up you have there. You mentioned you were coding. Are you building something?'

'Attempting to. I'm working on a recipe app, so I can open my own business one day. I've been going to night school to learn coding. That's another reason why this job suits me better than working in a restaurant.'

The egg timer once again pinged and Cross got to his feet.

Birdie sucked in a breath and resisted the urge to exchange a look with Seb.

Not only had the chef been inside two of the houses prior to the burglaries, but he knew his way around computers. Did he have the expertise required to program a jammer and find the perfect spot to position it?

They really needed the forensics report on the jammers. How they'd been activated and could they be traced back to a particular

IP address – and, most importantly, were there any fingerprints on them?

'Thank you for your time,' Seb said, getting to his feet, though once again he was looking at the back of the room. 'Good luck with the app you're building.'

'Thanks, mate.' Cross walked them to the door, closing it behind them.

The car was parked around the block and once they were well away, Birdie turned to Seb. 'Can someone learn how to code jammers?'

Seb nodded. 'I think he's more advanced than he was letting on. His computer set-up wasn't from any old high street store. It was clearly custom built.'

'So he could be our guy. But we still need to place him at Nigel Kaye's house and even without the list, we know it was only media personnel. I didn't want to ask in case he clammed up. Damn, maybe I should've risked it.'

'You didn't have to.'

Birdie came to an abrupt halt and stared at her partner. 'What are you talking about? Have you heard back from Nigel Kaye? Is Cross on the list?'

'No, I don't have the list yet, but I can confirm that Cross knows who Nigel Kaye is.'

'How?' Birdie asked.

'Apart from the Green Meadows box and his computer, did you notice anything else?' Seb asked.

She thought for a few seconds. 'It's the artwork on the wall, isn't it? Those bright splotches of colour were made by Nigel Kaye.'

'Correct. They were from Kaye's last exhibition. The one that put him in the million-pound orbit,' Seb confirmed.

'You reckon Cross paid millions of pounds for them?'

'No. His were only signed prints. Although being signed means they wouldn't be cheap.'

'Why didn't you say anything?'

'For the same reason neither of us pushed him on being a computer coder. Because I didn't want to alert him.'

Birdie grinned. 'Right. Now we need to investigate Isaac Cross in a lot more detail. Who his friends are, does he have debts, and more importantly, where was he on the nights of each burglary.'

'I couldn't agree more. Let's get back to the office.'

ELEVEN

Thursday, 25 June

'Hello, girl.' Birdie dropped to her knees and patted Bonnie, who had rushed out into the hallway to greet them. The young dog was followed more slowly by Elsa, who nudged her head into Seb's leg. Keira appeared from the study wearing a flowery maxi dress, one foot clad in a brown sandal, while the other was encased in a strappy, heeled wedge. A wide-brimmed sunhat was on her head and in her hand was a pair of cut-off denim shorts and a sleeveless T-shirt.

Clearly they weren't the only ones who'd had a busy morning.

'Thank goodness you're back.' Keira blew a strand of long hair off her face and waved the denim shorts in the air. 'I'm having a fashion disaster. Does this dress give too much of a mum-vibe? Shall I wear my shorts and go more casual boho-chic, instead?'

'Mum-vibe? Dare I ask what that is?' Seb's face was blank and Birdie burst out laughing.

'You know... looking too old, as if I'm more interested in being comfortable than anything else,' Keira patiently explained.

'There's nothing wrong with feeling comfortable.' Birdie patted her own wide-legged trousers and plucked the denim shorts from

Keira's hand. 'And I'm not your dad, but even I can see these are designed for a child.'

Keira grinned. 'See, now *that's*... mum-vibe.'

'Behave. Why are you having a fashion meltdown before lunch?' Birdie threw the shorts back at her and laughed. But secretly she was pleased to see that Keira was once again her usual bouncing self.

'I'm seeing Sara – I mean Zara... She's asked me to call her that, because everyone does now. We're meeting at the pub this afternoon. After I called, we started texting each other. It's been awesome. You know there are some friends where it doesn't matter if you haven't spoken for one day or one year. Well, it was like that with us.'

'Did she say why she changed her name?' Seb asked as they headed into the kitchen to prepare lunch.

'There's another influencer with the same name. Zara reckons that changing her name was the best thing she's ever done. It's like turning over a new leaf and becoming an entirely different person. I can't tell you how buzzed I was to talk to her... It's hard to remember to call her Zara. Let's hope I don't mess it up at the pub.'

At the mention of the pub, Seb frowned. 'Remember not to bring up the burglaries.'

'But if Zara mentions them, definitely play along and sound interested,' Birdie clarified.

Keira gave them both an exaggerated eye roll. 'Relax, you two. I know what I'm doing.'

'Says the girl wearing two different shoes,' Seb retorted, a smile tugging at his lips.

'I don't mean to put a dampener on your preparations, but how did you get on with the research?' Birdie asked.

Keira immediately put down the clothing in her hand and retrieved her phone from somewhere in the folds of the maxi dress. 'Out of the three of them, Nigel Kaye is the most prolific poster. Often you can tell if they use a social media specialist because the posts are colour coordinated tiles, and come out in a schedule to make sure they all match when you're scrolling through the profile. But Nigel seems to do his own and is forever posting photos of himself and the kids.'

She held up the phone. The social media account was indeed peppered with numerous images of his two young children running through the woods and mounted on horseback, while a glamorous woman watched on. His wife, Bianca. There were photos of bright artwork, like those hanging on Isaac Cross's wall. And among the posts were details of the school play that was on the night of the burglary.

Sighing, Birdie straightened up. 'He basically told his entire audience that he'd be out on the night of the burglary.'

'Yeah,' Keira agreed, pointing to a number on the screen. 'All three million of them.'

'Were there any comments that stood out?' Birdie asked.

'No. Just a whole lot of, "so adorable" and "break a leg" comments from people. I've compiled a list of those who publicly engaged the most with his posts. We can use them to cross-reference with who went to Kaye's house the week before the burglary.'

'That's great.' Birdie gave an approving smile. Keira was every bit as smart as her dad and a real asset to the team. 'Do Cynthia and Susannah have any followers in common?'

'Cynthia has an account but it's set to private, which makes me suspect it's only for friends and family. She also has a LinkedIn profile but there are no posts and she doesn't seem to engage with anyone. She's a closed book, for sure. I had a little more success with Susannah.' Keira tapped at her phone and held up a page that had the banner *Green Meadows* across the top.

Birdie frowned. 'It's all about her recipes and reasons for becoming vegan.'

'That's right. Her focus is clearly on public health and advocacy. There's some great content here. And before you ask, I have a list of her most active followers, especially those who commented on the posts in the last month.'

'Excellent work,' Seb told her. 'Anything else?'

'Actually.' Keira began to hop from foot to foot, something she often did when she was excited. Or nervous. 'You know I've considered becoming vegetarian in the past? Well now I'm thinking of being vegan.'

'Is that before or after you eat all the ice cream in the freezer?' Birdie wanted to know.

'This isn't about what tastes nice, it's about what's good for my body and the planet,' Keira informed her in a serious voice. 'I've ordered Susannah's new book. And Dad, I think we should get a subscription for a meal box.'

Birdie bit back a grin. She'd been right.

'If that's what you'd like, then that's fine with me. Do you have time for lunch before you leave?'

'Lunch? Crap. Is that the time? I still haven't decided on my outfit.' Keira put her phone away and scooped up the discarded clothing. 'I need to finish getting ready. Fill me in later on how it went, okay? Please will one of you take Bonnie for a walk?'

'We live to serve,' Birdie said, giving a bow, as Keira had disappeared back to her room.

Birdie and Seb sat down for a quick lunch and by the time they'd finished, Keira had flown down the stairs and out the door, only stopping to give them a list of instructions regarding the newest addition to their family.

'You'd think I've never owned a dog before,' Seb commented, though his eyes were twinkling.

They headed into the office and Birdie collapsed into her chair and picked up her phone. 'Twiggy should've heard back from forensics by now.'

'Talk of the devil. I was about to call you,' the officer said after answering on the third ring.

'Of course you were,' Birdie replied well used to her old partner's excuses. 'Have you heard back about the devices?'

'*That's* what I was going to call about,' he explained. Birdie put her phone on speaker so Seb could listen. 'According to the report, the devices found at the burglary sites can definitely jam the security signals. There's also a lot of techie mumbo jumbo here that's way above my pay grade and I have no idea what it means.'

'Please email it to me. I'd like to go through it,' Seb said.

'Better your brain than mine,' Twiggy said. They heard the clatter of a keyboard and then Seb's computer pinged with a new email. 'Now, if you don't mind, I need to grab some lunch. I'm starving.'

Birdie opened her mouth to speak but before she could, he'd gone.

She doubted she'd have done much better than Twiggy when it came to going through the technical elements, but Seb didn't have an issue with it, judging by the way he studied the screen. Finally, he looked across at her, his mouth set in a tight line.

'Well?'

'The devices are extremely sophisticated. They're designed to intercept and block the security signals, which use radio frequencies, while at the same transmitting a false signal to the monitoring company. If they'd used something more basic, it would have been picked up immediately. It's ingenious.'

'By ingenious, I hope you mean terrifying. The fact someone can plant a device that takes out the system without anyone knowing is concerning.'

Seb rubbed his chin. 'It is indeed. The reason they planted the device prior to its use is for it to learn the security system's normal signals, and then mimic them. This, in turn, prevents it being picked up by anyone monitoring the property.'

'Do they have any idea where these devices come from?' Birdie tapped her fingers against the desk. 'Can they be bought on the dark web?'

'It's possible, though this report suggests they've been at least partially handmade. It's not something you can learn from a YouTube tutorial. Whoever built them is extremely knowledgeable, and has money to spare. The parts are expensive.'

Birdie jumped to her feet and began pacing. 'It takes us right back to Cross. Do you think he could have built them? He could have been lying about creating an app.'

'Possibly, but he'd need more than a computer. There was no sign of a soldering iron or the other equipment he'd need.'

'They could have been in his bedroom, or in the garden in a shed. We need a search warrant to check.'

'Together with enough proof to convince Sergeant Weston to *apply* for said warrant,' Seb added. 'Nothing about the burglaries was left to chance. I doubt whoever's behind them would leave evidence scattered around for us to discover.'

'Except, they left the devices behind.'

'Because they had to,' Seb reminded her.

Birdie stopped pacing and sighed. 'You're right. But that doesn't mean we can't find out more about Isaac Cross and Deanna Church. They're connected to two of the properties and Cross has Nigel Kaye's prints on his wall.'

'You want to pay them both another visit?'

Birdie shook her head. 'Not yet. Let me have a snoop around and see what I can unearth about the two of them.'

'While you do that, I'm going to find out if the jammers' parts are traceable. If they are, it will give us a better chance of discovering where they came from and who bought them.'

TWELVE

Friday, 26 June

'Can you believe that Zara's been to Crete and even stayed in the same villa I've seen online? Okay, so it's not one Hamish and I can afford to book, but surely it's a sign we were meant to meet up again,' Keira announced the following morning as she and Seb strolled around the garden, the grass still glistening with dew against the pale sunlight.

Seb could in fact believe that Zara had been to Crete and stayed in a particular villa, mainly because his daughter had talked of nothing else since she'd met with her old friend. To think he'd been worried that Keira might spend the whole summer being dismal from missing Hamish.

It appeared that a new dog and an old friend were the perfect remedy to her malaise. When she'd returned from university without her usual sparkle it had upset him, more than he'd have thought possible. He'd wondered if it was because he'd missed the earlier years of her life and hadn't witnessed the ups and downs that were a part of growing up. But then a part of him whispered that he wasn't equipped with the parenting skills he needed to support her during this important time in her life. He'd never struggled like this with anything before. Most things had come easy. But he wouldn't change a thing. Having Keira in his life was beyond anything he could've imagined.

'She might be able to recommend places to visit when you go overseas next summer,' Seb suggested, as Bonnie drifted ahead of them, sniffing and exploring her new home, her dark eyes bright with curiosity.

'That's exactly what I said. It's amazing how much she's travelled in the last two years. Zara says her focus is on making memories rather than making money. Isn't that awesome?' Keira bounced along beside him, energy radiating off her.

'Travelling's a good way to learn about the world.' Seb tempered his voice, still not sure how he felt about someone working as an *influencer*. Correction. He wasn't sure how he'd feel if Keira chose that career. Thankfully, whilst it was clear Keira was proud of her friend, she didn't appear inclined to emulate her.

'It's a different kind of education,' Keira agreed, still beaming with happiness. 'It's so cool that we've reconnected. Zara's keen to hang out more. I was thinking she could come here this afternoon.'

Seb came to an abrupt halt. 'Here?'

'Well, yeah. Is that a problem?'

'I don't think it's appropriate, considering the case and that she was at Cynthia Thornton's charity event. You wouldn't have come across Zara if not for your research.'

Keira was silent for a moment. 'I suppose that makes sense. But that was before we caught up. I'd forgotten how much fun we used to have. Since her channel's started blowing up, she hardly has any real friends. She said most people just want to hang out because she's famous. What if she thinks that's all I'm doing?'

'Because you're not like that,' Seb assured his daughter firmly. 'You're kind and caring. But there's a line we must be careful not to cross.'

Keira sighed. 'Now you're sounding like my ethics lecturer. Do you think I should take a step back?'

Seb frowned, considering it.

Ethics aside, if Keira used the friendship to obtain information from Zara without her knowledge, it would impact the relationship going forward. Although it might help them piece together a timeline, or perhaps give them a clue, he wasn't prepared for his daughter to take the risk.

'No. But make sure you don't take advantage of the friendship by doing anything that might compromise your integrity.'

'Thanks, Dad. That makes sense. I didn't bring up the burglary when we were together but Zara did. She said she'd attended an event at a large house that was subsequently burgled. All I asked was if she knew anything else about it. You know... like any friend would do, I showed a natural interest.'

'What was her response?' Seb asked, curious.

'All she knew was the media mentioned some artwork and coins were stolen. She didn't say the event and burglary could be linked and I didn't pursue it. It's crazy to think we're the same age and she's getting invited to fancy events like that.'

'I didn't realise you were interested in these *fancy* events, because I'm sure your grandmother would happily take you to any number. You'd even get a frock out of it, I don't doubt.'

'A frock?' Keira groaned. 'No one calls them that, Dad. You're right, Grandma's always sending me invites, but they're her things, not mine. Not that I'm complaining. It just seems surreal that Zara has this grown-up life already and I'm still a student.'

'You're a student planning a great future. There's no rush.'

'Yeah, I suppose, but it's a weird feeling seeing other people getting on with their lives... Hamish, and now Zara, and I've still got to finish my degree.'

Seb rubbed his chin. He'd planned on discussing the idea of buying Rendall Hall with his daughter on her first night back, but between Hamish's change of plans and then welcoming Bonnie into the household he hadn't found the right time.

Was this it?

If he wanted an honest relationship with his daughter, he had to be open with her. He took a deep breath.

'Keira, I want to talk to you about Sarah.'

'Oh, no. Don't tell me she's coming back.' Now it was Keira's turn to come to a sudden halt.

Had it been a mistake to mention it? Why were conversations suddenly becoming like treading on eggshells?

'Would it be a problem if she is planning to?'

Keira let out a sigh. 'No, I suppose not. I mean it is her house, after all. It's just this is where I first met you and I love knowing it's always here to come back to. It will be weird not having it. Yeah, I know. It's totally selfish of me.'

Seb's worry dissipated and he let out a breath. He'd been so busy weighing up the pros and cons of his decision that he hadn't thought about his daughter's emotional connection to the house. It had the power of cutting through all the pros and cons that his spreadsheets had been throwing up, replacing them with something more tangible.

Keira loved it there.

'Actually, it's the opposite. Sarah's decided to stay in Canada and has offered to sell me the hall.'

'Can you afford it?'

He put an arm around Keira's shoulder. 'Yes. I might not be in the league of Cynthia Thornton, Nigel Kaye or Susannah Limbrick, but it's more than manageable. Even more so if it's something you would like?'

'Would I?' Keira replied, her eyes sparkling with excitement. 'But only if you want to,' she quickly added. 'When do you need to tell her?'

'In the next few weeks. There are still a few things to consider but I'm pleased you like the idea.'

'I *love* it,' Keira said as her phone rang. She studied the screen. 'It's Zara. Do you mind if I take it?'

'Of course not. But remember not to mention anything about the cases.'

'Duh.' She gave him a long-suffering sigh as she answered. 'Hey, how are you?' She paused. 'No way. Seriously? When did this happen?' Keira pressed a hand to her chest, her face breaking out into a grin. 'Zara, that's amazing. I'm so happy for you.'

Seb watched, trying to piece together the conversation from Keira's reactions. A new sponsor, perhaps?

'Okay, tell me everything. Start from the beginning and don't leave anything out.'

Keira disappeared into the garden, her free hand waving as she talked. Bonnie darted after her, while Elsa stayed at his side.

'Just you and me again, girl.' Seb crouched to pat his dog, letting the feel of warm fur relax him. He rolled his shoulders and the pair of them headed back to the house.

After receiving the details from Twiggy, he'd spent the previous evening researching into the jammers used but hadn't found anything specific that could be linked to a potential suspect. Birdie had concentrated on Isaac Cross, whose previous employers had been happy to talk about him and how reliable he was, which didn't help their investigation. However, Seb was going to spend the morning digging into Cross's finances. Something might turn up.

There was no sign of Birdie when he reached the house, which was hardly surprising since it was only nine in the morning and they'd both been working late, so he headed into the office and settled at his desk. He picked up his phone to make some follow-up calls to the three security companies who were responsible for the properties.

The next hour flew by. None of the companies had experienced computer breaches, and whilst they weren't forthcoming on the use of signal jammers, Seb had managed to discover that they were all developing systems to combat such interference. He'd also asked about their employees, and discovered there was no overlap between the companies.

He was about to make a coffee when his phone rang. It was Birdie.

'Hey. I've just finished a Pilates class. It's good for my flexibility, and as it's cricket season I need to make sure I don't pull any muscles. Sorry, I forgot to tell you last night I was going first thing.'

'No need to apologise. The last thing we need is you hobbling around. Are you coming into the office?'

'I was but Sarge called. He wants us at the station for a catchup.'

'Perfect timing. I've finished going through all the security companies and confirming that they didn't have any computer breaches nor were there any employees who'd worked at any of the other companies.'

'Well that puts them out of the frame, then,' Birdie said.

'Exactly. Our priority is discovering from where these jammers were bought.' Seb reached for his keys. 'If you're already in town, I'll meet you there.'

'Cool. See you soon. I'll even shout you a coffee. I'll pick it up on the way.'

THIRTEEN

Friday, 26 June

'Nice of you to finally join us,' Sergeant Weston growled from over his desk as Seb and Birdie walked into his office.

Seb glanced at what appeared to be total chaos and sat on one of the vacant chairs. It was clear from the officer's expression that he was looking for answers. Unfortunately, although they'd made progress, they weren't even close to naming a suspect.

'If you don't want the coffee I bought you, just say so,' Birdie retorted, placing the cup on the desk and sliding it over to him. She gave him an affectionate smile, handed another cup to Twiggy, and sat down.

Sergeant Weston took a sip of his drink and nodded to Twiggy. 'Tell us what you've got.'

'Forensics found tyre marks at the end of the woodland area by Nigel Kaye's property. They believe the tread is from a Ford Transit van,' Twiggy said.

'What about further into the woods? Did they look for tyre marks around the rest of the property?' Seb asked.

'Yes, but they couldn't find anything. The ground's very dry, so there's a possibility the burglars drove closer to the house and the tracks have disappeared.'

'At least we have a better idea of where they parked, and the vehicle they were driving,' Birdie said, jotting down some notes.

'CCTV footage?' Seb asked, placing his coffee on the desk and turning slightly to face Twiggy. 'Was anything found that matched?'

Twiggy shook his head. 'Not a sausage.'

'Not helpful,' Sergeant Weston snapped, confirming that he was feeling the pressure to get the case closed. 'What else do you have?'

'Plenty.' Twiggy flipped open a folder to reveal a messy stack of papers, which he began to shuffle through. 'Officers have been going house to house to see what else people remember. Including if they'd seen a Ford Transit van on the day of the burglary.'

'And?' Sarge made a winding motion with his finger, to encourage Twiggy to get on with it.

'No one saw a thing. Though it's no surprise since the closest neighbour is half a mile away.'

Sergeant Weston exhaled loudly, and then turned to Seb and Birdie. 'What have you two come up with?'

Seb gave him a quick rundown on where he'd got to with the security companies, then nodded at Birdie to take over.

'Yesterday we spoke to Deanna Church, whose company catered Cynthia Thornton's charity event *and* she was on the guest list for Susannah Limbrick's pre-book launch. Her head chef, Isaac Cross, was mainly running the Thornton event, and also attended the book event, in place of Deanna.'

'Is that so?' Sergeant Weston raised a bushy eyebrow. 'Have you interviewed him?'

'Yes. He said the charity event was so busy that he didn't notice anything but the food and drink. He said he only went to Susannah Limbrick's house because they're looking to offer more vegan options.'

'What's wrong with a good old-fashioned sausage roll?' Sergeant Weston muttered. 'Did you believe him?'

'Hard to say.' Birdie frowned. 'He's attending a course so he can build his own app and has a fancy computer setup. Seb's been researching to see if it's possible to build the jammers with that level of knowledge.'

'Is it?' Sergeant Weston said, turning his attention to Seb.

'It's unlikely,' Seb replied. 'He'd also need funds to buy the component parts, which are expensive.'

'So I've been informed by digital forensics. They couldn't trace any of the parts.'

Seb had come to the same conclusion but it was good forensics had confirmed it.

'There's one more thing,' Birdie added. 'Seb noticed that Cross had several Nigel Kaye prints on his wall.'

'That's it,' Twiggy said, excitedly. 'He's our common denominator. We need to bring him in for questioning.'

Seb frowned and gave a slight shake of his head. Birdie caught the motion and mirrored it. Clearly, they were both thinking the same thing but it was Sergeant Weston who spoke first.

'You want to question someone over a print on their wall? If Cross is involved, we don't want to pull him in until we have more to go on. Especially as it's unlikely he was working alone. Besides, aren't we waiting for a list from Nigel Kaye regarding who had access to the house? There might be several more of these *common denominators*.'

'I'll chase Kaye up again about the list,' Birdie quickly added, clearly trying to shelter Twiggy from Sergeant Weston's anger. 'I'll call him now.'

'Actually, there's no need,' Twiggy said, his cheeks the colour of someone who'd been too long in the sun. 'It came in late yesterday afternoon as I was leaving for the day.'

'Yesterday? *Yesterday?*' Sergeant Weston roared, his voice bouncing off the walls. 'Why am I only hearing about it now?'

'Because this case has lots of angles,' Birdie quickly interjected, again appearing to be protecting Twiggy from her old boss's wrath. If it had been anyone else who'd forgotten to mention the list, Birdie would probably be as angry as Sergeant Weston. But Seb knew she worried about Twiggy's illness and how it could affect his memory.

'Let's put Isaac Cross to one side for now and look at the list,' Seb suggested, not wanting them to become embroiled in petty squabbles. 'We can cross-reference it with the other two lists and take it from there.'

'Right. You get on with that and keep me informed of developments,' Sergeant Weston said, waving them out of the office.

As they left, Birdie gave Seb a grateful nod. He shrugged it off and followed her back to the main office.

When they reached the office, Twiggy dropped down into his chair and folded his arms in front of his chest. 'I suppose the pair of you think I messed up.'

'Pull your head in, Twig. No one thinks that,' Birdie said, dragging over a chair. 'The team's overworked which is why we were called in. It was Sarge being Sarge. You know that. So, stop sulking and show us the list.'

Twiggy's mouth slid into a mulish frown and he didn't bother to move. 'You think it's because I forgot, don't you?'

Birdie's shoulders stiffened, a flash of worry crossing her face. 'Don't put words in my mouth. And even if you did, it's nothing to be ashamed of.' She paused and stared directly at him. 'Has something happened with your health? You can tell us – we won't breathe a word to Sarge, promise.'

'There's nothing to tell,' Twiggy snapped, as he reached for a piece of paper. 'Here's the list. I'll send you a copy via email as well. That is *if* I can remember how.'

Birdie sighed but her eyes were still filled with concern. Seb realised it was probably best for them to give Twiggy some space. He took the list and straightened his shoulders.

'Thanks, Twiggy. We'll take this back to the office and start working through it.'

'Do what you want. I need to call forensics,' Twiggy muttered as he picked up his phone.

Birdie was silent while they descended the stairs and went out to the car park. It wasn't until Seb started the engine that she finally spoke.

'Did I make a total mess of that?'

Seb wished he could do something to ease the pain in her voice. It wasn't often that Birdie was out of her depth, but when it came to Twiggy's condition, she was finding it difficult to watch from the sidelines and not help.

'Not at all.' Seb turned onto the road and headed towards East Farndon. 'You were trying to look out for your friend.'

She sighed and tapped her foot. 'Yeah, but Twiggy hates when I ask him too much about it. As you witnessed. Before the diagnosis his personality had changed, and he'd become really snappy. I'm worried that might be happening again and that he's getting worse. Maybe I should talk to Sarge and remind him not to ride Twiggy too hard?'

'That could make it worse. How would you feel if Sarge suddenly started treating you like a long-lost friend?'

Birdie gave an involuntary shudder and stopped her tapping. 'You're right. That would be *much* worse. I worry about Twig so much. Maybe I should try talking to him on his own.'

'I think that's a good idea but not while you're discussing the case, because it's clear he's sensitive about people judging his performance.'

'What a mess.' Birdie ran a hand through her red curls and went back to her foot tapping. 'Still, at least we've got Nigel Kaye's list to work on. I feel like this case is going sideways instead of forwards.'

Seb suspected Sergeant Weston did as well, hence his bad temper.

But he also knew that breakthroughs come from being methodical and not following theories that couldn't be backed up. He swung into the driveway as the sun shone down on the slate tiles of Rendall Hall, making them gleam in the brightness.

'Sometimes I forget how gorgeous this place is,' Birdie said, also taking in the sight. 'Have you decided about buying it yet?'

'I spoke to Keira about it this morning and she's keen for me to purchase it. I hadn't realised how much she already considers it her home.'

'I get that.' Birdie nodded. 'Not that I grew up in a place like this. But knowing I always have a room at my parents' house is like a comfort blanket. Mind you... I'm still pleased to have my own place.'

'You don't miss sharing a bathroom then?' Seb teased, knowing this was one of the things she'd hated most, especially when her two younger brothers had been in residence. But instead of answering, Birdie's cheeks turned pink. Seb parked the car and turned to her. 'What's going on? Do you regret buying your apartment?'

'Not at all... but speaking of sharing bathrooms... I've been thinking of asking Melinda to move in with me. We've been dating for almost a year now, and her lease is about to run out.'

'Sounds serious,' Seb said, pleased for his partner. In the past, Birdie rarely spoke about her feelings and emotions but since she'd been dating Melinda, he'd noticed how relaxed she'd become. Of course she still raced down the hallways practising her cricket bowling, and tapped her fingers or toes when she was concentrating, but there wasn't as much restless energy exuding from her.

If she was happy, then he was too.

'It is,' Birdie admitted. 'I'm going to ask her before we leave to go out tonight. We're heading to the movies and then dinner. I might even light a candle or two.'

'Pulling out all the stops.'

'When you know, you know,' Birdie replied in a sage voice before grinning. 'Speaking of which, now that Keira and I are both sorted, we need to find someone for you.'

Seb inwardly groaned. The last time he'd allowed Birdie to set him up on a blind date it had been disastrous, and he wasn't about to repeat the experience. But Seb knew better than to protest out loud, because that would only encourage her. Instead, he climbed out of the car and walked back to the house where Elsa and Bonnie were waiting for him. Besides, they were in the middle of the case and he had more important things to worry about.

FOURTEEN

Friday, 26 June

Birdie frowned as she looked around her apartment. Were the candles too much? When she'd seem them in the shop it had seemed like a lovely romantic gesture, but now that she looked at the ten white, waxy cylinders, her palms began to sweat. She meant what she had told Seb on the drive home.

When you know, you know.

She and Melinda were perfect for each other. Not only was her girlfriend gorgeous and kind, but she was mature and willing to tackle any problems they encountered as they came up. It was refreshing and yet another reason why Birdie wanted to take things to the next level.

Except suddenly the candles seemed silly. After all, what kind of librarian would like naked flames? Candles were book killers. Birdie should have thought of that and got roses instead.

She glanced at her phone but there was no time to nip back to the shop.

Crap. The original plan had been to leave work an hour early, but she and Seb had got caught up researching the new names Twiggy had given them. They hadn't discovered any other connections between the three properties, but her gut told her to keep digging. There was something to be unearthed. She was sure of it.

She swore under her breath again as she blew out the candles and shoved them into a cupboard. The intercom buzzed and nerves made her legs tremble as she pressed for the door to open and let Melinda in. She quickly scanned the room. Her third-floor apartment wasn't large, but it was the perfect size for her and she loved how the late afternoon sun flooded the lounge and bounced off the pale wooden floorboards.

Combined with the blue sofa and scatter cushions, it made the whole place feel warm and cozy. She suddenly spied her cricket shoes poking out from under the armchair so she scooped them up and rushed into the bedroom, shoving them into the wardrobe, which was filled with her unfolded washing and the bits and pieces that she'd put in there earlier.

Birdie darted back to the front door and opened it just as Melinda appeared from the stairwell. Melinda had straight brown hair and a sprinkle of freckles that ran across the bridge of her nose and, as usual, there were several library books poking out of the bag on her shoulder. Birdie made a mental note to buy an extra shelving unit to house her girlfriend's extensive book collection. Grinning she stepped forward and hugged her.

'Hey, how was your day?' Birdie asked, drawing her further into the apartment. They'd first met almost a year ago on a night out and had hit it off immediately.

'Fine,' Melinda said, a little too quickly. 'How about you? Any leads on the case?'

'A few,' Birdie said without going into detail. It was something she'd always done with her friends and family to ensure that no lines were crossed. 'But I'm pleased it's Friday. I can't wait to see this film.'

'Yes, I've heard good things about it,' Melinda said. Her voice was flat and she dipped her head, as if to study something on her skirt. Birdie's skin prickled as she took in Melinda's pale complexion and the way her hands were fidgeting together, as if there was something crawling under her skin.

'Is everything okay?' Birdie immediately asked. She might not talk about her work, but when it came to the rest of her life, she preferred to be upfront. 'Did something happen?'

Melinda let out a watery sigh and tears glistened on her lashes.

Oh, hell.

Birdie's stomach dropped. Something *was* wrong. Suddenly she was pleased she'd put the candles away. There was silence as Melinda fumbled for a tissue and wiped her eyes. Was this about her lease? One of the reasons Birdie had decided to ask her to move in was because she'd visited a few of the one-bedroom apartments Melinda had looked at, and they'd been depressingly small, damp and overpriced.

'Sorry... I didn't mean to ruin our evening. Especially when you've tidied up. I can't even see your cricket shoes.'

'Don't check the wardrobe,' Birdie said, trying to keep her voice light. Then she remembered the candles. 'Or the cupboards.'

She'd hoped the confession would earn her a smile but instead Melinda's face crumpled. Hell. Whatever was going on, it was clearly serious.

'Maybe I should go home?' Melinda wrapped her arms around her torso, as if trying to soothe herself.

Birdie shook her head. 'You can't drive while you're this upset. Tell me what's happened. Are you mad at something I've done?'

'No, of course not.' Melinda sniffed as Birdie led her onto the sofa so they could both sit. 'It's a work thing. My manager told us today that the library is having to let people go. It's last in, first out. Which is me.'

'Mel, I'm so sorry. That sucks. Especially when you're so good at your job. Some of those old sourpusses you work with don't even like reading. Whereas you love books and are always helping customers to find the exact right ones to read. Even me.' Birdie swallowed hard, thinking of the brilliant book that now sat on the bedside table. 'Are you sure it's not just a rumour?'

Melinda sighed, her expression mournful. 'It's not a rumour. We've been hearing whispers about it for ages. The council's trying to cut costs. They think the library's overstaffed and doesn't give enough value to the community.'

'Tell them to go along to the literary quizzes you organise and then they'll see how many people turn up.' Birdie's skin bristled in annoyance on Melinda's behalf. It had been one of the many initiatives she'd started, but apparently it wasn't enough. Birdie's mind flashed back to the empty desks at Market Harborough police station and the reason she and Seb had been brought in.

It seemed that budget cuts were everywhere. Less money and more work to be done.

'I don't think they care about that.' Melinda sighed and squeezed Birdie's hand. 'But thanks for being so understanding. It's been such an awful day.'

'Will you get a redundancy payment?'

'No. That doesn't kick in until you've been somewhere for two years and I've been at the library less than a year. Another reason why it's so easy to get rid of me.' Melinda wiped her eyes again.

'It's their loss,' Birdie said firmly. 'One of the other libraries will snap you up. I'm sure of it.'

Melinda dropped her head, letting her straight hair fall like a curtain across her brow. 'I wish I could share your optimism. But that doesn't mean I won't be applying for anything that comes along.'

'You'll get something. I'm sure of it,' Birdie said, hating to see Melinda so upset.

'I'm worried about signing a new lease in Market Harborough when I won't be earning any money.'

Birdie sucked in a breath. Now was the perfect time to ask.

'Maybe you don't have to sign another lease.'

Melinda frowned. 'What do you mean?'

'I was going to ask you anyway, but with this happening it seems even more like a good idea. Why don't you move in here with me? There's plenty of space for you and it's not like you don't spend a lot of time here anyway.'

Birdie couldn't breathe while watching Melinda process her offer.

'I'm not sure. What if I can't find another job. I can't live here rent free – that's not fair on you.'

'You let me worry about that,' Birdie said, waving her arm dismissively. 'Anyway, you'll find something. Trust me. My gut's never wrong about these things.'

Melinda laughed. 'Okay, I'll trust your gut. Once the lease is up on my place in a few weeks, I'll move in.'

'That's fantastic. Come on, let's go out. We can talk about finding you another job later but, for now, we're going to enjoy ourselves.'

FIFTEEN

Monday, 29 June

There was no sign of Keira stirring from her bed first thing Monday morning, so Seb fed and walked both dogs. He'd hardly seen his daughter all weekend and had planned to catch up with her at breakfast, but before he could even crack an egg, Birdie texted to say there'd been another burglary and they were to meet Twiggy at the scene. She'd pick him up shortly.

Another burglary.

Seb rubbed a hand through his hair, trying not to imagine Sergeant Weston's grim face at the news. Soon the media would link the burglaries and go into overdrive. The headlines would go on for weeks until they were able to solve the case. The fact that they'd made relatively little progress would also be pounced on.

With no weekend plans, Seb had spent most of his time in the office, researching the numerous names on each of the lists provided by the victims. He'd paid particular attention to the journalists and photographers that were on Nigel Kaye's list.

Isaac Cross hadn't been there in person, but he may have known one of the visitors, and that was what Seb had spent time researching. Unfortunately, he found nothing.

The crunch of tyres alerted Seb to Birdie arriving. He gave the dogs a quick pat goodbye and pocketed his phone.

The sun was already bright despite it being early, and he squinted as he climbed into Birdie's car. She turned and beamed at him, her eyes bright. Did that mean everything had gone to plan with Melinda? He didn't want to ask. She'd tell him when she was ready.

'What do you know about the burglary?' he asked.

'It's in Sibbertoft and they took a garden sculpture worth one million pounds. Can you believe it? One million pounds for something you keep in the garden? It beats me. Well, each to their own.'

'Did Twiggy give you the name of the property's owner?'

'Eleanor and Martin Blackwood. They're in the building business. Have you heard of them?'

Seb nodded. 'They focus on sustainable building materials including precast concrete and recycled steel. They only work with builders who follow sustainable practices, including building carbon-neutral houses that are warm and healthy, affordable, and are built close to schools and public transport,' he said, reciting what he'd read. 'I researched them last year when I was seeking quotes for the replacement of Sarah's roof.'

'Business must be booming if they can afford to have a statue like that,' Birdie said.

'Their garden's almost as well-known as the business,' Seb responded. 'Part of the Blackwoods' ethos around sustainable building is that there should be no impact on the local environment. They've created themed areas in the garden that are based around different aspects of biodiversity and have been featured in several magazines. I believe that Eleanor is the gardener of the couple and she conducts tours of their garden several times a year.'

'Great.' Birdie groaned. 'So the thieves could have simply seen the sculpture in a magazine or done a garden tour. Whatever happened to hiding away your treasures?'

'Some collectors do that, but others believe that art is to be shared and experienced,' Seb said before frowning. 'Did Twiggy tell you anything about the statue?'

'It's a Jeff Smart. Even I've heard of him, and his work isn't exactly hidable. Who'd risk stealing something like that?'

It was a good question. Smart was best known for his stylised stainless-steel animals. Not something that blended into the background.

Seb retrieved his phone to do a quick search and it didn't take him long to find a photograph of the sculpture in question. It was a rabbit made from steel that had been rusted and had flowers growing out of it.

'It's a six-foot metal rabbit covered in flowers,' Seb told her and closed his phone.

'Wow... and that's worth a million pounds. By the way, how did you go with Nigel Kaye's list?' Birdie turned onto the narrow road leading to Sibbertoft.

'I found nothing of use. Kaye didn't use caterers and I couldn't connect Cross to anyone who was there.'

'I suppose that means we should park him for now. At least you did something useful.' She glanced in his direction, grinning. 'Seeing as you're not going to ask, my weekend was great, thanks.'

'I was waiting for you to tell me,' Seb answered truthfully.

'Honestly, you drive me crazy sometimes. Anyone else couldn't wait to hear the news. I have good and bad news. I'll start with the bad. Unfortunately, Melinda's going to lose her job at the library. But the good news is, I asked her to move in with me and she said yes.'

'That's marvellous, Birdie. I'm pleased for you both.'

'Initially Mel wasn't sure because she doesn't want to cadge off me if she can't get a job straight away, but that's ridiculous. It's not like I can't afford to live in my place so I'm not desperate for her contribution.'

Birdie turned onto the drive leading to the Blackwoods' property and Seb admired the thriving gardens. Unlike the tidy formal gardens that so many large houses had, these were built around biodiversity, with streams and pathways cutting through them. Rusted steel drums and wheelbarrows that were now part of the environment were filled with pollinating flowers and local shrubs, while the rewilded fields beyond were filled with clover, cow parsley, foxgloves and cornflowers.

Next to him Birdie let out a soft gasp.

'Impressive, isn't it?' Seb said, admiring the way the landscape shifted and changed to show each separate theme. Beyond the garden was a high bricked wall, and small solar panels gleamed in the sunlight, suggesting that might be how the security system and garden lights were powered.

'It's gorgeous. It shows that they really walk their talk. Or... should I say that they grow their talk.' Birdie said, laughing. 'Maybe you could do something similar with the front lawn of Rendall Hall.'

'Maybe,' Seb agreed as Birdie parked the car outside a modern, two-storey house that had been cut into the side of a sloping hill, with thick slabs of concrete and wood seamlessly weaving together, almost making it part of the landscape. It was the style that Blackwood Industries was known for. Twiggy appeared around the side of the house as they climbed out of the car.

'Thanks for getting here so quickly,' the officer said, with no hint of his usual banter. Either Sergeant Weston had given him another dressing-down or the stress of the case was getting to him. 'The Blackwoods are inside. I wanted to wait until you got here before we question them. We've already found the jammer.'

'Where was it?' Seb asked.

'In the garden. I'll show you.' Twiggy gestured for them to follow along a path made of railway sleepers and through to the side of the stream. A glass wall stood between the path and the stream and behind it was an empty plinth. 'It's hooked up to the security system, but of course the jammer prevented it from going off.'

Seb scanned the area, searching for footprints, but the path was covered in old leaves and mulch. 'Have forensics arrived?'

'Yes. They've already checked this area and are now searching for somewhere a van and trailer might have accessed the property.'

'In that case, let's go inside to speak to the Blackwoods,' Birdie said, her sharp eyes sweeping the area before marching back towards the house.

Martin and Eleanor Blackwood were waiting by the front door and Twiggy made the introductions before they were led inside into a large, open-plan kitchen/dining/sitting room. Light flooded through the bi-fold doors and it was pleasant and relaxing.

'Would you like a cup of tea?' Eleanor asked, as she gestured for them to sit on the two navy, corduroy sofas in the sitting area. She was in her forties, with long dark hair tied back at her neck. Her skin was tanned, suggesting she spent most of her time outside in the garden. Martin was tall and lean with calloused hands. Seb had read that he'd been a builder, and was distressed at the amount of wastage in the sector. It was what prompted his business venture.

'No thanks,' Birdie said. 'We need to get on. Please could you tell us when you noticed the statue had gone?'

'It was yesterday evening,' Martin explained. 'We'd been out all day at a sustainability expo. I gave a speech and sat on a couple of panels. They're excellent for our profile but exhausting. When we got home, Eleanor and I went for a walk through the gardens.'

'It's our way of relaxing.' Eleanor reached for her husband's hand and squeezed it. 'At first we were both so shocked we thought we were hallucinating. I mean, who'd steal a giant rabbit? There was no sign of the security glass being tampered with, or that the system had been taken offline.'

Seb nodded. A virtual carbon copy of the other thefts.

'You have other sculptures in the garden. Are any of them of greater value than the one stolen?' Seb asked.

'We have four others and all of them are worth more than the

Smart.' Martin raked a hand through his dishevelled hair. 'That's what we couldn't understand. Why not steal one of them?'

'Are they all insured?' Birdie asked.

'Yes. It was our insurance company that insisted on the glass barrier,' Eleanor explained. She let out a small sob. 'It was the first piece of art I bought for the garden. I can't believe this has happened.'

'How long have you had it?'

'We bought it five years ago. Even if someone was targeting it, why wait so long to take it?'

Yet another question they didn't have an answer for.

'We're unsure at this point in the investigation. Was anything stolen from the house?' Seb asked.

'No. We've searched thoroughly,' Eleanor replied.

'We'll still be checking for fingerprints, just in case,' Twiggy added, his voice sounding almost defiant.

'Can we circle back to the expo?' Birdie cut in. 'Where was it and why did you both attend?'

'It was in Northampton. We went together, so Eleanor could network while I was on stage,' Martin answered.

An hour round trip, plus the time they'd spent at the expo. It gave plenty of time for the burglars to act.

'Mrs Blackwood, were you also on the programme?'

'No. I was asked to participate but didn't have time to prepare anything because I was so busy prior to it.' Eleanor increased the grip on her husband's large hand.

Birdie tensed, her eyes bright as she studied Eleanor. 'Why were you so busy?'

'Because Saturday was our annual summer open day. We run one each season. We not only fundraise for a local climate action charity, but also aim to educate people and show them that creating eco-friendly gardens isn't nearly as daunting as they might think.'

Seb and Birdie exchanged a glance and Twiggy let out a groan.

Once again it meant that anyone could have got close enough to the security system to plant the jamming device without being detected.

'Is that a problem?' Martin asked, picking up on their concern.

'It means we have a large suspect pool,' Birdie explained. 'Do you have a list of everyone who attended?'

The couple looked worried as Eleanor shook her head. 'No. People pay at the gate but we don't give receipts. It would be ironic to hand out tickets when we're trying to reduce our carbon footprint,' she explained.

Seb sighed. It wasn't the answer he'd been hoping for. 'Do you know how many people attended?'

'Oh, yes. As part of the ticket price, we provide an organic, locally sourced afternoon tea, so we cap the number of visitors to two hundred and fifty.'

Next to him, Birdie stiffened. 'Which caterers do you use?'

'Slow Harvest from Lutterworth. We always use them,' Eleanor responded then frowned. 'You don't think they're behind it?'

'It's important we get an accurate picture of who was at the event,' Seb said, not being drawn into answering the question. 'Please will you email me a list of everyone who was working on the day, both catering and other staff?' He held out his card, which she took.

'I'll have to contact Slow Harvest for the catering staff but I do have names of the volunteers who worked on the gate and also acted as guides, which I'll email to you straight away. Once the caterer gets back to me, I'll forward their list.'

'Thank you. Could you also add to the list the names of visitors you did recognise. I assume there were some celebrities there?'

'Yes, of course. Do you think there's a chance you'll find the statue? It has such sentimental value to us.'

'We'll do our best,' Seb promised, not wanting to give them false hope.

The three of them said their goodbyes and headed to their cars.

'I need to get back to the station but I'll call you as soon as anything comes back from forensics.' Twiggy fumbled for his keys and unlocked his car door. 'So don't go thinking I've forgotten.'

Birdie rolled her eyes. 'Let it go, Twig. You know we won't think that. We need your full focus on the case and this isn't helping.'

SIXTEEN

Monday, 29 June

'What about over there?' Birdie pointed to a shaded clump of trees down the road from the Blackwoods' property. 'The thieves could have waited until Eleanor and Martin left for the expo and that way they could be sure that both went. The expo promo would have listed Martin as being there, but not Eleanor.'

'It's possible. We'll ask Twiggy to extend the search around the perimeter.'

'Speaking of Twiggy, do you think it's weird that he's still so touchy about his memory? I'm wondering if it's getting worse and he doesn't want to admit it in case he's asked to stop work. Or be chained to his desk, which is as bad, if not worse, as I can vouch.'

'It can't be easy for him. But the fact he's aware of it is a good thing,' Seb pointed out.

The tightness around Birdie's jaw loosened. 'Yes, you're right. I didn't think of that.' She sighed. 'I still can't believe someone had the audacity to steal such a huge sculpture. It seems so risky.'

'It would have needed extensive planning. I think we should assume, therefore, they knew beforehand that Eleanor was going to the expo. She could've mentioned it to someone.'

'Yeah. I mean it's not like it was some state secret.'

Birdie sped up, as the road cleared ahead of them. They spent the rest of the journey going over what they'd learnt. It was almost ten-thirty by the time they pulled into Rendall Hall and climbed out of the car.

'Unless you give me coffee immediately, I won't be able to function.' Birdie made a beeline for the kitchen.

'We can't have that,' Seb replied, stepping in behind her.

Elsa was curled up in her bed asleep, while Bonnie was next to her, in her own bed, one paw hanging over the side and the other wrapped around the large stuffed penguin Birdie had bought her as a welcome-to-the-family gift. Keira was sitting at the long wooden table nursing a mug of coffee. Her hair was rumpled and she was in her pyjamas.

'Woah.' Birdie came to a halt and widened her eyes. 'You look like you've been on a bender.'

'Stop talking so loudly,' Keira groaned and took another gulp from her mug. 'I didn't even drink much... but it was a late night.'

'Tell your Auntie Birdie all about it.' She pulled up a chair and rested her arms on the table. 'Come on. Spill the beans.'

'You're so melodramatic.' Keira gave a playful roll of her eyes and put down her mug. 'I went to the pub with Zara and we ended up at someone's house. It was very low key, I swear.'

'Way to ruin my chances of living vicariously through you.' Birdie tutted and sat back in the chair.

'Sorry to be such a bore.' Keira yawned and rubbed her eyes. 'Where have you two been?'

'I left you a voice note,' Seb said, frowning. He never interfered with Keira's social life but it wasn't like her to sleep in or not check her messages. Then he caught himself. She'd just finished her second year at university and had every right to kick back and celebrate. 'There was another burglary yesterday.'

'Oh, no. That's terrible. Did they steal more artwork?'

'A Jeff Smart sculpture worth over one million pounds,' Seb said.

'Jeff Smart?' Keira's fatigue fell away and her face drained of colour. 'You're kidding?'

'That's not your dad's MO, as you well know,' Birdie quipped. She appeared to study Keira more intently. 'Why? What's going on?'

'Sorry, it's just so weird. I was at this open garden tour on Saturday and saw a Jeff Smart sculpture. It was of a giant rabbit. So amazing.'

'You were at the Blackwoods' on Saturday?' Seb sucked in a sharp breath, not quite managing to keep the incredulity from his voice. 'Why didn't you tell me?'

'I don't have to tell you where I am every minute of the day. Besides, you were busy working on the case.' Keira's confusion turned to annoyance and she folded her arms.

She was right. Yet he'd thought their relationship was one in which they did mention their plans for the day.

Clearly not.

Birdie went over to them. 'I think your dad's just surprised, since garden tours don't seem like your regular weekend thing. Not counting giant Jeff Smart sculptures.'

Keira threw up her hands. 'Okay, fine. So I don't usually get off on wandering around gardens, but it sounded fun when Zara invited me – and it was.'

'Each to their own,' Birdie retorted. 'Tell us what you did there and whether you noticed anyone suspicious hanging around the sculpture?'

'I wasn't paying much attention,' Keira admitted. 'We were having such a laugh watching all the society women schmooze up to Eleanor Blackwood like they were best friends. Loads of them were in high heels and then couldn't walk on the paths. I was pleased I had on my trusty Docs.'

'Eleanor estimated there were two hundred and fifty people there during the whole day. Was that your take?' Birdie asked.

Keira nodded. 'That sounds about right. We were there from around twelve until three. There was a lovely terrace set up with teas, coffees and all this amazing organic baking. So good.'

'Are you sure you didn't see anyone casing the area, perhaps checking for other ways onto the property?' Birdie pushed.

'No.' Keira shook her head then clutched at her temple, as if suddenly remembering her headache. 'But I did take photos. Do you want to see?' She glanced at Seb in a way that suggested she'd calmed down from her earlier show of temper.

'Yes, please. I was going to ask you to check for any photos people had posted online.'

'I can do that,' Keira agreed and picked up her phone. She thumbed the screen for several moments before bringing up a folder. 'I'll forward these so you can see them on the computer.'

'Thanks,' Seb said.

'Now, back to Zara. Why did she want to go to the open garden?' Birdie asked.

'*Why did she want to go?*' Keira blinked, as if confused by the question. 'I'd have thought that was obvious. Because she's passionate about sustainable living. She's visited the garden several times in the past and always films content while she's there. It's her way of helping fight climate change. The media was there and Zara needs to be seen at important events.'

'How convenient,' Birdie muttered.

Keira flinched. 'Do you think she had another reason for being there?'

Birdie sucked in a breath and gave Seb a concerned look.

It was clear they were both thinking the same thing. Zara had now been at two of the victims' houses. Birdie opened her mouth, as if she was going to push Keira on it, but he quickly shook his head, not wanting to upset his daughter.

It was also a reminder of why it was dangerous to get personally involved with anyone connected to an active case.

'What do *you* think?' Seb asked in a diplomatic voice. It was a conciliatory question and the fire in Keira's eyes dimmed.

'I think it's ridiculous. Zara's so straightlaced. At school she wouldn't miss a single class. She's doing amazing things with her career. There's no way she'd be involved in any art burglaries. You do believe me, don't you?'

'Of course we do,' Birdie quickly said. 'But she might have noticed something that would help. Especially if she often goes to these kinds of events. If there was someone acting strangely, for example.'

Understanding filled Keira's eyes and she lost her defensive pose. 'Sorry, I should've thought of that. Do you want me to interview her?'

Definitely not.

Seb shook his head. 'We need to keep a clear divide between working the case and you being friends with a potential witness. Zara mustn't be aware of our involvement. Birdie and I will speak to her. She shouldn't connect you to me because you use Austin, your mum's surname.'

'Good point. I swear I haven't mentioned anything about the investigation.'

'We believe you,' Seb assured her.

'I hate to break it to you both, but even without the name, you're both ridiculously tall and have more than a passing resemblance to one another.' Birdie waved her hand in Seb's direction. 'Plus, you went to every school function you could, so Zara might recognise you from them.'

Keira chewed her lip as if considering it, then nodded. 'Birdie's right. You don't exactly blend in.'

Seb pinched the bridge of his nose, accepting the truth of the statement. He could hardly counsel his daughter to not put the case at risk, and then do something that could result in being equally problematic.

'Fine. Birdie, you can go alone.'

'Right, that's settled. Keira, please text me Zara's details? Birdie said.

'Doing it now,' Keira replied as she tapped her phone.

A moment later Birdie's phone pinged. 'Thanks. I'll ask

Twiggy to come with me and follow up with him on getting the area around the outside of the house searched.'

'I'm going for a shower and will then start looking through social media for photos of the day.' Keira darted out of the room, seeming more like her usual self.

Once she was gone, Birdie started scrolling through something on her phone.

'What are you looking for?' Seb asked.

'I'm going through one of ZaraH's social media accounts to get a feel for what we'll be walking into.'

'Thank you for not pushing it with Keira,' Seb said.

'There's no point making things awkward,' Birdie said, holding out her phone for Seb to see a series of glamorous photos.

Zara was shorter than Keira, with blonde hair and tanned skin. She appeared to be always photo-ready, and had the same smile as she stood in front of historic buildings, country fields and even when she was visiting a recycling plant. Seb recognised her from his visits to the school, and nothing about her screamed evil genius.

'Make sure you're careful not to say anything that connects you back to Keira,' he said.

'Ye of little faith.' Birdie rolled her eyes. 'This isn't my first rodeo. After I've called Twiggy, I'll contact Zara. I'd prefer it if we can go in as private investigators rather than the police, in case it freaks her out.'

'She might not be up, considering the late night she had.'

Birdie grinned. 'Then let me fix that. She's already missed most of the morning, so really I'm doing her a favour.'

SEVENTEEN

Monday, 29 June

'Okay, just say it,' Twiggy commanded as Birdie pulled out of the police station and headed towards Leicester, where Zara lived.

'Say what?' Birdie frowned and sneaked a glance in his direction. His arms were folded across his chest and his jaw was tight, which was at odds with his normally casual expression.

'You've been watching me like a hawk ever since we started this case.' He slumped back in the car seat. 'I'm surprised you haven't called Evie yet for an update on my blood tests.'

Damn. Was it that obvious?

Guilt caught in her throat and she swallowed.

'Twig, I'm sorry. I don't mean to make you feel uncomfortable but please tell me how you *really* are. Even if it's not the news I want to hear. You know I won't blab to anyone. Promise.'

He let out a breath and twisted slightly in his seat so he was facing her. She forced herself to keep her eyes on the road, but the pressure in her throat increased and she tightened her grip on the steering wheel.

'Some days are harder than others,' he finally admitted. 'I keep pretending that I only forget things when I'm busy or stressed but the truth is that sometimes they just disappear from my mind. I'm working really hard to fight it but... but it's exhausting.'

'That sucks.' Tears prickled the corners of Birdie's eyes but she forced them back. She'd long ago promised herself not to make Twiggy's journey harder by having him worry about how she was coping with it.

'Yeah, you're telling me,' he said sounding more like his usual self. 'The reason I get cranky when people fuss over me is because I don't want Evie and the girls to worry. That's why I must keep working. Because otherwise we might have to sell the house and I couldn't do that to them. I can't let them down.'

'You could *never* let them down. But I hope you're not keeping things from them. If you need support, you must let them know.'

At this he let out a soft laugh. 'Don't worry about that. Evie makes you look like an amateur. But she also knows that I need my space and don't want to talk about it every second of every day.'

There was pain in his voice and Birdie again pushed back her worries. Twiggy was telling her how she could support him, so it was the least she could do. She straightened her shoulders and merged into the traffic.

'Well, if you don't want to talk about it so much, then you'd better stop winding up Sarge. Otherwise, you might find yourself twiddling your thumbs at home on the couch. Then where would you be?'

'Winding up Sarge is my favourite pastime,' he responded. 'But I suppose for *you* I could try and mend my ways. Now, what do we know about this influencer?'

Birdie, pleased they were back on good terms, gave him a quick rundown on Zara as they pulled into an upmarket apartment block in the centre of town. It was a modern building with floor-to-ceiling glass doors that led into a foyer with a long reception desk running across the marble-tiled floor. To one side was a modern seating area that looked out onto a courtyard full of ornamental trees and walking paths.

A uniformed concierge stood behind the desk, his eyes fixed on them.

Twiggy held out his warrant card and gave Zara's name. After a quick phone call announcing their presence, the man directed them to the elevator, instructing them to go up to level eight.

'I'll take the stairs, thanks,' Birdie said, patting Twiggy's arm. 'Wait for me before you go inside.'

'I do remember your lift aversion. It's not that long since we worked together.'

His eyes twinkled. A clear sign he'd forgiven her. She poked out her tongue, the way she always used to, then disappeared into the stairwell.

She was out of breath by the time she stepped out into a spacious hall with striped, thick-pile carpet on the floor and expensive-looking prints hanging on the walls.

The apartment door was open and a smiling Zara was waiting for them.

Up close she was shorter than she appeared in her photos and videos, and her blonde hair was pulled back in a ponytail, while her body was swamped in an oversized beige tracksuit, making her look more like a regular person.

'You took the stairs?' Zara's gaze swept over Birdie's trim figure. 'My PT's always telling me to do that. It's great for a quick cardio hit.'

'PT?' Twiggy frowned.

'Personal trainer,' Zara explained, giving a rueful grin. 'Sorry, I hate it when other people use jargon and here I am doing the same thing.'

'We appreciate you making the time to meet us,' Twiggy said, showing his warrant card. 'This is Birdie; she's a consultant who's working with us on a case.'

'Nice to meet you.' Zara gave them both a warm smile. Her teeth were bright white and perfectly straight. They had to be veneers. 'Come in.'

'Thanks. It's nice to—'

She broke off as Zara led them into a huge apartment with high ceilings and long glass doors that looked out onto the city. It would be amazing at nighttime with all the lights. It must have cost a packet. Amazing for a twenty-year-old. At that age, Birdie had still been living in her childhood bedroom, eating pot noodles and hoping her rust bucket car wouldn't break down.

'This is a lovely apartment,' Twiggy said, covering for Birdie's stunned silence.

'Isn't it just. Sometimes I have to pinch myself, to realise that it's really mine. Let's sit down.' She led them to two long velvet sofas.

'We're investigating a series of burglaries and it appears you were at events held by two of the victims.'

'Two?' Zara's brow wrinkled and she tucked her bare feet under her legs, so that she was sitting in a lotus position. 'I read about what happened to Cynthia Thornton but I had no idea there was another burglary. That's dreadful.'

'There have been several,' Birdie said, retrieving her notebook from her pocket. 'The latest was yesterday at Martin and Eleanor Blackwood's property. A Jeff Smart sculpture of a rabbit was taken.'

'That's impossible.' Zara stared at them blankly. 'I was there on Saturday and saw it. It was stunning… but how could someone even attempt to steal it? It was massive.'

Birdie ignored the question and continued. 'Why did you go to the open day? Are you interested in gardening?' As she spoke she looked around at the several pot plants dotting the room. But they had an artificial look about them.

If Zara had green fingers, she was hiding it well.

'I adore both the Blackwoods. Eleanor's such a leading light in the sustainability movement. She talks about how we can all reclaim our environment and create more sustainable ways to live from the land. We've caused so much damage over the years and it's up to my generation to do something about it.'

'Eleanor mentioned they do four open gardens a year. Was this the first time you attended?'

'Oh, no. I've been going for the last couple of years. I've followed her on social media for a long time. She's one of the reasons I became a climate activist.'

If the Blackwoods bought the sculpture five years ago, it meant Zara would have seen it numerous times. As would anyone else who'd attended one of the previous open days.

'Did you go alone, or did you take a photographer and makeup artist?'

She laughed. 'I wish. Unfortunately, my budget doesn't stretch that far.' She reached up for her phone and gave it a wave. 'I do all my own filming and editing. The only person with me was an old school friend.'

'Can we have their name and contact details, please,' Birdie said, knowing it was important to not appear to cut corners.

'Sure. It's Keira Austin.' Zara rattled off Keira's number without looking it up. Then shook her head. 'I still can't believe the Smart was stolen. It was such a statement about how we interact with the environment.'

'Yes indeed,' Twiggy said in a dry voice before flipping a page of his own notebook. 'Could you talk us through the day?'

Zara nodded. Her account was almost identical to the one Keira had given Birdie. It didn't put them any further ahead in the investigation.

'The Blackwoods' event was pay at the door, but Cynthia Thornton's was by invitation only. Is it usual for you to have received an invitation to that sort of event?'

'Yes,' she admitted, almost looking embarrassed as she gestured at a neat pile of invitations on heavy, quality card, with gilt edging. 'I get invited to many more events than I can attend.'

'How do you decide which ones to accept?' Birdie asked, curious.

'It all comes down to what the event is for. A lot of them are just restaurant openings or film premiers where they want as many celebs as possible to walk the red carpet. Not that I'm considered an A-list celebrity by any stretch of the imagination. I'm not interested in those events. I only attend those I'm passionate about. My dad died of cancer a couple of years ago...'

'Which is why you agreed to attend Cynthia Thornton's fundraiser,' Birdie finished off. 'Did anyone go with you?'

'No, I was on my own.'

'Did you go inside the house?' Twiggy asked.

'No. I stayed in the garden.' Zara stretched out her legs. 'Sorry I'm not being much help.'

'This is very useful,' Birdie assured her. 'Because you go to so many events, did you notice anyone who didn't seem to fit in?'

'No.' Zara shook her blonde ponytail then looked upwards. 'Actually, come to think of it. There was a guy who made me think he shouldn't be there.'

Birdie and Twiggy both straightened.

'In what way?' she asked.

'He kept disappearing into the house and each time he came out he looked... well... shifty. I feel bad saying that because it sounds so judgy. I'd hate to get him in trouble when for all I know he donated thousands of pounds and was just going to the loo.'

'Was he wearing a chef's uniform?' Birdie's skin prickled as her mind went to Isaac Cross, who was still the only real connection they had between the events. Although Eleanor Blackwood had used a different catering company, Cross could have attended.

'No. He was in black trousers and a blue shirt. He was about six feet tall with red hair... maybe the same colour as yours... and green eyes.'

Birdie let out a reluctant sigh and made a note of the description. It definitely wasn't Isaac Cross. But it was still useful.

'He might not be guilty of anything, but if he can help us with the investigation, it will make our job easier,' Birdie explained. 'What about the Blackwoods' open day. Did you see him there?'

'No. I would have remembered.'

'Have you ever been to Nigel Kaye or Susannah Limbrick's house?' Birdie asked.

'No. But I love Nigel Kaye's art and Susannah Limbrick's my queen. I adore her recipes and already have her new cookbook. It's so lit. Wait...' Zara paused. 'Have they been burgled too?' She raised a hand to cover her mouth.

'Yes, but please don't discuss this with anyone else,' Birdie said. 'It might hamper the investigation.'

'Of course, I understand,' Zara said as an alarm beeped from the watch on her wrist. 'Sorry, I need to start getting ready for another function. Unless you want me to cancel. I can if you want.'

Birdie shook her head. Apart from the description Zara had given them, she clearly didn't know anything about the burglaries, though at least she was trying to be helpful, which was more than they often got when interviewing people.

'No, it's fine.' Birdie stood and pulled out a business card, but instead of following suit, Twiggy leant over and tapped a finger on the pile of invitations for upcoming events.

'Actually,' Twiggy said, his tone more serious than usual. 'Can you give us a list of all the invitations you've received in the last month and let us know which events you'll be attending.'

Zara drew her brows together. 'How will that help? You don't think someone's following me do you?'

'No,' Birdie quickly assured her, while giving Twiggy an impressed glance. 'But it might help us predict where they'll strike next. It seems you're on a lot of mailing lists.'

'It's an occupational hazard. I work hard to be seen. I have a million followers but, these days, brands want more. I'm considered a macro-influencer but the ones who get the massive deals are considered mega-influencers. That's where the real clout is.'

'By clout you mean money?' Birdie asked.

Zara gave a fierce shake of her head. 'It's not all about the money. It's about changing behaviour. That's what I want my legacy to be. Anyway, I'll get that list to you as soon as I can. I enter every invite into a spreadsheet – so I can look back at those I've attended or declined – so it's easy to forward.'

'Thank you,' Birdie said as Zara escorted them to the door.

Once they were outside, Birdie turned to Twiggy and patted his arm.

'Nice work, that was a mic drop moment if I've ever seen one.'

'Mic drop?' He wrinkled his brow. 'Now you're sounding like my daughters.'

He gave her a familiar Twiggy-like smile and the last of her worries about him faded. At least for now she knew her friend was still capable of doing his job in the same way he always had.

EIGHTEEN

Monday, 29 June

'I can't believe the number of events Zara's invited to,' Keira said an hour later as she held up the printed list of upcoming events Zara had emailed through. 'No wonder she has to turn down so many.'

Seb nodded, pleased that Twiggy's idea had worked. Getting the list of upcoming events had given them something concrete to work with, enabling them to anticipate rather than react.

'Poor thing, having to scoff down caviar and champagne every afternoon,' Twiggy said, a crumb from the scone he'd just consumed sticking to his chin.

'It's not like that,' Keira bristled.

'He's teasing. Ignore it,' Birdie cut in, shooting Twiggy a warning look.

Seb was grateful to Birdie. Keira wasn't yet used to Twiggy's particular brand of humour.

'Oh. Sorry.' Keira blinked, sounding uncertain.

'Let me take a look at the list,' Seb said, walking round to the other side of the kitchen table where they were finishing off a late lunch. 'If we can predict where they might strike next, it will give us the advantage.'

'I'm surprised you're not invited to some of these, Clifford,' Twiggy said, brushing away the crumb from his chin and leaning over to study the piece of paper. 'A lecture on how to keep your own beehives sounds right up your alley.'

Seb raised an eyebrow but didn't comment. He had, in fact, received invitations to several of these events but hadn't accepted. Such gatherings had never appealed to him, regardless of the subject matter.

'Can you see any that look like potential targets?' Birdie asked, feeling hopeful.

'A few are standing out.' Seb circled a name on the list. 'I think we should start here. It's one that Zara has indicated she'll be attending.'

Birdie frowned and read it out loud:

'Heritage and High Tea. This is a not-to-be-missed opportunity to view Leonard and Rose Castle's collection of Chelsea Porcelain Factory ceramics. The collection has been thirty years in the making and they will be joined by the esteemed expert Tim Richards, who will take us through the fascinating history of the much sought-after pieces. After, guests will be invited to stay for a charming afternoon tea. All proceeds will go to The Eco Friends Trust.'

Twiggy pulled a face and even Keira gave her father a sceptical look. 'Pottery? That sounds a bit dull. I wonder why Zara's going to that one?'

'Probably because they're raising money for a local environmental group,' Birdie pointed out. She turned back to Seb. 'Do you really think our thieves might be interested in this pottery?'

Seb nodded. 'Some of the pieces in this collection are incredibly rare.'

'And yet I've never heard of it,' Twiggy replied with a shrug.

'Neither have I,' Birdie admitted. 'What makes it so fancy?'

'The Chelsea Porcelain Factory was the first important porcelain producer in England. They specialised in soft paste and were set up in 1744 to compete with the likes of Meissen and Sèvres. At the time a lot of money was spent on luxury items and they wanted their share. Prince William, the Duke of Cumberland, was a huge supporter from the start. The pottery's highly collectable and Leonard and Rose Castle are very well-known.'

Twiggy frowned. 'The other burglaries were more than a million pounds. Are you telling me a bunch of cups and saucers are worth that much?'

'One particular vase sold for a quarter of a million pounds recently. The Castle collection has over two hundred pieces and is renowned,' Seb replied, drumming his fingers on the table. 'We can't know for certain they're the next target, but they could be and we need to act.'

'I agree,' Birdie said. 'We'll interview them and check if any devices are already on the property.'

'We'll also request a list of people who visited the property last week, and ask to be added to the guest list,' Seb continued.

'You're assuming they'll be willing to work with us. Especially as we have no evidence they're potential victims,' Birdie said.

'I'd be surprised if they refused,' Seb replied. 'The Castles have spent over thirty years building their collection; ensuring its security will be a priority. If we're all in agreement, I'll call and arrange a visit.'

'Ready and waiting,' Birdie replied. 'Twiggy, if we get the okay from the Castles, can we leave it to you to arrange surveillance? We need photos and car reg of every vehicle entering the grounds.'

Twiggy winced. 'That's going to cost a bomb and we don't even know if they're the next target. God knows what Sarge will say.'

'We don't know they're *not*,' Keira reminded him. 'I think I should go as well.'

Seb's stomach lurched. 'Absolutely not.' The words came out harder than he'd intended.

'If Zara sees you speaking to us, the whole thing will be blown,' Birdie added. 'It's way too risky.'

'Yes, but I won't be going *with* you two. Zara's already invited me to several upcoming events saying that I make even the biggest yawn fest fun. She didn't say which ones they are specifically but did mention one of them was next Sunday.'

'I don't like it.' Seb's jaw tightened. 'It's one thing to spend time with her, but you might find it a lot more difficult if we're in the room and you have to pretend that we've never met.'

'It's called character acting, Dad. Think of how much more we can cover if the three of us are there. I promise you can trust me.' Keira's eyes were bright and it was clear she was desperate to prove her worth.

'This isn't about trust,' Seb said, even though as the words left his mouth he knew they weren't entirely true. He did trust Keira. What he didn't trust was the situation itself. The variables he couldn't control and the people whose intentions remained unknown. What if she inadvertently kept looking at Birdie and was observed? That could put her at risk. He'd spent many years witnessing what criminals did when they felt threatened. They didn't issue polite warnings. They eliminated problems. 'I'm not prepared to have you rushing into danger.'

'It's not going to be dangerous though, is it? You and Birdie will be there and Twiggy will have a surveillance team with him. I'll be as safe as houses. Please, Dad. Please.'

Birdie caught his eye and gave him a cautious nod. 'It's up to you, but I think it'll be okay. Also, you don't need to ignore each other, just don't act like you're with me, Seb. You could have been invited there anyway.'

What Birdie said made sense.

'Okay. But you must promise to be careful. Don't tell Zara that I'll be there, though. We can act surprised to see each other if necessary.'

Keira let out a small squeal and hugged him. 'Thanks Dad. I'm going to call Zara now and ask what we are meant to be doing on Sunday. It might not even be this event. Plus, it will be good to hear what she thinks about your visit today. If she tells me, that is.'

Once Keira had disappeared into the garden, Seb headed over

to the window watching his daughter as she held the phone to her ear.

He'd made the right decision. He was almost certain of it.

Almost.

'What did you and Keira find out while we were gone?' Birdie asked, cutting into his thoughts.

He turned back to face her. 'Not much. Keira went through social media and found plenty of photographs from the Blackwoods' open garden, but nothing's standing out.'

Birdie frowned. 'We might have to go through them again. Zara remembered someone at Cynthia Thornton's fundraiser. She described him and said he was acting suspiciously. But she didn't see him at the Blackwoods'.'

'Interesting,' Seb said after Birdie gave him the description. 'Keira's already managed to get photos for most of the guests at the fundraiser, so I'll ask her to check if there's anyone who matches this man.'

'I'm impressed she managed to do that.' Birdie whistled. 'I must admit that's the kind of work I find tedious. Let's hope it pays off.'

'It certainly makes my life easier,' Twiggy said as his phone rang. He studied the screen and got to his feet. 'It's forensics. *Yeah... what have you got?*'

Seb and Birdie exchanged a hopeful look as Twiggy walked to one end of the kitchen and then pivoted and paced in the other direction. Most of the conversation was one-sided with the occasional 'uh-huh' and 'what else do we know'. Finally, he finished the call and pocketed his phone as Keira walked back in.

She gave them a thumbs up. 'It is the Castles' high tea. Zara's replied to the invite and included a plus one. So, I'm officially going.' Then she looked at Twiggy, whose eyes were bright. 'Do we have more news?'

'I hope so. Twiggy's been speaking to forensics,' Birdie replied.

Keira's eyes lit up. 'Excellent. My favourite subject. Now I feel like we can really get started on this investigation. What did they say?'

'They've confirmed the jammers at each house were home-made, which is what we suspected. Like Clifford, they've been trying to trace the parts but have hit a brick wall,' Twiggy explained.

'Anything else?' Birdie demanded.

'I'm getting to it. One of the devices had a partial fingerprint. We've put it through the database but haven't been able to get a match.'

'Even a partial fingerprint's useful,' Keira cut in. 'I studied them last semester. A lot of the prints that are retrieved are only partials and even low-quality prints can help establish the identity. Though after the 2011 inquiry, it was decided they could only be used as opinion and not fact.'

'Why have one walking encyclopaedia when you can have two?' Twiggy quipped.

Keira grinned and bobbed in a mock curtsey. 'It makes sense when you consider that even experts who use the same equipment and techniques can still make different judgements, which means it can't be considered factual. The outcomes are classified into four different groups depending on the quality. If there's sufficient quality and quantity of the mark, the expert can use it to identify the suspect. The second group is when enough features don't match, which excludes the suspect. The third is if there aren't enough quality marks to make the comparison, that makes it inconclusive, and the fourth group is when it's low quality or been compromised by something to make it unreliable. That is known as insufficient.'

Seb listened with quiet pride to his daughter speak. She knew her stuff and was capable. She'd be fine.

He had to believe that.

'The problem is, the fingerprint's no use to us without having something to compare it with,' Birdie said.

'What about Isaac Cross?' Keira asked. 'You parked him because he wasn't on Nigel Kaye's guest list but now we have a print it would at least confirm if we're looking in the right direction.'

'It's worth a shot,' Birdie agreed. 'Twiggy, can you find out if he has a criminal record?'

'Already done,' Twiggy said. 'After you mentioned him the other day I did a background check. There was nothing on him.'

'So it could be him?' Keira's eyes were thoughtful. 'But how will you get his prints?'

'By finding out if he's a suspect,' Twiggy said in a dry voice. 'Shall we bring him in for questioning?'

'What do you think, Seb?' Birdie asked.

Seb considered it for a moment. Bringing in Cross might spook him if he was involved. Or it might yield nothing and waste valuable time. It was worth the risk, though.

'Bring him to the station. Birdie and I will observe the interview. Does tomorrow work?'

'It should be fine.' Twiggy checked the time on his watch and then rolled his shoulders. 'I'd better go back now and give Sarge an update. Hopefully this will keep him off my back. I'll text you when it's confirmed.'

'Thanks, Twig,' Birdie responded.

As Twiggy headed for the door, Seb glanced at Keira. She was scrolling through her phone, completely at ease and totally unaware of the dark scenarios still playing out in her father's mind.

He'd keep her safe. Whatever it took.

Even if it meant putting himself directly in harm's way.

NINETEEN

Tuesday, 30 June

Seb took his place beside Birdie in the observation room at Market Harborough so they could watch the interview.

Isaac Cross had been brought into the station half an hour ago and judging by the rigid set of his body, he wasn't happy about it. He glared directly at Sergeant Weston and Twiggy, whose backs were to them, making it impossible to read their expressions.

'Cross looks angry. That won't endear him to Sarge,' Birdie said in a low voice.

'I can't imagine much would endear him to Sergeant Weston, short of a confession,' Seb replied, staring at the back of the officer's salt-and-pepper head.

'You're getting to know him well,' Birdie said, laughing. 'Twiggy mentioned that Cross volunteered to give his fingerprints. Let's hope they're a match and we can crack this case.'

Twiggy started the recording equipment and Sergeant Weston went through the formalities before beginning the interview. 'You're here to answer questions regarding the recent spate of burglaries in the area.'

'This is a total waste of time. Some of us have work to do,' Cross growled, folding his arms across his chest.

Seb winced.

One of the reasons he hadn't wanted the police to show their hand too early with Cross was that he might clam up.

'And it's costing me a headache in paperwork,' Sergeant Weston responded in his gruff voice. 'So, let's cut the dramatics and get on with it. You were at Cynthia Thornton's charity event and Susannah Limbrick's pre-book launch. In both instances, they were burgled not long after.'

'Like I told those other two detectives, I was working at the first, and the second I was there in a professional capacity because we're looking to expand our menus. Anyway, both events were crammed with people so what makes me so special? It could have been any one of the attendees. Did you drag me in here because I'm not loaded like most of the others who went are?'

Sergeant Weston's back straightened. Clearly, he didn't like what Cross was implying.

'You're right, it could have been any of them,' Twiggy said, retrieving a plastic bag from under his chair and placing it on the table. 'As long as that person knew how to make one of these.'

Cross's sulky expression fell away and he studied the bag with interest. Inside was a black ridged case with a small antenna poking out of one end.

'That's a ballsy move, showing him the jamming device.' Birdie let out an approving breath.

'It's working.' Seb gestured to Cross, who had unfolded his arms and was now tapping his fingers against the table, as if fighting the urge to open the bag. 'They've hooked him.'

'I've no idea what that is,' Cross muttered, though his eyes were fixed on the wall, rather than looking directly at Sergeant Weston and Twiggy.

His attempt at lying wasn't convincing.

'Really? I'd have thought an expert like you would know,' Twiggy said.

Cross's eyebrows raised. 'Who said I was an expert?'

'You did, when Birdie and Clifford paid you a visit on Thursday the twenty-fifth of June,' Twiggy replied, his tone indicating that he was enjoying himself.

'I didn't say I was an expert,' Cross said, glaring at Twiggy. 'I said I'm learning to code. Not quite the same thing, as you well know.'

'So why can't he take his eyes off the jammer?' Birdie said nodding at the man.

Seb stared at Cross, whose gaze was still fixed on the jamming device in the middle of the table.

Sergeant Weston picked up the evidence bag and held it in the air. 'This is how the security systems were breached. It intercepts and blocks the signals that go out to the security company and creates a fake one. Though, of course, you already know that. You will also know that it's not something that can be bought online. This was built for the job.'

'You seriously think I'm behind this?' Cross blinked then let out a laugh. 'Yeah, I like computers but I'm not some mastermind burglar who knows how to build a device like that. You've got the wrong person.'

'Have we?' Sergeant Weston said in a cool voice. He took the device out of the evidence bag and slid it across the table. 'You seem very interested in it.'

'Well, yeah. Of course I am,' he admitted. 'But if you think I'm going to put my fingerprints on it, then you've got another think coming. Especially since you've already taken my prints. I'm not stupid.'

'Noted. And while we're at it, we're not stupid either. *And*... we're not in the habit of setting people up,' Twiggy said, pulling some disposable gloves from his pocket. He threw them across the table. 'Satisfied?'

Cross didn't answer as he pulled on the gloves and picked up the device. There was silence as he studied it, turning it carefully over and even examining the tiny screws that held the case together.

'What's he looking at?' Birdie asked.

'Possibly trying to decide how it was made, or where the parts came from. Though I think the real evidence will be on the circuit board, which isn't visible.'

Finally Cross put the jammer down and peeled off the gloves.

'I take it you know what it is?' Sarge pushed.

'I know about them in theory,' Cross admitted. 'They use software-defined radio components and a digital signal processor with a microcontroller that has a time function. But I've never seen one before, let alone built one.'

'Of course you haven't,' Sarge snapped.

Twiggy's phone pinged with a text message. He stared at the screen and showed it to Sergeant Weston.

'It must be about the case,' Birdie said.

Sergeant Weston shifted in his seat.

Even Cross seemed to pick up on the shift of focus. 'What is it? Your bosses telling you to stop wasting my time?'

Sergeant Weston ignored him. Moments later Birdie's phone pinged and she studied the screen. 'It's from Twiggy. Cross's fingerprints aren't a match.'

'Disappointing but not entirely unexpected,' Seb said.

He avoided getting attached to the different theories and instead liked to focus on where the evidence took them.

'You said you've heard about these devices. From where?' Sergeant Weston continued to push, even though the man was no longer a suspect.

Cross stiffened before shrugging. 'Just around. The internet's a big place.'

'It is indeed. But I think you're holding out on us,' Sergeant Weston said. 'Do you know the person who built it?'

'Not as such,' Cross finally said, after seeming to consider the question.

'Nice work, Sarge,' Birdie said. 'I think Cross has realised he's off the hook and that his life will be easier if he cooperates.'

'What's that meant to mean? Either you know or you don't,' Sergeant Weston said.

Cross gave a low sigh. 'Ummm... Well... There's a girl who works at Powerhouse Electronics. She's a genius when it comes to stuff like this. You could try her.'

Birdie snatched up her phone and tapped in the name of the store. 'It's in Oadby and looks massive. They sell everything electronic you could possible want.'

'What's her name?' Twiggy demanded.

'Pip Range,' Cross said, a guilty flush crossing his face.

'How well do you know this woman?' Twiggy asked.

'She's not a mate if that's what you're asking. But I know her well enough to buy an iPhone from,' Cross countered, his previous snarky attitude returning in full force. 'Is that all?'

Next to Seb, Birdie bristled. 'I knew he was holding out on us. Twiggy's never going to let me hear the end of this. They got the woman's name and we got zilch.'

'But without us we wouldn't be this far,' Seb responded in a mild voice.

Birdie reluctantly chuckled. 'I suppose so. We linked him to the case in the first place. Still, it bugs me that we didn't get a name out of him.'

Seb didn't reply and turned his attention back to the interview room.

Sergeant Weston was drumming his fingers on the table. 'Where were you on Sunday between ten am and four pm?'

Cross glanced up towards the ceiling. 'Hmmm... Let's see... on Sunday I was with my kid. He lives in London and I don't get to see him much. We spent the day at Wacky Warehouse. You can ask the ex. She'll confirm it. Why? What happened on Sunday?'

'Nothing you need worry about,' Twiggy said. 'Text us your ex-wife's telephone number so we can follow up on your alibi.'

Sergeant Weston got to his feet. 'That's it for now but don't leave the area without first checking with us. Are we clear?'

'Crystal,' Cross snapped, also standing.

Seb and Birdie waited several minutes, giving the police time to escort Cross to the station's entrance, then made their way to Sergeant Weston's office, where he was waiting. Twiggy joined them not long afterwards.

'Do you think he's trying to fob us off?' Sergeant Weston rested his arms on his desk. 'Perhaps we should have held him until after we'd spoken to Pip Range?'

Seb considered it then frowned. 'I think we're safe. When he gave his alibi, his shoulders were relaxed and there was no tension around his mouth.'

'Not to mention he looked directly at you, despite your renowned stare, which I'm assuming you were giving, because we couldn't actually see.' Birdie dropped into one of the swivel chairs and spun around.

'Can you not sit still for one minute. I'd forgotten how annoying you can be,' Sergeant Weston said, with a frustrated sigh.

'Okay, for you I'll stop,' Birdie replied, dropping both feet and coming to an abrupt halt.

'Thank you. Right, I'll leave you two to question Pip Range. Twiggy, you've got some urgent admin to finish.'

'I can't catch a break,' Twiggy said with a rueful grin. 'I guess I'll be chained to my desk this afternoon.'

'We'll head over there now,' Birdie said, tapping the arm of the chair. Then her eyes drifted to the jamming device on the table. She picked it up. 'Can I take this? It might help jog her memory.'

'Be my guest,' Sergeant Weston said, gesturing with his hand.

'I'll let forensics know you've got it,' Twiggy added. 'Be careful.'

'Don't worry about us.' Birdie's eyes gleamed and Seb got the feeling she was going to enjoy the upcoming interview. He would too, if it gave them the answers they needed.

TWENTY

Tuesday, 30 June

Powerhouse Electronics was in a sprawling building with a large customer car park to one side. Seb pulled into a free space and they crossed to the entrance. Several customers were milling around and three assistants were close by, in grey and yellow uniforms.

'There's the information desk. If Cross has phoned and warned this woman, he'll regret it.' Birdie marched over to the long counter.

'Can I help you?' A young man appeared from a back office, brushing crumbs off his shirt. He flushed. 'Sorry, just finishing lunch. It's been a busy morning.'

'No need to apologise. We can't have you fainting on the job,' Birdie said, in a jokey tone. 'We're here to see Pip Range. Is she working today?'

'Yes, but she's with a customer right now.' The young man nodded towards the back of the store. 'Can I help instead? Are you looking for something particular? We have some great specials on this week.'

Birdie shook her head. 'Sorry, we need to speak with Pip. She's been recommended to us.'

'Yeah, you and the rest of the world.' His shoulders slumped as he glanced to the back of the store where a woman in uniform, in her mid-twenties with purple hair, was having an animated conversation with a couple.

Seb eyed him. 'What do you mean?'

'She's got a reputation as a genius when it comes to computers, and since we get paid on commission, she earns double what the rest of us do.'

'Is she really that good?' Birdie asked, sounding sceptical.

Seb knew it was to draw out the young salesman. Because if Pip Range was as talented as her colleague reported, she was more than capable of building the jamming devices.

'She's better than good. Ask anyone who comes in here. I don't mean to sound jealous. She's awesome and— Hey... it looks like you're in luck. She's finished with her customers.'

Seb peered over as a couple walked away holding a large box. Birdie thanked the young man and they made their way through the game consoles and huge TV screens until they reached the purple-haired woman, who was busy putting a laptop back onto the display cabinet.

She looked up and smiled. 'Hello. Can I help you with anything?'

'That would be great.' Birdie gave a beaming smile. 'We'd like to talk to you about home security systems?'

'Let me fetch Noah. He's the expert when it comes to surveillance.' Pip matched Birdie's smile and waved to a tall man standing by a tower of food blenders.

'That won't be necessary. We were told you're the best person to help,' Birdie pushed.

'Are you sure? I mean I can show you how to download an app to run your smart home. Or help with a device, but for the security side, I'm not that knowledgeable.'

'What about when it comes to jamming security systems?' Seb stepped closer and for the first time Pip's smile faltered.

'Jamming? Ummm... I have no idea what that even means.' She thrust her hands into her pockets, not quite returning their gaze.

'Really? So, you don't know what this is?' Birdie withdrew the black-cased jamming device and held it out. It had an immediate effect and colour rose up Pip's neck.

'Should I?' the saleswoman countered as she took a step backwards.

'That's what we're here to find out,' Seb said in a cool voice. 'Please answer the question.'

'Who are you?' Pip took another step back but she was hemmed in by a rack of computer consumables.

'I'm Birdie and this is my partner, Sebastian Clifford. We're private investigators who are working on a case with the Market Harborough police. If you don't want to answer our questions, we'll simply ask our colleagues to take you to the station for questioning. I'm not sure how your boss would feel about that, though?'

Pip's eyes filled with alarm. 'The police? But I haven't done anything wrong.'

'That's not how it looks,' Birdie said.

Seb folded his arms. The combination of this and Birdie's words seemed to work and Pip's shoulders dropped.

'Is there somewhere quiet we can discuss this?' Seb asked, aware of the interested glances coming from around the store.

'We have a table in the far corner. Go over there and I'll be with you in a second. I've got to put this lot back first,' Pip said, gesturing to several laptops that were out on a counter. 'Can you put that thing away,' she added, nodding towards the jammer.

'Of course. Though I am pleased it helped jog your memory,' Birdie replied as she accompanied Seb to a round table half hidden behind a wall of printer inks.

They sat and Seb turned to watch Pip Range pick up various boxes and load them back on shelves.

'I've a good feeling about this,' Birdie said.

'Let's take it one step at a time,' Seb said, turning back to Birdie.

'I can't see her,' Birdie said, a worried expression on her face. 'Can you?'

Seb stood, but the woman was nowhere to be seen. 'She's gone.'

'Crap,' Birdie said. 'She's done a runner.'

They moved quickly, weaving through the maze of display stands and promotional banners.

'You take the back,' Seb said. 'I'll cover the front entrance.'

Birdie nodded and disappeared down an aisle of washing machines, while Seb strode towards the main entrance, scanning the area as he went. There was no sign of Pip Range. He approached a young man in the same uniform who was straightening a display of phone cases.

'I'm looking for Pip Range. Where would she go if she's not on the shop floor?'

The man blinked. 'Um, I don't—'

'Where are the staff rooms?'

'If you go through the home appliances section there's a room there, but you need a pass to go—'

Seb hurried off before the man could finish. He cut through the fridge/freezer section and pushed open a door marked *Staff Only*. A narrow corridor stretched ahead, lined with notice boards. He heard a banging sound and headed in that direction. He saw Pip Range slamming her shoulder against an emergency exit, but the door wouldn't budge. She rattled the handle, swore and then spun around.

'I imagine it's alarmed,' Seb said calmly. 'Now I suggest you come with me and you can answer some questions.'

'I haven't done anything,' Pip said, sounding breathless, as her eyes darted past him, presumably looking for another escape route.

'Then why run?

'Because I know how this goes. You're looking for someone to blame for something and I'm the one.'

'But you don't even know what we want to know.'

Pip flushed. 'I—'

'There you are.' Birdie's voice came from behind him. 'Well caught. Now you can answer our questions,' she said, turning her attention to the woman. 'We'll stay here. Over to you, Seb.' Birdie folded her arms and stood in front of Pip Range to make sure she couldn't escape a second time.

'There have been a series of burglaries in the area and jamming devices, like the one you were shown, were found at each property,' Seb explained, scanning the woman's face for any micro tells. He was rewarded when the tiny muscles around her mouth tightened and her breathing quickened. 'Millions of pounds' worth of artwork have been stolen.'

'You don't think I was involved, do you? I don't even steal paperclips from this place. I swear.'

'It's not paperclips we're concerned about,' Birdie snapped. Usually his partner managed to keep her temper under control but it was clear she was running out of patience with Pip Range. She wasn't the only one.

Seb locked eyes with her. 'Did you, or did you not, make the jamming device we showed you?'

The colour drained from Pip's face and she gave a faint nod. 'Okay, yes. I made it but I never used it. I take orders for all kinds of specialised computer equipment.'

'Even when that equipment is going to be used for illegal activities?' Seb said, keeping the hard edge in his voice.

'That's like blaming an off-licence for selling alcohol,' Pip protested in a sullen voice. 'Most of the orders are for custom-built gaming computers.'

'Tell yourself that if you want, but don't expect a judge to fall for it,' Birdie retorted, her eyes narrowed. 'Who ordered the jammer and how many did you make?'

Pip swallowed. 'I'm not sure. Can I see it again, please?'

'Does that mean you've made more of them for other people?' Seb asked as Birdie retrieved the device and held it out for her to see.

'Like I said, people order various things from me. But I've made a few different kinds of radio frequency jammers.' Pip took it from Birdie and this time took her time studying it, before sighing. 'I made this one a few months ago. The customer ordered ten.'

'Ten?' Birdie growled and Seb winced.

Damn. He wasn't often rattled but the news was not welcome.

So far there had only been four burglaries but if there were six more devices, did that mean there were six more planned? That could potentially push the stolen goods into tens of millions of pounds.

'Did you use the same black casing for each device?' he asked, realising it would make things more difficult if the remaining six were different.

She nodded. 'Yes. I used the same housing for all of them.'

Good. At least that was one less thing to worry about.

'We need a name, address and phone number,' Seb said, not bothering to mince his words. Birdie wasn't the only one losing her patience.

'I don't know how to contact him. He only ever gave me his first name. It's Ewan.'

'Let me get this straight, you sold ten devices that would allow someone to bypass complex security systems and you only have a first name?' Birdie's fists clenched by her sides, turning her knuckles white.

'My business has always worked like that. People give me the order and pay up front. I try to keep it simple.'

'How do they know about you?' Seb growled.

'Word of mouth. I don't ask questions.' Pip's lip began to tremble. It seemed the implications of her side hustle were belatedly occurring to her.

'That's abundantly clear,' Birdie said. 'I suggest you tell us as much as you can about *Ewan*. You said you charged him up front. Did he pay into a bank account?'

'I only take cash and don't do anything over the phone or by email. I met him once and it was dark so I couldn't see his face. He wore a hoodie but I got the feeling he was in his fifties. The only thing I can tell you is that he's tall, over six foot, and has a Scottish accent.' Her face crumpled but Seb couldn't muster any sympathy.

Avoiding any kind of electronic trail suggested she was aware of the potentially dangerous impact her products might have.

Birdie looked equally grim as she glared at Pip. 'Where from? Glasgow, Edinburgh, Highlands?'

'I don't know. It was just Scottish.' Pip wrapped her arms around her body in a protective gesture.

'How much did you charge him?' Seb pushed.

'Five hundred pounds each. Am I in trouble?'

'That's not our call.' Seb fixed her with a stern glare.

'You mean the police?' Pip said, her voice hardly audible.

'That's right,' Birdie replied. 'Now you can tell us what you were doing on the following dates.'

Birdie called out the date for each burglary and Pip, who'd lost all pretence of playing it cool and was crying, went through her phone calendar. She had an alibi for each of the dates, but it was something they'd be following up.

'Can I go back to work now?' Pip asked.

'You may. But don't think of disappearing because the police will want to talk to you,' Birdie responded.

'I won't,' Pip promised.

They all walked back into the store and parted company when they reached the computer section.

'Bloody hell,' Birdie spluttered, once they were outside.

It summed up Seb's feelings perfectly. He'd come face to face with a variety of criminals but there was still something disturbing about Pip's lack of acceptance of her own culpability.

'She's either very naive or living in denial,' Seb responded.

'I'm not sure which one's worse.' Birdie sighed. 'I wonder if she'd even thought about the ethics of what she was doing. Or was she happy to say yes to whatever request came her way?'

'Let's hope this is the wake-up call she needs. She might still find herself in trouble depending on how Sergeant Weston wishes to progress the case.'

'Which won't happen until we solve it.'

Seb pulled out his phone and checked his messages. There was a text from Leonard Castle.

> My wife and I will be home all afternoon and would be happy to have a chat with you. We've met your parents several times and look forward to making your acquaintance.

'Good news?' Birdie asked as she checked her own phone.

'The Castles have invited us over.'

'Excellent. Let's go straight there. I'll call Twiggy on the way and ask him to check if they've got a six-foot Scottish man called Ewan on the records. If that's his real name.'

The thought had occurred to Seb.

There was no reason not to give his real name if Pip Range didn't do any background checks or even ask basic questions. He hoped their visit would have frightened her enough to think twice before doing anything like this again.

They climbed into the car and headed back towards Great Bowden, on the outskirts of Market Harborough, to speak with Leonard and Rose Castle. Knowing there were still six more jammers in circulation made it imperative to prevent another burglary.

TWENTY-ONE

Tuesday, 30 June

'I bet ten pounds it was built during the Edwardian period,' Birdie announced as Seb pulled up outside a lovely, three-storey red stone house.

Deep bay windows flanked the front door, while dormer windows peered out of the tiled roof and a newer extension sprawled out along one side of the property.

'It's hard to imagine a time when you didn't know your flying buttresses from your Doric columns,' Seb responded in a mock deadpan voice.

'Ah, yes. That's all a distant memory now. I could probably do my very own Posh Houses of Leicestershire guided tour.' Birdie grinned.

Before she'd met Seb, she had as much interest in architecture as she had in the reproductive cycle of a gnat. But, probably because of his upbringing and his impressive memory, Seb was a font of knowledge when it came to historic houses and she was absorbing it without even trying, as if by osmosis.

'I'm sure it would sell out,' her partner assured her.

'Thank you.' She gave a mock bow and then sighed. 'But I'm

afraid that when it comes to cups and saucers, you're on your own. I'd never even heard of the Chelsea Porcelain Factory before. How do you know about it?'

'Courtesy of my grandmother, on my father's side,' Seb acknowledged as they reached the door. 'She had several figurines displayed, including Summer and Autumn. It was a stunning piece and she loved talking about it. I learnt a lot that way, but then did my own research, knowing how much it pleased her.'

'Are you sure you weren't just sucking up?' Birdie teased, though secretly she could easily imagine a young Seb diligently reading everything he could get his hands on to increase his knowledge.

'I did get extra homemade shortbread to take back to boarding school, as a reward for my efforts. Much to my brother Hubert's annoyance, I might add,' Seb confessed in a dry voice.

'Homemade? Your gran did some baking? No way.' Birdie shook her head.

'She didn't bake it herself, obviously. But she instructed Cook to bake extra and pack them for me to take.'

'Oooh. That's more like it. Being the son of a viscount certainly has its benefits. No one baked shortbread for me.'

Okay, that was a slight exaggeration. There was always homemade baking in the house, thanks to her mum, but admitting it would ruin the joke.

'It also has its issues, as you're fully aware.'

'Yeah, right... *Issues*,' Birdie said with a dismissive wave of her hand. 'Now let's get on.' She took hold of the large, circular brass door knocker and rapped it three times on the dark-red door.

It didn't take long for a housekeeper to open it and lead them through a panelled hallway, that had been painted white, giving it a fresh modern feel, to a sunroom at the side of the house where the Castles were waiting.

Leonard was a tall man in his mid-sixties with very little hair and a large moustache covering his top lip. Rose was almost as tall, with thick auburn hair and bright green eyes. Like the hallway, the sunroom was painted white, with an array of prints hanging on the wall.

'Sebastian, it's a pleasure to see you again.' Leonard Castle crossed the floor and shook his hand. 'How are your parents?'

'Very well, thank you. They send their regards.'

Did they really? Seb hadn't mentioned he'd told his parents they were visiting their friends.

'That's very kind of them. And you are?' Leonard Castle said, looking at Birdie and quirking an eyebrow.

'I'm Birdie, Seb's partner. It's very nice to meet you, Mr Castle.'

'Please call me Leonard, my dear. This is my wife, Rose.' He gestured to the woman, who remained seated on one of the floral sofas on the far side of the room. 'Come and sit down.'

'Sorry I didn't get up,' Rose said, once they were all seated. 'I tripped yesterday and have sprained my ankle.'

'Oh no,' Birdie said. 'I hope it's not too painful.'

'It's a lot easier today, thank you.'

'We appreciate you letting us visit and we're sorry for the mystery,' Birdie said, taking in the couple's concerned faces.

Had they guessed the reason for the visit? She'd agreed with Seb that it was best to disclose it in person, because they didn't want to alarm them more than was necessary.

'We thought it must be something serious, but weren't sure what exactly,' Leonard said.

'Are you aware of the recent spate of burglaries in the area?' Seb asked.

Rose nodded. 'When it comes to fine arts, it's a small world and I must admit to being alarmed when I read what happened to poor Cynthia. She's a friend.'

'We're working with the police on solving these crimes,' Seb added.

'Are we a target?' Leonard asked, frowning. 'We didn't think we would be because of our security system. It's supposed to be impenetrable.'

'We have no proof that you are,' Seb quickly assured them. 'However, we do know that there are at least six of the devices used to disable the security systems in the other properties still in circulation.'

Leonard's eyes widened. 'A device? There was no mention of that in the papers.'

'This information hasn't been released to the public,' Birdie explained.

'Our plan is to pre-empt where they'll next target in the area, and we believe it could be your event,' Seb added. 'We're hoping you'll allow us to search your property to ascertain if a device has already been planted. We'd also like you to take us through your security set-up for the day.'

Leonard and Rose exchanged a worried glance.

'Yes, of course,' Rose said. 'Our Heritage and High Tea is an annual event, but we've never had any problems in the past. Part of me thinks we should cancel it, but I can't bear to do that when we're also raising funds. We've arranged for a speaker to come up from London to introduce some of the new pieces we've added to the collection.'

'Tim Richards,' Seb said. 'I've attended several of his lectures and very much admired the show he curated for the V&A Museum several years ago.'

'I'm impressed you've heard of him. Despite his knowledge and passion, he isn't one for the spotlight,' Leonard admitted. 'Which is why we were thrilled he agreed to join us.'

'I suspect he was the one who was thrilled. From what I've seen of your existing catalogue, he'll be looking forward to inspecting the three Goat and Bee jugs you have,' Seb added.

'You sound like an aficionado. People who don't understand this world find our obsession a little strange,' Leonard replied.

'We're all drawn to different things,' Seb said diplomatically.

'We'll show you the collection,' Rose said, standing and taking hold of a bottle-green walking stick that was leaning against the sofa.

They followed Rose and Leonard into the hall and through to a large room with glass cabinets running along the walls.

'How did you get started?' Birdie asked as she headed over to a cabinet which was filled with delicate figurines dressed in eighteenth-century outfits, with gold detail running through the designs. They stood on sculpted bases. They were too ornate for her taste. Still, like Seb had said, each to their own.

Leonard led her to the next cabinet and gave a fond sigh. 'See that tall blue vase? John Donaldson painted the centre panel. I inherited it along with several other key pieces from my grandmother. It's after that my interest began.'

'You and Seb have something in common.' Birdie glanced over to Seb, who was deep in conversation with Rose as they inspected a teapot covered in botanical flowers.

'A man after my own heart. It's quite a treat for us to have someone as passionate as we are examining the collection,' Leonard said. 'I collected other pieces as and when I could afford them. I worked in international corporate law, which allowed me to fully indulge in my hobby.'

'I think we've moved past it being a hobby,' his wife chided as she came over and stood beside them, with Seb following. 'Sebastian has been telling me about his visit to view the Andersons' collection.'

'It doesn't rival yours, but they do have a nice Hen and Chicks tureen.'

'Tell me about it. They outbid us for it at an auction a few years ago.' Leonard let out a rueful sigh then rubbed his hands together. 'Maybe you'd be interested in giving a lecture here, Sebastian. As well as our annual fundraiser we do have private events, mainly for PhD students and collectors.'

'I'd be honoured,' Seb replied. 'But first let's ensure your collection stays intact. Please will you walk us through your security system.'

'The main panel is this way.' Rose took them back to the hallway, indicating where the sensors were situated. As they walked,

Birdie let Seb pay attention to the details, since he would have no trouble recalling them, and she used the time to check for a jamming device.

By the time they returned to the sunroom, Birdie hadn't found anything. 'I haven't seen a jammer.'

'That's good news, isn't it?' Rose said.

'Yes,' Seb agreed although he was frowning. 'We haven't been able to establish detailed timelines but we suspect the jamming devices were fitted when someone had easy access to the property. Unfortunately, that doesn't mean one won't be fitted here.'

'Most likely at our fundraiser.' Rose shivered.

'It's a possibility,' Birdie admitted. 'Do you have a list of everyone coming?'

Rose nodded. 'We send out invitations to a select number of people, and sell tickets online. We have the name of the person buying the tickets, but not any of their guests.'

'That's assuming they give their correct name,' Leonard added. 'We've never thought to ask for identification in the past.'

Birdie let out a frustrated sigh. It would be easy enough for someone to book under a false name and walk straight in. She tapped her fingers against her leg. 'Could you still provide us with a full list of the guests you do know. Who else will be coming and going from the house between now and Sunday?'

'Well... let's see, the caterers and of course our regular staff. They've all been with us for a long time so are used to the preparation involved. We'll get cleaners in beforehand, but I let Mrs Ainsley organise that. She's our housekeeper,' Rose replied.

'You said caterers. Do you use The Curated Feast?' Birdie asked on the off chance, though wasn't really surprised when Rose shook her head.

'No. I know Cynthia uses them, but I prefer to keep to our regular caterer.'

'That's understandable.' Birdie nodded in agreement. 'Along with the guest list, please could you provide us with the names of all your personal staff as well as the caterers, cleaners and anyone else who'll be visiting here before Sunday.'

'I'll email it to you later,' Rose said. 'I feel on a knife's edge right now, worried something might happen.'

'I know it's alarming, but try not to dwell on it,' Seb said. 'You might not even be a target. This is a good opportunity for us to ensure nothing happens. What are your own plans for the rest of the week?'

Leonard flushed, suddenly appearing concerned. 'We're heading to our house at the Lakes tomorrow morning. We usually go there for a few days before the high tea. We call it our own annual retreat. I suppose we should cancel.'

Seb shook his head.

If the Castles made any changes to their expected itinerary it might scare off the burglars, which meant they'd be back to square one.

'We understand your concern,' Seb said. 'But it would be better for you to keep to your plans, so as not to alert the burglars that you're expecting them.'

'Especially if people already know of your plans. Who else knows you're going?' Birdie asked.

'It's common knowledge,' Leonard admitted. 'We're on several committees and are very open with our calendar. Every year after the high tea we head to London for two weeks. Do you wish us to still do this?'

Birdie resisted the urge to swear. If she was a burglar, she'd be thanking her lucky stars for the Castles and their travel plans. Not only were they giving people direct access to their house, but they were also leaving it unattended for days both before and after their event.

Still, if it *was* the next target, at least Birdie and Seb would know the window of opportunity.

'Please don't change your plans,' Seb said. 'You can trust us to ensure your collection remains safe.'

The married couple seemed to be having an entire conversation with their eyes. Finally Leonard nodded. 'If you think that's for the best, we'll do as you ask.'

'What about the actual event? You'll both be here, won't you?' Rose asked, wringing her hands.

'Absolutely,' Birdie said, her tone resolute. 'Please add us to the guest list so it doesn't look suspicious. We'll also arrange for the police to have surveillance teams set up. If someone does attempt to break in, they won't get away with it.'

Birdie and Seb left not long afterwards and the mood was sombre during the journey back to their office.

'What happens if we've got the wrong place?' Birdie finally spoke. 'It would be awful if we've caused them so much stress for no reason.'

'It's always a risk. But the idea of them losing part of their collection doesn't bear thinking about. I'm pleased we're being overly cautious.'

'I guess that's one way of looking at it,' Birdie said as her phone buzzed with a text message. She studied the screen and grinned. 'It's from Twiggy. He might have discovered who bought the jammers from Pip. He's on his way to Rendall Hall now.'

Seb pressed his foot down on the accelerator. 'Then we'd better get our skates on.'

Birdie agreed and she leant back into the car seat, pleased they were finally getting somewhere.

TWENTY-TWO

Tuesday, 30 June

'Since when do you have a second dog, Clifford?' Twiggy asked as Bonnie stood behind Seb, peeping out at him.

'This is Bonnie. She's a new addition to the household,' Seb explained as he ushered Twiggy inside.

Bonnie turned and then zoomed back into the kitchen.

The two of them followed, and Seb watched Bonnie join Elsa, who was curled up in her bed, and snuggle up to her. He'd initially worried that Elsa would soon tire of the younger, more energetic dog but thankfully it wasn't the case and they already seemed to be the best of friends.

'Hey, Twig. I've made you a cuppa,' Birdie said from the other side of the room. 'But I'm afraid there's no sugar.'

'You mean it's hidden because you've been speaking to Evie,' Twiggy said. 'I knew I should've had an extra cup at the station before I left. Stupidly I thought you'd want to know what we've discovered as soon as possible.'

'We *do* want to know,' Birdie replied, as she pushed the cup towards him. 'And this is for your own good. Now, what have you got?'

'Ewan Thomas, aged fifty-six and originally from Dundee, has a record. He now lives in Newton Linford.'

'Newtown Linford?' Birdie blurted out. 'You mean the place that was once named the most upmarket place to live in England. Not where I'd expect to find your average burglar. Last time we played cricket there I swear the cutlery used in the clubhouse was silver.'

'Whoever we're dealing with isn't average,' Seb reminded her, though he had to agree it was a surprise. Properties in the village were almost as expensive as in London. 'Why does he have a police record?'

'He was arrested for handling luxury stolen goods. He got off with a caution because he claimed it was accidental,' Twiggy explained.

'You do know we could've done this over the phone, to save you coming out here,' Birdie said with a frown.

'You're right... but this way I get away from Sarge asking me every five minutes how it's going. I get it, he's under pressure from up top but, seriously, he needs to give it a rest.'

'You're welcome here anytime. You know, this is promising. Do you have anything else on him?'

'He's divorced with two kids and his ex-wife is a journalist working for a TV production company in Norfolk.'

'What does he do for a living?' Birdie joined him at the table.

Twiggy flipped open his notebook and skimmed through it. 'He's a wine merchant. He got a classics degree from the University of Edinburgh and from there went into banking before moving into wine. You're right, he doesn't sound like your average burglar. But if he is our guy, why on earth would he use his real name when buying the jammers?'

'Stupidity?' Birdie suggested as she toyed with her mug. 'Or arrogance. Maybe he thinks he's too smart to get caught?'

'He wouldn't be the first criminal caught out by their own hubris,' Seb said, which earnt him an eye roll from Birdie.

'In plain English please,' Birdie said with a grin. She looked at Twiggy. 'Do you see what I have to put up with?'

'It's Greek and means—'

'I know it means self-confidence... I was teasing. Honestly, it's so easy to wind you up.'

'Point taken. Back to Ewan Thomas. He wasn't on any of the guest lists,' Seb said.

'Could he have sold wine to the victims?' Twiggy suggested.

'You read my mind,' Birdie added. 'It's certainly a good starting point.'

'Yes—' Seb was interrupted as Keira walked into the kitchen.

She'd texted last night to say she was staying over at Zara's and, judging by her bright eyes, she'd had a good time.

At least she didn't appear hungover this time.

Bonnie zoomed over to greet her and Elsa opened an eye in recognition.

Once Keira had finished greeting the dogs she pulled out a kitchen chair and collapsed onto it, staring at each of them in turn. 'What's going on? Birdie, you're practically bouncing out of your chair.'

'Plenty. And it's not bouncing, it's creative processing,' Birdie retorted with a grin. She explained what they'd discovered. 'Which means you're just in time to start researching.'

'Sure. Shall I start with Ewan Thomas?'

'Yes. Thomas wasn't on any of the guest lists, but that doesn't mean his associates weren't. Let's find out who he's in business with,' Seb said.

Keira retrieved her phone from her shorts pocket and began searching. 'Here we go. Thomas and Co Fine Wine Merchant and Broker. He's been in business for ten years. There's no mention of him going to any public events or fundraisers but he does have a social media presence.' Then she wrinkled her nose. 'Whoever does his socials needs firing. Some of these photos are rubbish.'

'Unfortunately, that's not a crime.' Birdie sighed, leaning over to view Keira's screen. 'Though the price of that wine is. Five hundred pounds for one bottle?'

'I'd be too scared to drink it,' Keira admitted as she continued to scroll. 'There's no mention of his associates, but I'll get a quick shower and then do a proper search on the computer.'

'Excellent. I'll haul him in for questioning,' Twiggy said but Birdie shook her head.

'If you do that, then it'll ruin our chances of catching them red handed. Let's at least wait until after the high tea on Sunday.'

Twiggy glared at Birdie.

'She's right,' Seb said. 'This is our chance to spot the person planting the devices and, assuming Sergeant Weston gives the go-ahead for a surveillance team, we'll have enough eyes on the property to apprehend the burglars.'

'It's risky. What if Thomas is behind it and we have the wrong venue? There are two other events going on this weekend. It could be either of them,' Twiggy pointed out.

Seb rubbed his chin. 'I agree it's a risk but the Blackwoods have by far the most valuable collection.'

'It's also risky to pull him in just because his name's Ewan,' Birdie added. 'I might not play poker but even I know not to show my hand too quickly. Seb and I can visit his business and pretend we're there to buy wine.'

'You think he stocks Blue Nun?' Twiggy said, with a chuckle.

'Haha, very funny,' Birdie retorted.

'That's an excellent idea, Birdie,' Seb said. 'I'll say my parents are looking to expand their wine cellar. We'll have to make an appointment to visit – it won't be possible to drop in.'

Birdie's face fell. 'Damn. I was hoping to go today.'

Seb suppressed a smile. Birdie was by far the more impulsive of the pair of them. And while he appreciated her focus, it would give them more time to fully research into Thomas and discover his connections.

Twiggy stood up. 'I'd better go back to the station before Sarge sends out a search party. Once I'm there I ll contact the victims to see if any of them have bought wine from Thomas.'

'Thanks,' Birdie said.

After he'd left the room and they heard the front door close, Keira put down her phone.

'Last night Zara and I went to the pub and she told me all about when you went to see her. I didn't want to mention it until we were alone, in case you hadn't told Twiggy about our friendship.'

'He knows,' Birdie said. 'What did she say?'

'She was excited to help an investigation because she wants to make a positive difference in the world. She said it made her understand why I adore my studies so much.'

Seb frowned. It sounded a little hyperbolic, but he supposed that's what people of her age were like.

'Did she make any connection between me and your dad?' Birdie asked.

Keira shook her head. 'No. She knows that Dad's an investigator but thinks he mainly deals with cases in London because he used to be in the Met.'

Seb nodded in approval. 'Good. The less you talk about me the better.'

Keira tutted. 'We didn't spend the whole night talking about the burglaries, you know. Zara explained how she makes her content. I had no idea how much work goes into filming each episode. She knows all about cross-cutting and matching the eyelines and parallel editing. And of course we discussed what to wear on Sunday.'

At the mention of the high tea, Seb coughed. He hadn't been thrilled with the idea of Keira going and nothing they'd discovered had changed his mind.

'Keira, I'm not sure about you attending the Castles' event,' he finally said.

'I can't pull out now. I promised Zara,' Keira protested, her lower lip falling into a pout. 'Besides, now we've got a lead, isn't it better if you have more backup? And don't tell me you can get more police to go undercover because Twiggy's already said how short-staffed they are, and if they have a surveillance team outside, they won't have enough people to send inside and mingle as guests.'

'Part of going undercover is remembering not to blow it,' Birdie said, her tone unusually serious. 'If you're going as Zara's guest, then that's all you can be. So no following anyone... or doing anything Zara wouldn't do.'

'I swear I won't,' Keira said, turning to Seb, her eyes pleading.

He let out a breath and nodded. 'Okay. But Birdie's right about not taking any chances.'

'Thanks,' Keira said, jumping up, her mood restored. 'Now, I'm going to find out everything I can about Ewan Thomas.'

'Great.' Birdie got to her feet and pretended to bowl a cricket ball, as was her habit when she was thinking. 'Seb, you can book us an appointment to talk fine wines.'

TWENTY-THREE

Wednesday, 1 July

The following morning Seb slowed down as a tractor pulled out in front of them. Next to him, Birdie let out a long groan and he bit back an amused laugh. It appeared that Newtown Linford and East Farndon had a lot in common. Still, they'd left early to make sure there was plenty of time for their appointment.

Ewan Thomas had been all too ready to fit them in at eleven.

Seb suspected it was because he'd introduced himself as Viscount Worthington's son. It was something he loathed doing but with time running out, it had seemed the best way.

'Could that thing go any slower?' Birdie complained as they crawled past the ivy-covered hedgerows which flanked the narrow road. Ahead were road cones and a temporary set of traffic lights. Birdie's groans got even louder.

'I think that's answered your question.' Seb brought the car to a halt as Birdie impatiently tapped her foot and scanned the documents in her lap.

It was the information Keira had discovered yesterday afternoon. Apart from being prosecuted for handling stolen luxury goods, Thomas had kept a low profile. There had been very little on his social media channels and his website focused on wine auctions and current sales. Keira hadn't been able to discover his business associates. There was very little information on his family either, other than his estranged ex-wife and children.

With a sigh, Birdie shut the folder just as her phone rang.

Her mood instantly improved. 'It's Twiggy. I'll put him on speaker... Hey, Seb and I are in the car on the way to see Thomas. I hope you're not going to tell us we're on a wild goose chase.'

'Not a wild goose in sight.' Twiggy chuckled. 'It's much better than that. It turns out that Thomas sold wine to Cynthia Thornton for her fundraiser, Susannah Limbrick for her pre-launch party and to the Blackwoods for their open day. Also, Nigel Kaye and the Castles buy wine from him on a regular basis.'

'Bingo.' Birdie grinned, punching the air. 'We have our missing link.'

'It also suggests the Castles are next on the list.' Seb eased his foot down on the accelerator as the light turned green. 'Twiggy, please could you contact people putting on future events in the area and enquire if they have dealings with Thomas?'

'No problem. It will help give us an idea if you're right about the high tea being the next target... Are you sure we shouldn't bring him in for questioning? I didn't mind holding off until we had more evidence, but surely this is enough to pursue him further.'

'We *are* pursuing it further,' Birdie reminded him before glancing over to Seb. He gave a quick shake of his head. Like Birdie, he believed jumping in too soon wasn't the correct way to proceed.

'Put a tail on him, instead,' Seb suggested, as he pulled up outside a stone building with a thatched roof and arched windows. A sign hung from the fence with the words:

THOMAS AND CO FINE WINE MERCHANT

'Good idea,' Birdie added.

There was silence as Twiggy seemed to consider it. 'Fine. I'll see what I can arrange.'

'Thanks, Twig. We've just got here... And you're right. There's no way this place sells Blue Nun.'

'Okay, let me know how it goes.'

'Will do,' Birdie agreed.

As she tapped the screen to end the call, Seb parked the car and they climbed out. Despite the warm weather, he'd elected to wear a suit to create a more formal impression. He adjusted his tie and next to him Birdie smoothed down the wide-legged, navy trousers that she'd teamed with sandals and a plain T-shirt. At first they'd considered having her dress up and pretending to be his assistant but, as Keira had pointed out, if Thomas had any brains he'd google Seb in preparation for the meeting, and he'd soon figure out who Birdie was. They'd revised the plans and decided Birdie would be herself and ask a lot of questions.

'You don't scrub up too badly,' Birdie commented, running her fingers through her red curls. 'Remember to leave all the awkward questions to me. You can complain about how I never stop working even when I'm off the clock.'

'As you wish.' He rubbed a hand across his jaw. 'I'd like to see his response to the burglaries, if you can bring them up in conversation.'

Birdie winked. 'I'm sure I can segue into it. Now, it's time for your eleven o'clock appointment, Mr Clifford.'

'Thank you, Miss Bird,' he replied as they entered the building through a freshly painted black door. It had the same arched top as the windows and a bell chimed as they stepped inside.

The walls were lined with floor-to-ceiling shelving, each containing bottles of wine. Several wine barrels were placed in the centre of the room, presumably to be used as tasting tables.

Ewan Thomas stepped out from behind the counter and gave them a warm smile. His hair was brown and streaked with grey. It was pushed off his face and highlighted a tanned complexion, suggesting he'd recently spent time overseas in the sun. His suit appeared to be bespoke and he wore a heavy signet ring on his finger.

At the far end of the counter was a younger man with a long white apron tied around his waist, holding up a bottle for a couple to inspect. Thomas glided over to them and held out a hand.

'You must be Sebastian Clifford. I'm delighted to meet you.'

'Thank you. This is Birdie, my business partner. We're on our way back from visiting a client in Leicester.'

Birdie blew one of her curls out of her face and looked around. 'Nice set-up you've got here.'

'Indeed,' Seb agreed, resisting the urge to smile as Thomas's face scrunched up, a series of emotions flashing in his eyes. Clearly he wasn't sure what to make of Birdie's manner.

'Thank you.' Thomas straightened and turned away from Birdie, as if deciding that was the best way to deal with her. 'You mentioned that your father, Viscount Worthington, is planning a charity event. I'm honoured you're considering partnering with me.'

'Their previous broker was involved in the Bordeaux fraud case. My father's now on the hunt for a new broker, who can also manage his cellar.'

'Oh, dear. It was shocking to read about the case. Fortunately none of my clients were affected. I'd be honoured to work with the viscount. Could you please tell me more about the fundraiser. We offer a full menu-matching service for the wines. Will he be wanting Champagne?'

'Yes, my mother insists on it.'

'A woman of excellent taste. I was in Champagne last month and secured some excellent varieties,' Thomas said before glancing at the wine fridge. 'Can I interest you in a tasting?'

'Not for the moment.' Seb held up his hand. 'I'd like to know more about the merlot?'

'Of course.'

Thomas spent the next ten minutes talking about several bottles, of which Seb was already familiar.

'Excellent. There is one other issue.' Seb cleared his throat. 'My father is insistent on discretion. He will not work with anyone who attempts to use his name as a calling card.'

'Discretion is my middle name,' Thomas said in a delicate voice. 'I have numerous clients who feel the same as your father. I see my role as the person behind the scenes, providing wines that only years of experience and connections can obtain.'

'That's all very well, but if no one knows who your clients are, how do we know you're any good?' Birdie, who'd been walking around, reappeared and gave Thomas a questioning stare.

The broker flinched and struggled to hide his irritation.

'I'm sure that's not the case,' Seb said in a mild voice, while making a note to congratulate Birdie on her excellent timing. 'Mr Thomas might refrain from boasting about his prestigious clients, but that doesn't mean he has none.'

Thomas gave Birdie a sour glare before coughing. 'Thank you for being so understanding. I'm happy to provide a list of my clients who don't mind it being known. Let's see, recently I provided a full bar for Cynthia Thornton She's very well known in the area and had a very successful fundraiser.'

At the mention of Cynthia's name, Birdie's eyes brightened. 'I've heard of her. Wasn't she burgled recently? We don't tend to work on cases like that, but I did read about it in the paper. Must have been terrible for her.'

'I didn't know that. I hope nothing too valuable was taken,' Thomas replied in a curious voice, that was at odds with his clenched jaw.

Interesting.

'I'm afraid there was. I believe they took several pieces of artwork and a valuable coin collection,' Seb pushed.

Thomas's nostrils flared and his eyes dilated before he rolled his shoulders and plastered a saddened expression onto his face. 'I'm sorry to hear that. Now, about the merlot, would you like to sample some? Or perhaps your parents would like to visit for a tasting? I would ensure the shop was closed, so they're not subjected to any interruptions.'

Seb clamped down on his lips. There was nothing his parents would hate more than to be treated differently because of their title. It didn't mean his father couldn't be proud at times, and occasionally cold, but he still preferred to earn his reputation rather than have the word 'viscount' speak for him.

Birdie stepped in front of Seb and faced Thomas directly. 'That won't be necessary. I know their calendar is quite full at this time of year and they have no immediate plans to visit Leicestershire, which is why they asked Seb to come by. You haven't explained your delivery schedule. I can see you don't have room for a large cellar here, so where's all your stock kept?'

'I have a warehouse in Glenfield ensuring delivery isn't an issue,' Thomas replied in a haughty voice. 'Now, if you would like to go over the details—'

'I'll need to consult with my parents first,' Seb said, forcing his voice to sound neutral, despite being tired of having to play the charade.

He'd met enough men like Thomas over the years. Sycophants who'd say anything to get ahead. Still, the visit had proved useful.

If Thomas was their man, he wouldn't be working alone. It wouldn't be enough to catch someone planting a jamming device at the Castles' house; they needed to find the stolen artwork.

Presumably that was why Birdie had asked the question about storage.

Disappointment crossed the man's face but he hid it quickly and flashed Seb a smile, while still ignoring Birdie. 'Of course. I look forward to hearing from you soon.'

It wasn't until they were back in the car that Birdie let out a disgusted sigh. 'What a slimy creep. Did you see the way he acted when I mentioned the burglary?'

'I did. Well done for managing to get under his skin.'

'I like to think it's my superpower.' Birdie beamed and brushed her shoulders as if congratulating herself. 'All I had to do was be myself. Though I'm sure if I said my dad was a baron general, he'd have changed his tune.'

'Baron general, eh?' Seb said in amusement as he pulled out of the car park. He was fairly certain Birdie knew that wasn't an actual title.

Further down the lane was a red car with a young couple sitting in the front seat peering down at their phones.

'Hey, that's PCs Dermot Quinn and Natalie Moore,' Birdie explained as they drove past. 'Twiggy obviously didn't have a problem convincing Sarge we need to tail Thomas, which is good, because now I've met the man I'm totally convinced he's tied up in this. Do you think he's storing everything at his warehouse?'

'I do. Even if he has buyers lined up for the stolen goods, it would be dangerous to move them too quickly. We need to discover its location.'

Birdie nodded and tapped away at her phone. 'Hmmm, it's not mentioned on his website and not coming up in a Google search, either. Damn. Maybe I should've asked him outright?'

'It's better that you didn't since it would have sounded suspicious.'

'True,' Birdie conceded. 'I'll call Twiggy and give him an update. Then we can start searching for the warehouse. If we find the stolen goods, this case will be halfway solved.' Before she called, her phone pinged. 'Oh,' she muttered.

'What is it?' Seb asked.

'Melinda has asked to come round this evening, even though we haven't planned on seeing each other until Friday. She hasn't said why.'

'Does she need a reason?' Seb asked, tossing a quick glance in her direction and trying to reassure his partner.

'I suppose not. Maybe she's got a surprise up her sleeve. Yes, I bet that's it,' Birdie responded with a smile. 'Anyway, I'll soon find out.'

. . .

'That's the thing, Birdie. I've spent ages hunting and there are literally no jobs around here. Librarians don't tend to leave often. I was pinching myself when I got this one.'

'Yes, but I've already said you can live here for as long as you like rent-free until you find something,' Birdie responded, trying not to sound desperate.

'I don't think anything will come up. I've thought long and hard and... well... it looks like I'll have to move back to London where there are jobs.'

London?

The word echoed around her flat, bouncing off the walls, before hitting Birdie square in the face. Her throat tightened and her mouth went dry. Melinda wasn't going to move in with her anymore because she was leaving the area.

Leaving me.

'But you hate it there.' Birdie finally managed to form the words. 'You said it drains away your soul.'

'Not to mention my savings account.' Melinda sighed. 'I need to work and don't want to waste my qualifications. The only good news is that an amazing job has come up at the British Library. A friend forwarded it to me a little while ago and I applied, on the off-chance, and got an interview. I couldn't believe it because I thought they'd be inundated with applications. Anyway, the interview's tomorrow.'

Oh. Why was this the first time Melinda had mentioned this particular job?

Birdie felt like she'd been punched in the stomach. She closed her eyes, trying to compose herself. This was the first time she'd really allowed herself to like someone, and now it was blowing up in her face. Except it wasn't fair for her to make a fuss. Melinda hadn't planned it, and as much as Birdie didn't want it to be true, she knew that there weren't many library jobs around. Especially ones that paid a decent wage.

'Where does that leave us?' She forced the words out, though her throat was tight.

'Nothing needs to change.' Melinda shifted so that they were facing each other. 'I might not even get it.'

But she would. Of course she would. Melinda was brilliant and smart and articulate and they would snap her up. And even if she didn't, it seemed clear that she was going to move back to London.

'Let's assume you *do* get it. We'll have to break up, won't we?' The words caught in her throat like glass, and she hated the way her hands began to shake.

'Break up with you? No, that's not what I want. I love what we have together.' Melinda seemed to notice the way Birdie's hands were shaking and wove their fingers together. 'I can still come up on weekends. Or you could come down to me. Not during cricket season of course. But I'm sure we can make it work.'

Birdie forced a smile onto her face but the lump in her throat grew bigger. It wasn't just the cricket season. It was the agency. When she and Seb were in the middle of a case, there was no chance to take off to London for a few days.

It was clear by Melinda's quivering lip that she was already upset enough, and the last thing Birdie wanted to do was make it worse, so she couldn't say anything.

'Sure.' She nodded, trying not to think about how close she'd come to having everything she'd ever wanted. 'Long distance won't be so bad. I'm sure we'll make it work.'

TWENTY-FOUR

Thursday, 2 July

Birdie bounced from foot to foot while standing on the platform at Market Harborough train station. Next to her, Melinda smoothed down the new skirt and top she'd bought for the interview. It was still early and a chill clung to the air.

Or was that just Birdie's mood?

Melinda must have sensed the shift and squeezed her hand. 'You could be worrying about nothing. I might not even get it.'

'Of course you'll get it. You're awesome and they'll see that straight away,' Birdie said, trying to ignore the lump in her throat. She wasn't a crier, but right now she felt dangerously close to bawling like a baby. 'This job's perfect for you.'

Melinda rubbed her lips together, causing her lipstick to smudge. 'I wish I didn't feel so conflicted about it. Why can't my dream job be based here with you?'

'Because the universe has a sick sense of humour,' Birdie retorted with a brittle laugh.

Again, the unwanted emotions tried to work their way up her throat. She swallowed them down. Besides, even if Melinda didn't get this job, she'd be applying for others in London, and had arranged to look at two different studio apartments later today while she was down there.

Whether Birdie liked it or not, the move was happening and her life was about to change.

Melinda's brow furrowed as she studied Birdie's face. 'I feel bad leaving you when you're right in the middle of a case.'

'It's fine. Let's face it... when am I *not* in the middle of a case,' Birdie reasoned, hating the way Melinda always seemed to know how she was feeling, regardless of whether the words were spoken out loud. Was that what made her such a good librarian because she was able to read people and know exactly what books to recommend? 'Seriously, you don't need to worry about me.'

'You're better than fine. You're amazing,' Melinda said as the train pulled up and the doors slid open. 'Don't you forget it.'

'I'll try my best. Try not to worry about today. You'll be brilliant and they'd be daft not to bite your hand off.'

'Thanks. I hope so.' Melinda took a deep breath and gave her a quick kiss. 'Okay, this is it. Wish me luck. I'll text you when it's all over.'

'I'll be thinking of you,' she promised, watching Melinda step into the carriage along with the other travellers.

Birdie shivered, the empty platform suddenly seeming too much like a metaphor of her future. Standing alone as the people she loved disappeared.

Stop with the dramatics, she admonished herself.

This was hardly the worst thing that had ever happened to her, and if she and Melinda were meant to last as a couple, they would. End of.

Feeling better, Birdie jogged out of the station and climbed into her car, forcing herself to think about the day ahead. Twiggy had confirmed yesterday that none of the other events in the area at the weekend were using wine supplied by Thomas. Seb's prediction that the Castles' high tea would be targeted seemed likely.

She drove out of the car park and headed to work. The drive wasn't impeded by any roadworks or tractors and she was soon pulling up outside Rendall Hall. She opened the front door and Bonnie raced over to greet her, the penguin in her mouth.

Birdie stroked the dog's smooth reddish-brown fur. 'Hello, girl. Aren't you full of energy.'

Bonnie trotted at Birdie's heels as she walked through to the study, where Keira was hunched over her laptop and Seb was behind his desk talking on the phone. He finished the call as she sat down at her desk.

'Morning. Is everything okay?'

'Yes. Why?' Birdie bristled.

'No reason. We were expecting you earlier, that's all.'

Crap. That was right.

'Sorry. I went to the station with Melinda... She's going to London for a job interview at the British Library.'

'I see. Was that why she wanted to see you yesterday?' She'd forgotten that Seb had been with her when she'd received the text.

'Yeah. But I don't want to talk about it now. We have work to do,' she replied, opening her laptop, signalling that the conversation was over.

'Of course, whatever you want.' The concern in his voice was matched by the worry in his eyes and almost caused her to totally break down, which she wasn't prepared to let happen.

'What's going on here? Any updates? Has Twiggy called to say how the tail went?'

'No. Our friendly DC hasn't been in touch,' Keira said before a smug smile appeared on her face. 'But yours truly has found the warehouse. It's under a different company name but Thomas is listed as a director, and a little more snooping confirmed it.'

'Excellent. Where is it?'

'Mill Lane Industrial Estate, Glenfield, which is close to Leicester. I've sent you a link to Google Maps,' Keira replied. 'I'd suggest we should go there now but there isn't much we can do without a police warrant.'

'And the police, themselves,' Seb added with a wry smile.

Birdie studied the location on her screen. It was about a thirty-five-minute drive, and Seb and Keira were right. It was pointless visiting when they couldn't get inside. 'I take it that's my cue to call Twiggy.'

'Your mindreading abilities are getting better by the day.' Keira grinned.

Seb gave his daughter a look then turned to Birdie. 'I agree, do you?'

'Consider it done. I'm in the mood for a raid.' Birdie flexed her arms, pleased to do something that would shift the weight of emotions still churning through her body.

She called Twiggy, but it went straight through to voicemail. Knowing he was rubbish at checking it, she sent through a text with the address. Her phone pinged a moment later with a reply from him. Her brow furrowed. If he could reply to a text, why couldn't he have picked up the phone? She clicked on his message.

Are you alone? Can you speak?

Birdie frowned. What the hell? Twiggy wasn't one for being so mysterious. Her stomach tightened. Despite their conversation the other day, she couldn't help worrying that this was another sign of his illness taking hold.

She quickly tapped out a reply to him.

I'm in the office and we're discussing the case. Why?

'Was that Twiggy? What did he say?' Keira asked.

Birdie quickly looked up.

Keira's dark brows were pushed together in puzzlement and Seb was also frowning. Damn. While she might be fine acting when they were out of the office trying to get information, it seemed she wasn't quite so good at hiding things when she was around her colleagues.

Not that she knew what she was trying to hide.

That Twiggy was acting strangely? Or that she was worried about him?

'It wasn't Twiggy,' she improvised, not happy about lying, but not wanting to say anything until she'd spoken to her friend. 'It's Annie. Our coach has decided to leave Lily out of the team and replace her with Marnie. Which is crazy. Okay, Marnie might be a great spin bowler but Lily's not only our fastest bowler, but she's great at batting, too. I don't get it.'

At least this part was true, even if it was based on the conversation she'd had with Annie the other evening when they'd met at the pub.

At the mention of cricket, Keira's eyes lit up. 'Are you playing at home this Saturday? I'd love to come along.'

'Sure. Melinda will be there if you want to hang out. We need as much cheering as we can get,' Birdie added. 'But there'll be no late-night celebrating if we win because we have the high tea the following day.'

'Trust me, after last weekend I have no intention of being hungover anytime soon,' Keira promised, then caught the concerned look that Seb was giving her. 'Not to mention I'll be working, so it wouldn't be appropriate.'

'I'd still prefer it if you refrained from going on Sunday,' Seb reiterated. 'So, if you do want to go out with the team and celebrate, that's fine.'

Colour rose in Keira's cheeks. 'I promised Zara I'd go. I meant what I said about wanting to have a break from partying too much.'

Birdie frowned, wondering if she'd have to play referee again, but before she could decide, her phone pinged with another text from Twiggy.

> Can you come to the station? We need to talk.
> Alone.

Alone?

Her stomach tightened and once again she glanced from Seb to Keira before going back to her phone. Whatever the hell was going on, it wasn't to her liking. But if she tried to call him back now, Seb and Keira would wonder why she hadn't put her phone on speaker. And if she slipped outside to call, there was the risk that Twiggy would clam up or get defensive.

For the second time in as many minutes she had to lie to her business partner. She got to her feet and reached for her denim jacket. 'I need to go to Market Harborough to pick up a prescription for my dad. Sorry about that. I'll bring back coffee.'

'I'll have a mocha thanks,' Keira piped up.

'Americano for me,' Seb added.

'Got it,' Birdie said and hurried out the door.

Twiggy had better have a bloody good reason for making her lie to Keira and Seb.

TWENTY-FIVE

Thursday, 2 July

The sun was bright in the sky as Birdie drove to Market Harborough. She'd tried calling Twiggy as soon as she'd pulled away from Rendall Hall but, like before, he hadn't answered.

What the hell was he playing at?

Irritation and panic competed as the fields flashed past. Damn. She slowed down, realising the last thing she needed was a speeding ticket. She drummed her fingers against the steering wheel as time seemed to stretch out forever. But finally, she reached the station.

There was no sign of Twiggy in the foyer, and as she climbed the stairs her mind was still whirling. Was he simply excluding Seb because of his dislike for her partner? Or was it to do with his FTD? She didn't like either option – and hoped there was a third alternative.

She increased her pace and finally pushed through the door and into the large open-plan office.

Much like her last visit, several of the desks were empty, but she found Twiggy leaning over his computer screen, his lips set in a thin line. Her annoyance evaporated and was quickly replaced by worry.

'Hey, what's with the cloak-and-dagger dramatics?' she asked, trying to keep her voice light as she crossed the room and sat on the chair next to his desk.

'Thanks for coming,' he said by way of answer, his expression still grim.

Birdie's stomach tightened and she tapped her foot. Whatever was going on, Twiggy was genuinely concerned.

'You didn't leave me much choice. Since when did you start being secretive?'

'I'm not being secretive, I'm being discreet.'

Birdie frowned. 'Well, I don't like it. Whatever you want to discuss should have included Seb. We're partners and don't have secrets. You'd better not be trying to score points against him.'

'I wish I was.' Twiggy sighed and gestured for her to look at his screen. 'Sorry for the mystery. I thought it was best for you to see these first.'

'See what?' she complained as she joined him and stared at a photo of Ewan Thomas sitting in a café, wearing the same expensive suit as yesterday.

Her eyes dropped to the time stamp.

It was yesterday.

'Was this taken by Quinn and Moore?' she asked, recalling the two officers who'd been waiting close to his premises.

'Correct. About an hour after you and Clifford left, Quinn and Moore followed him to this café. Thomas took several phone calls before someone joined him.' Twiggy clicked the mouse and another photo flashed up on the screen. It was of someone walking towards the table where Thomas was sitting. Their back was to the camera and a dark hoodie was pulled over their face.

'Who is it? Did they get a shot of their face?' she asked impatiently, tilting her head as if it would somehow give her a better view. It didn't, but all the same her mind automatically tried to sift through who it could be.

Isaac Cross?

Despite ruling him out, this person had a similar build. Then again so did Deanna Church. Isaac had overseen the bar at Cynthia Easton's fundraiser, so it was entirely possible there was a relationship between The Curated Feast company and the wine merchant.

'We did get several shots, which is why you're here,' Twiggy retorted and brought up another photograph, this time from a different angle so the person in the hoodie was now clearly visible.

Crap.

Her stomach dropped as she took in the familiar face of Keira's old school friend turned influencer. Zara.

Birdie sank back into the chair, running her fingers through her thick curls.

What did it mean? Surely they couldn't be friends. Thomas was old enough to be Zara's father, yet as Twiggy continued to click through the photos, it was clear they already knew each other.

But how? And why?

Birdie closed her eyes, trying to tease out the answer. What if Thomas wanted to hire Zara to promote some of his wines? Or maybe Zara was trying to organise her own event and needed to provide the wine. Both were plausible. It could even be that Thomas was a family friend and they'd bumped into each other.

She opened her eyes, a spark of hope flaring in her chest but it quickly extinguished as she recalled how Thomas had kowtowed to Seb, almost falling over himself trying to impress. If Zara was a client, then surely they wouldn't be meeting at a café. It would be at his premises, where he could use the surroundings to prove his social worth. Also, there was nothing about their body language to suggest it was a business meeting.

Well... she corrected... not a legitimate business meeting. Birdie had met Zara and viewed enough of her content to know that covering herself in a black hoodie wasn't her usual attire.

Twiggy continued to scroll through the photos and it was clear that the conversation was tense but there was also a familiarity in the way they interacted. Several times Zara looked up and peered around the café, as if worried she was being watched. Thomas didn't seem as bothered, though the tight clench of his jaw suggested he was nervous about being seen with the younger woman.

It wasn't an affair, of that much Birdie was certain.

'Is there any video footage? Can we hear what they're saying?'

'No, sorry. Even if there was, I doubt Sarge would spring for someone to lip read the conversation.' Twiggy closed the laptop and drummed his fingers on the desk. 'There's definitely something fishy going on, that's for sure.'

'You're telling me. I hate to say it... there's only one explanation that makes sense.'

'Zara is working with Thomas and they're both involved in the burglaries,' Twiggy replied, before she had time to voice her thoughts.

What a mess. Birdie let out a long sigh and rolled her neck. 'I appreciate you showing me first. Can you show me the rest of Quinn and Moore's report?'

'I've made a copy for you.' Twiggy handed over a folder. 'After the meeting, Zara left in a Mercedes and Thomas returned to his shop where he spent the afternoon working. He then went to a wine bar before going home for the evening.'

Birdie flicked through the report before frowning. 'Do you think Thomas is paying Zara to plant the jamming devices?'

'It makes sense. Thomas gets a wine order from a potential victim and he visits the house to make an initial assessment, on the pretence of seeing where the wine will be situated.'

'If he thinks it's worth it, he then pays a young influencer to slip in a jamming device,' Birdie said, picking up the thread. 'After all, she's always filming content so even if someone catches her wandering around the property, she can use her channel as an excuse. It's perfect.'

'We certainly wouldn't have made the connection if not for these photos,' Twiggy added. 'How friendly is Keira with Zara?'

Too friendly.

Birdie swallowed, trying not to think of Seb's reaction to all of this. 'They lost contact after school, which was two years ago. But lately they've become close again. Keira had planned to go travelling through Europe with her boyfriend this summer, but he got offered some work in Africa. She was very disappointed, so when she started hanging out with Zara, it seemed like a great way for her to take her mind off things. Seb'll go ballistic when he finds out.'

'Can't say I blame him.'

Birdie swallowed. 'Are they tailing Thomas today?'

'Yes. That's why I wanted to give you a heads-up.'

'Thanks, Twig, I really appreciate it.'

'What do you want to do about it?'

'As much as I dislike the idea, we need to tell Seb,' Birdie said firmly.

'I figured as much. Well, I guess we'd better get this over and done with. Will you call Clifford?'

'I can't explain over the phone. Even if Keira isn't in the room, she has this uncanny knack of knowing everything that's going on. She's like a bat with supersonic hearing. Most of the time it's impressive, but right now it could be an issue.'

'I live in a house with three women and while I don't understand *how* they always know everything I'm doing, they always do,' Twiggy said as Birdie dragged her phone from her pocket and brought up Seb's number.

He answered on the first ring. It was as if he'd been expecting the call. Her stomach tightened.

'Hey,' she quickly said before he could get a word in. 'Are you on speaker?'

'No.' His voice was tight. 'What did Twiggy have to say?'

Birdie flinched. 'How do you know I'm with Twiggy? I said I was going back to collect a prescription for my dad.'

'So you did,' he retorted. 'Now, please explain what's going on?'

'It's not something I can tell you over the phone. Can you come to the station, now. Alone,' she quickly added.

There was silence and she could imagine Seb gripping the handset. He didn't often show his emotions. Had he guessed that it had something to do with his daughter?

He let out his breath. 'I'm on my way. I'll be there in twenty minutes.'

'Thank you. Drive carefully and we'll see you soon.' Birdie ended the call and sucked in a breath. She wasn't looking forward to this.

TWENTY-SIX

Thursday, 2 July

Seb sighed and remained seated in his car. After driving far too quickly into town, now he was at the police station, he was reluctant to move. This behaviour wasn't like him, but when it came to Keira, he wasn't always rational.

It was obviously something to do with his daughter, or why else would Birdie have asked whether he was on speaker and then requested he come to the station alone?

He'd been concerned from the moment Birdie had started rambling about her cricket match, and it hadn't taken him long to realise she'd been speaking to Twiggy. At first a wave of anger had coursed through him that she'd gone on her own. But he'd quickly got over that. He trusted Birdie with his life and had forced himself to wait until she'd contacted him.

The only good news was that Hamish had called Keira and his daughter had disappeared to her bedroom for a video chat with him.

His chest tightened and he swallowed hard. Whatever this was, he needed to face it now. He climbed out of the car and headed to the station. Once inside, the officer on the front desk waved him through, and out of habit he took the stairs to the room where Birdie and Twiggy would be waiting for him.

Unsurprisingly, Birdie was standing. She looked as if she'd been pacing the room.

At the sight of him she exhaled loudly. 'You're here. Good. Did Keira say anything?'

'No,' he said in a cool voice, marching over to her. 'Please explain what this is about.'

'You need to see these.' She picked up a folder and opened it. 'You know the tail that Twiggy put on Thomas yesterday? Well this is what they found out.'

Seb peered at the photos in the folder, one at a time, all showing Thomas in a café. He came to one showing Zara's face and he sucked in a breath, while remaining very still.

Keira's friend was tied up in this?

'Sorry, Clifford,' Twiggy said, sounding genuine. 'I don't like being the bearer of bad news.'

'It might not be bad news,' Birdie quickly added, but he could tell she didn't believe it. Neither did he. Whatever the explanation for these two meeting up, it wasn't anything he wanted his daughter caught up in.

He dropped the folder onto the table. 'Did anyone follow Zara after the meeting?'

Twiggy shook his head. 'The budget wouldn't extend that far and it wasn't until I saw the photos this morning that I even knew about the meeting.'

'Nothing else came up when they tailed him, but they're following him again today,' Birdie explained. 'We need to work out why the hell a twenty-year-old influencer is having secret meetings with a wine merchant in his fifties.'

'There's no good reason I can think of,' Seb said, bluntly. 'We can't connect Zara to all the events where there were burglaries but we know she was at two of them and has accepted at least half a dozen others. She told Keira it was to network, make content and raise her profile, but is it possible that Thomas paid her to place the jamming device at Cynthia Easton's house and at the Blackwoods' garden party?'

Birdie gave a glum nod. 'That's what Twiggy and I were discussing. But why invite Keira to go with her to the gardens? Wouldn't it have been easier if she was on her own? The same with the high tea. If that was me, I'd want one less problem to deal with.'

Seb had been thinking along the same lines. Unless—

Hell.

He stiffened. 'Unless she *wanted* someone with her to blame.'

Next to him Birdie went rigid and swore under her breath. 'If that's the case, then the next time I see her, I'm going to—' She broke off. 'Let's assume you're right, there's no way Keira can go to the high tea on Sunday. She can't be anywhere near Zara until this is over.'

'Agreed,' Seb said, managing to bring his anger under control. He should've put his foot down about the friendship right at the beginning of the case. 'But we're left with the issue of how to stop Keira from attending.'

Twiggy shuddered. 'My girls are about the same age and are total sweethearts until they're crossed. Evie keeps reminding me it's all part of growing up, but sometimes it feels like walking through a minefield.'

Seb nodded.

There was no way he'd allow Keira to attend the event if it put her in danger of being caught up in whatever it was Thomas and Zara were involved in.

'Why don't you tell Keira the truth?' Twiggy pondered. 'That ll stop her going.'

Seb rubbed his chin, trying to examine the problem from all angles. Except his usual detachment had deserted him. He couldn't remain impartial when his daughter's future and safety was at risk. There was also the niggle that Thomas and Zara knew his involvement in the case and were using Keira.

'There's too much at stake to risk telling her the truth,' he finally answered. 'It might change the way she acts around Zara, which could be a tip-off. It might impact the case, or something worse...' He tailed off, trying not to think of what could happen if they suspected Keira of working for him and the police.

Twiggy's eyes widened. 'You're going to let her go?'

'Absolutely not. I'll explain that the police have decided her presence might interfere with the proceedings. She's aware of how many moving parts are involved in these operations and how easily things can escalate.'

Birdie frowned and shook her head. 'Keira's an adult and will appreciate if we're honest with her. Surely you owe her that. If I found out something like this had been kept from me, I'd be furious.'

'My first duty is to keep her safe, which I hope she'll understand. If she doesn't then I'll have to deal with it.'

'I agree with Clifford on this one, Birdie. Parenting isn't all ice-cream cakes and sleepovers. Sometimes you need to make tough calls.'

'I know,' Birdie retorted. She turned to Seb, the fire fading from her eyes. 'It's your call, not mine. I'm just pleased I won't be the one to tell her.'

Birdie was correct. Keira wasn't going to like it. 'I do expect some pushback. Will you sit in on the conversation? It will give more credence to the request.'

'Of course. I always have your back even if we don't agree,' she said, her voice fiercely loyal.

Some of the tension in Seb's neck dissipated. 'Thank you.'

'When are you going to do it?' Twiggy asked, checking his watch.

'I think we should wait until tomorrow afternoon,' Birdie suggested. 'Because even if we don't tell Keira the whole truth, there's no saying how Zara will react when she hears the news. Or Thomas for that matter. They could've already made the connection between Keira and Seb, and somehow found out we're on the case. The more we can minimise that risk, the better.'

'Agreed.' Seb's jaw ached. 'It's better to sleep on it, which will mean less time for Keira to react. We've a lot of work to do between now and then.'

'Yes,' Birdie said. 'We need to find out as much as we can about Zara, but it's not something we can do at Rendall Hall. If Keira sees us working on it, this whole conversation could be moot.'

'With fireworks on top.' Twiggy wriggled his fingers and made a swooshing noise to indicate an explosion.

Seb was devastated that Keira was inadvertently caught up in the case. He realised she was old enough to make her own way in the world, but he felt responsible, and would do whatever it took to keep her safe.

'Can you work at your apartment?' Seb asked Birdie.

'You mean my tiny apartment that doesn't even have room for a computer desk?' She raised an eyebrow before her gaze drifted to the desk next to Twiggy's that had once been hers. It was barely visible under piles of paper, boxes and a motorbike helmet. Clearly in her absence it had become a dumping ground.

Twiggy followed her gaze. 'I take it you'd like to work from here instead.'

'Let's see, it has bad coffee, smells funny and has Sarge stomping around in a rage most of the time. All my favourite things.'

Twiggy shrugged and turned to Seb. 'I'm not sure I'll ever understand her humour.'

'Who says I'm being funny?' Birdie retorted.

'Sometimes it's easiest to roll with it.' Seb gave Twiggy a sympathetic look.

'Tell me about it. Next she'll be searching my drawers to see if I have a secret stash of doughnuts.'

'You'd better not,' Birdie warned, waving her finger in his direction. 'Now, let's get to work. I want everything we can get on Zara.

Seb, let me know if you or Keira discover more about Thomas. If this is going to work, we need to be prepared.'

Seb couldn't agree more and after listening to Birdie and Twiggy bicker over the Wi-Fi code, he made his way downstairs and returned to his car. He wasn't looking forward to the conversation with Keira, but it had to be done.

TWENTY-SEVEN

Friday, 3 July

Birdie stared at the screen on her temporary desk at the station but, try as she might, she was finding it hard to focus. Melinda had arrived back from London late last night and they'd stayed up discussing the interview. Despite her girlfriend's concerns, Birdie gathered the interviewing panel had been impressed, which was great for Melinda, but not so great for her.

Not that she should be thinking about that right now.

She took a long gulp of coffee and got back to work just as her phone pinged with a text message from Seb wanting an update.

He was usually so patient but now he was texting like a teenager, desperate for news or at least a response. Her heart went out to him. It was like he was getting a crash course in parenting, and the only way she could help was to find out everything she could about Sara Hunt before she became Zara. They'd already built a background profile of her alter ego, ZaraH the influencer, but all they knew about Sara was what Keira had told them.

Birdie knew Seb would be itching to research the young woman himself, but it wasn't something he could risk. Hence the text messages. She opened a new tab on her computer browser and ignored the rising voices as Sarge tore strips off a young PC.

Wincing in sympathy for the unknown officer, Birdie typed in Sara's name, age and the school she'd attended. Multiple articles came up, and she scrolled through all the entries until she came to a photograph of the girl with her arms around a bunch of school friends.

Gotcha.

Birdie followed the link directly through to one of the less popular social media sites.

She frowned. The site had been promoted as the next big thing a few years ago but after a huge scandal involving the owner's beliefs around climate change, most users had deserted it. For someone like Zara, who'd grown her platform on sustainability, it seemed an incongruous fit. It was also a surprise that the account wasn't set to private, especially for someone who had a large online profile.

With luck on her side, Birdie began working her way through the account. The most recent update was from two years ago when Sara was still at school and suddenly it made sense. The account had been started and discarded before she'd branded herself as ZaraH, and she'd either forgotten about it, or didn't care.

Birdie's fingers tapped the keyboard as she sifted through the numerous school photographs. Most of them were composed of schoolgirls wearing the Churchill School navy uniform from when they were in year eleven. Some of them were of Sara holding a violin and beaming at the camera.

She was musical?

There had been no sign of a violin in the minimalist luxury apartment, or on her ZaraH platform. Had it been a schoolgirl phase, much like when Birdie had momentarily been interested in learning the guitar before getting bored with it?

As the girls moved up to sixth form, Keira started appearing in the group, which was when she'd enrolled at the school.

Birdie pressed her lips together as she studied Seb's daughter, her long arms wrapped around her friends. The group of girls became smaller and soon the photos were made up of Sara and Keira in a series of poses.

Continuing her search, Birdie came across a photo of Sara with two other girls. She followed the tags and found out their names.

Juliet Mackay and Imogen Thomas.

Thomas? Hairs rose on Birdie's arms at the familiar name.

The girl in the photograph had the same sharp features as Thomas with a deep tan and brown streaky hair. Could they be related? Why hadn't it come up when they'd done a search on Thomas? She flicked back through her notes on the wine merchant. He had an ex-wife and two children who lived in Gloucester. But they hadn't found the names of the children and, with limited time, they hadn't pursued it further.

Crap.

Birdie clicked through from Sara's profile to see what she could find on Imogen Thomas. But unlike Sara's account, Imogen's was set to private. Birdie tried several different platforms but kept meeting the same privacy blockers.

She pressed her lips together and put the photo into facial recognition and suddenly, as if she'd unlocked a safe, a series of photos populated the screen. Including one of Imogen standing next to a beaming Ewan Thomas. They were at a racecourse and were both dressed up and holding glasses of champagne. The tagline read:

Father and daughter enjoying a day out. Ewan Thomas, local wine merchant, was a proud father as he and daughter Imogen spent a day betting up a storm.

Birdie let out a long whistle.

Her phone pinged again with another text message from Seb, but she ignored it and began working her way through Churchill School's old newsletters and found Imogen's name mentioned numerous times for awards and scholarships she'd won, as well as being named head girl. Birdie looked at the dates and began to make notes.

Imogen Thomas was two years older than Sara and Keira and had been in the school choir and orchestra, where she played the cello.

Cello? Birdie thought of the photograph of Sara and the violin and began scanning through the newsletters looking specifically for mentions of the orchestra.

Finally, she came across one of Sara, Imogen and Juliet, all sitting together with their instruments.

Birdie quickly searched for the three names together and several photographs came up of the girls playing together in a small string group. Excitement grew like a bubble in her chest. She did a quick background search for Juliet but couldn't find any connections to the recent spate of burglaries, so kept her focus on Thomas's daughter.

Imogen was currently studying for an MA in Art History and Museum Curating at the University of Edinburgh. The same university that her father had attended. Birdie flipped back to the photograph at the races. They were obviously close. Close enough to work together?

But how did Zara and Ewan Thomas fit together? Had Imogen introduced them before she moved to Scotland?

It seemed the most logical explanation, and Birdie continued to work through all the online links. There were several photos of Imogen kissing a man who appeared older than her. He had a strong jaw and dark hair, but Birdie couldn't discover his name. She flicked back to ZaraH's current accounts to see if Imogen was following them or leaving comments but she wasn't.

Giving a loud sigh, Birdie got up from her chair, her mind whirling.

This had to be the connection but how did it come about?

Birdie toyed with several ideas but they were all speculation. Then another thought hit, firing a dart of panic through her.

Had Thomas guessed there was more to Seb and Birdie's visit

than merely to discuss wine? Would he make the connection? Or, worse, discuss it with Zara? Who would then piece together that Seb and Birdie worked together?

It might be nothing... but it might be something and they couldn't ignore it because Keira could be in danger.

Birdie sent Seb a quick text to let him know what she'd discovered. His reply boomeranged back.

Damn.

A second text came through.

How do you think it started?

Birdie frowned and let her fingers move across her screen with the reply:

Hard to tell. The last photo of Sara and Imogen together was in a string group playing at a private event. But that was before Imogen went to university.

Seb's reply came back immediately.

Maybe Thomas was at an event and recognised his daughter's school friend?

Birdie considered it:

Or... Zara approached him about it? When Twiggy and I spoke to her she seemed very competitive and focused.

Two ticks appeared to show Seb had read the message but there was a delay before his next one arrived:

It's a possibility. Keira has returned from walking the dogs. It's time we had the conversation. When can you get here?

Birdie's finger hovered above the screen. In light of this new information, it was increasingly obvious Keira couldn't go to the high tea on Sunday. But surely now it made sense to tell her the truth so she'd understand the seriousness of the situation. But she'd given Seb her word, and had to go with his decision. If he didn't want to explain fully then there was nothing she could do. After all, she was his daughter, which meant it was his call.

On my way. Be there in twenty.

She pocketed her phone and looked around. Twiggy hadn't returned from a meeting, and Sarge was in his office on a phone call. She turned off her computer and headed for the stairs, only to hear Sarge's gruff voice.

'Where are you off to in such a hurry?'

Coming to a halt, Birdie winced. So much for a quick getaway. 'I've found the connection between Thomas and Zara.'

Sarge raised one thick brow. 'Do share.'

'His daughter, Imogen, went to the same school as Zara, when she was known as Sara.'

'And Keira,' Sarge added, immediately managing to home in on the dilemma.

'Correct. There's nothing to make us think that Keira knows Imogen. But Zara does. They were in a small string group together.'

'Where's this Imogen now?'

'She's at university in Scotland. I can't access her social media accounts to see if she's home for the summer break, but we must assume it's a possibility.'

'And that she's involved with her father,' Sarge finished off.

'It's the theory that makes the most sense. I'm on my way to Rendall Hall. Seb's going to talk to Keira.'

Sarge's expression darkened. 'What's he going to tell her? If this operation's at risk, I need to know.'

'You, Seb and Twiggy are all on the same wavelength. All Seb's going to say to Keira is that she can't go to the high tea on Sunday.'

'Make sure it goes okay. There are many staff hours on the line and this might be our only shot. We'll get slaughtered by the press and the insurance companies if this gets messed up.'

'Tell me something I don't know.' Birdie sighed and said goodbye.

She took the stairs two at a time but the exercise did nothing to lessen the sense of dread coiling in her stomach.

TWENTY-EIGHT

Friday, 3 July

'What?' Keira's voice rose an octave as she pushed back her chair and stood up, her brown eyes flashing with anger. 'You can't be serious.'

'Yes, I am.' Seb's blood began to heat. He'd had several arguments with his daughter since she'd come into his life but they'd been quick to pass and had been part of the way they'd established boundaries. He'd known the conversation would be difficult, but had expected Keira to do as instructed when it came to work decisions.

He was convinced it was the right thing to do, especially as Birdie had discovered the existence of Imogen Thomas, the person connecting Zara and Thomas. Just one passing comment from Keira could cause them to join the dots and conclude that Keira was acting as a spy. Especially given the coincidence of when she got back in touch with Zara.

'You're being totally unreasonable,' Keira retorted.

'I'm sorry you see it that way,' he replied.

Keira made a snorting noise. 'Birdie, please tell him I can be trusted and that I'm not going to do anything to jeopardise the operation. You don't think the same as him, do you? You get why I should go on Sunday, don't you?'

On the other side of the table, Birdie put down her phone, which she had been fidgeting with, and gave Keira a reassuring smile.

'I'm sorry, Keira. This isn't your dad's call to make. I've just come from the station and was talking to Sarge. His budget's tight and if this operation goes sideways, it might be our last shot. He told me he doesn't want any added complications.'

'I'm *not* a complication.' Keira folded her arms, her temper still shimmering in waves. 'I'm not stupid, either. Of course I won't get in their way. But if I don't go, Zara will be disappointed. Dad, you were the one who told me I could go in the first place. You need to tell your sarge that.'

'It's not my place to do that, and even if it was, I wouldn't because I happen to agree with Sergeant Weston,' Seb responded, making a concerted effort to keep his voice calm. 'Part of working on a team means sometimes having to do things you'd rather not.'

'What bollocks. Isn't that why you left the Met? Because they moved you to another team and you didn't like it,' Keira flung back at him.

Tears glistened on her lashes. She was becoming overwrought. The last thing Seb wanted to do was upset her, but right now he needed her to comply with his instructions.

'That's enough, Keira. The decision's been made,' he said firmly, placing both hands on the desk.

'Yes, but it wasn't made by me. What am I meant to say to say to Zara? "Sorry I can't come because my paranoid father is worried that we *might* be somewhere a jamming device *might* be planted." We don't even know if this is the next place to be targeted.'

'I understand how frustrating this is,' Seb said, trying to sound reasonable, despite annoyance creeping through him. He wouldn't have dared speak to his father in this manner.

'I'm not frustrated. I'm pissed off. It's so hypocritical. If you're really worried about the operation being dangerous then surely I should persuade Zara not to go?'

'Keira, that's enough.'

'Why shouldn't I worry about my friend?' Keira snapped, her brows drawing together, as she thought. 'None of this makes sense. Why would Sergeant Weston care if I'm there or not? Unless you all think I'm going to do something stupid and screw it up. I'm right, aren't I?'

Seb glanced at Birdie, and gave a tiny nod, indicating for her to answer. 'Of course not. Your dad and I both think you should sit this one out.'

'Huh. You're happy for me to stay in the background researching but don't want me to step outside of the box? This is my summer break and I've been in the office researching my arse off. Don't I deserve some respect?'

Seb's jaw flickered but he sucked in a calming breath. 'We do respect you and understand how awkward it is. Why don't you tell Zara that something's come up and you have to go to London. I'm sure your grandmother would love to see you.'

'So now you're trying to send me away. You're so annoying.' Keira spun to face Birdie. 'Surely you can see how ridiculous this is.'

'Look, Keira, I get why you're feeling annoyed, really I do. But your dad's right. This operation's complex, and it's best that you keep away.'

'I thought you'd understand, Birdie,' Keira retorted, rolling her eyes. 'But clearly I was wrong. You're the same as Dad and don't trust me. It's obvious you don't see me as part of the team anymore, even though I've worked with you both for ages.'

'I know you have, and you've been a huge help. But you've never been out in the field with us. It's a very different dynamic and not something you can learn in one day. Your dad and I worked on the force and have had training which ensures we know how to respond in high-stakes situations.'

'But this isn't even field work,' Keira snapped.

She glared at them both before storming out of the room. The door slammed behind her and her footsteps could be heard as she ran to the front door and outside. A moment later an engine revved and her silver car flashed past the window, heading down the drive.

Damn.

That hadn't gone well.

'When she calms down, I'll speak to her again about it,' Seb said.

'Will you consider telling her the truth?' Birdie asked, staring at him.

'When the case is over. Her behaviour supported my belief that it would be too risky. If she wants to be treated like an adult, she needs to act like one.'

Birdie's eyes widened. 'That's a bit harsh. Okay, she shouldn't have stormed off, but I do get it. Don't you remember when you were that age and the rage would simmer inside until you wanted to scream?'

'Regardless of how I might have felt at that age, I wouldn't have acted on it. It would never have been tolerated when I was growing up. I appreciate that Keira's childhood was different from mine, but she needs to learn that having a tantrum isn't the way to get across her point of view.'

'Hey, I'm on your side. But remember, she's only twenty and she actually does have a point. For the last two years she's worked for us and has been included in everything but now she's told she can't be part of the investigation, and she's not being given a good reason why.'

'If she ever wants to be part of a team, she needs to learn that sometimes you put aside your own wants to do what's necessary,' Seb said.

Birdie opened her mouth but clamped it back down, as if she was stopping herself from saying something. He arched an eyebrow at her but she shook her head.

'Let's move on to Imogen Thomas.' Birdie opened her laptop.

'Good idea.' Seb joined her.

It didn't take Birdie long to walk him through the backstory she'd pieced together. He then shared his worry that Thomas and Zara might be grooming Keira to implicate her.

'I don't like unanswered questions,' Birdie growled. She stood up and began pacing, as was her habit when she needed to think. 'Especially when they all point to danger.'

'We need to keep researching to find those answers,' Seb retorted in a tight voice.

'You're right. Let's concentrate on Imogen. Was she on any of the guest lists? Usually, I'd ask Keira to check—' She waved a hand towards the empty desk. 'But under the circumstances I think it's easier to use your super brain.'

Seb gave a grim smile. 'She wasn't on any of them, but if she's a student, she could be in the area for the summer. You said that you couldn't get into her social media accounts but I wonder if anyone else has posted photos of her recently.'

Birdie marched back to her laptop, her eyes bright. 'I'd started looking into that when I was at the station. Let's see what else I can find.'

'Also, assuming Thomas is still under surveillance, they might have seen Imogen with him.'

'Let me check my inbox for an update.' She tapped on the keyboard and then studied the screen. 'Thomas has been at his shop all morning. There have been three visitors but no one matching Imogen's description. Of course that doesn't prove she isn't here. I'll keep digging.'

'I'll continue working through the Castles' guest list. We've also got the names of people who visited the house when they were away. It's mainly tradespeople.' Seb returned to his own desk, still mulling over Keira walking out rather than staying to help. Once it was over, and they'd discussed it rationally, he was convinced she'd understand his reasons.

In the meantime, he needed to focus on the case.

TWENTY-NINE

Sunday, 5 July

Birdie climbed out of her car, flinching as the warm breeze caught the hem of her skirt, blowing it against her knees. She hated wearing stupid outfits like this and she pushed the skirt back into place. Seb hadn't mentioned a dress code, but she'd gone online and looked at photos from the high tea last year and the women all wore floral, floaty things, along with loads of heavy gold jewellery.

Although she wasn't big on flowers or too much bling, she'd reluctantly worn the dark floral cami-dress, with ruffled trims, and a light cardigan over the top, that she'd bought for a family wedding last year. She'd almost taken it off until Melinda said how cute it looked. Now, as she looked at the row of European cars parked outside the Castles' Edwardian manor, and the queue of expensively dressed guests, she was pleased with her choice.

They'd come in separate cars, in case Zara saw them together but Birdie couldn't see her.

She spotted Seb and hurried over. He was wearing a dark navy suit, crisp pale blue shirt and a paisley tie. With his towering height and air of confidence he stood out and for the first time since the argument with Keira on Friday, Birdie totally got why he hadn't wanted her there. His daughter was almost as tall as he was, and had striking good looks, which meant she, too, would always stand out in a crowd. It wasn't something you wanted if you're working undercover. Although Seb had learnt to use his height and upbringing as its own kind of armour, Keira didn't yet possess those skills. In other words: she was an easy target.

'How's it been with Keira?'

'Not good. She avoided me yesterday. Not that she was in much.'

'She'll get over it,' Birdie said, trying to reassure him. 'She turned up at the match but was gone before we came off the field. Melinda chatted with her and said she seemed fine.'

'That's good to know. Was Zara with her?'

Birdie shook her head. 'No, she was on her own.'

'I see,' Seb said, his tone flat.

'Try not to think about it. You need to look like you're enjoying yourself.'

Seb nodded and smiled. 'You're right. Come on, let's split up.'

The queue at the door had disappeared and as they walked towards the entrance she wished she'd worn her Docs instead of the heels. She felt ridiculous wobbling on them.

Inside, the large hallway was filled with huge vases of summer flowers, lending a sweet perfume to the air. Birdie peered at the garden, which was visible through the long windows. Small round tables had been set up for the high tea and staff were at work putting the final touches in place.

The Castles were at the far end of the hall, ushering people into the huge room where their collection was housed. As she got closer, she overheard people talking in delight about the porcelain. Seb wasn't the only one to go all gaga over it. Birdie still couldn't understand what could possibly make the collection worth so much money, but maybe the upcoming lecture would enlighten her.

To one side of them was DS Bell, and elsewhere were two DCs Birdie didn't know, who'd been brought in from the Wigston station. None of them so much as glanced at her as she blended into the crowd, and Birdie gave a tiny nod of approval. As she'd driven towards the house, she'd also spotted Quinn and Moore parked along the road. They must have been taken off Thomas's tail to ensure all bases were covered today.

Birdie's eyes scanned the crowd. When Twiggy had the house checked yesterday there wasn't a jamming device which meant it might be planted during the afternoon.

The lecture was due to start in ten minutes and as she glanced at Seb, to make sure everything was okay, she saw anger filling his eyes.

She followed his gaze in time to see Keira walking through the door.

Her long dark hair trailed down her back and her cheeks were flushed, while her companion's blonde hair was in a high ponytail and her face was perfectly made up.

Zara.

Birdie's jaw clenched as Keira scanned the room and her eyes landed on Seb. She immediately put up her chin in a defiant gesture before laughing at something Zara said as they stepped further into the crowd.

Birdie moved towards him. 'Pretend not to notice her,' she muttered under her breath. 'Let's check the room. You go that way.' Birdie nodded to the wall of glass cabinets that were nowhere near his daughter. 'I'll do the other side.'

Seb gave a clipped nod and walked away. The tension seemed to melt away from his posture completely, allowing him to slip through the crowd without drawing attention, despite his height. It was impressive how he managed to control his emotions. Although she was getting better at doing the same, she doubted her hot-headed temper would ever be fully doused. Which meant she should also avoid Keira in case she said something stupid to her.

It didn't take long to make her way around the room, feigning interest in the display cabinets while scanning the faces. She recognised many of them because of the hours she and Seb had spent doing background checks on the attendees, but everyone seemed focused on the porcelain and exchanging gossip.

Birdie spotted Seb in conversation with a woman with a flushed complexion. As she headed in their direction, a man with a strong jaw and dark hair strode past her, almost knocking her over. Rude. She stepped to the side and frowned. There was something familiar about him.

She craned her neck, hoping to place him. At that moment he turned to speak to someone and she caught the angle of the jaw. An image flashed into her mind. Imogen Thomas was kissing him in a photo on her social media account. Was Imogen there, too?

A murmur went through the crowd and people began making their way to the many seats that had been set up in rows, all facing the makeshift stage.

Birdie and Seb exchanged a glance and followed the sea of guests. Seating wasn't allocated but Seb used his long stride to secure himself one at the end of an aisle, and Birdie sat behind him.

Keira and Zara were seated several rows in front of them and their heads were bowed together as if in deep conversation. Seb didn't react to them being in sight but before Birdie could ask if he was okay, Leonard and Rose Castle stepped onto the stage, smiling broadly.

The chatter stopped and Leonard opened his arms in appreciation. 'Friends. Rose and I are so pleased you could join us for our annual event, which is the highlight of our calendar. We're delighted to have Tim Richards here to talk about the huge impact the Chelsea Porcelain Factory had in such a short space of time.'

The man with the square jaw appeared on the stage and was met by a round of applause. He smiled in acknowledgement and stepped onto the podium, tapping the mic.

The hairs on Birdie's arms prickled. She leant forwards. 'That's Imogen Thomas's boyfriend,' she said quietly in Seb's ear. 'I found a photo of them on social media. I'll check him out on my phone.'

Surely this confirmed their suspicions that this was the burglars' next target.

Birdie zoned out of the lecture and pulled out her phone to research him. Her suspicions increased the more she read.

After years of working at the British Museum he now lectured at the University of Edinburgh, specialising in fine arts. So he was Imogen's lecturer. And boyfriend. Birdie slipped her phone over to Seb for him to scan then put it away, trying to ignore the twitching sensation in her legs as the lecture continued. She wanted to act, not sit there listening to him drone on. But they were all trapped until it was over.

Her eyes drifted to Keira just as Zara leant in and whispered something in her ear. Zara then left her seat and headed out of the room. Birdie's heart rate quickened and in front of her, Seb gave a miniscule nod, confirming she should be the one to follow.

Birdie left the room by a different door from the one Zara had taken. The advantage of having already visited the house was that she knew her way around. She headed through the empty hallway to where the security panel was housed.

There was a small alcove and Birdie stepped into it as Zara came into view, her flowery dress floating around her. She was wearing pale grey lacy gloves and had a slim, silver bag hanging from her shoulder. Birdie inched her way closer as Zara unclipped the bag and let it slip down her arm and onto the floor. Birdie put her phone on silent and began videoing.

If Birdie hadn't been watching so closely beforehand she'd have assumed it was an accident, but as Zara dropped down to retrieve the bag she took out a jamming device and tucked it down the side of a bookcase, hidden from sight.

Excitement washed over Birdie as she halted the video and pocketed her phone.

Their theory was correct about this event being the next target.

Thomas must have convinced Zara and Imogen to join him. But where did Tim Richards fit in? Had Imogen brought him to help value the pieces?

Zara stood up in one fluid motion, and Birdie saw that her lace gloves were enclosed with satin, meaning she couldn't leave fingerprints. Zara headed in the direction of the bathroom just as applause rang out from the room next door and guests began drifting back into the hall. The whole thing had taken less than a minute and if Birdie had been any later, she'd have missed it.

She grinned to herself and sent Twiggy a text.

As tempting as it was to arrest Zara immediately, if they did, it could mean forfeiting the chance of catching the burglars in action. But knowing the jammer had been planted meant that as soon as the Castles left for London tomorrow morning, the house would need to be under full surveillance.

'Where is she?' Seb was suddenly by Birdie's side, and her excitement at having caught Zara in the act faded as the reality of the situation hit her. If Zara was involved, then Keira was in danger of being accused of being an accessory.

'She went to the bathroom, but not before planting a jamming device.' Birdie quickly told him what she'd seen, and that she had video evidence.

Seb's expression darkened as his gaze settled on his daughter, who was emerging from the lecture. Birdie suspected it was taking all his effort not to march straight over and say: 'I told you so.' Then again, his stony glare conveyed the message and, after locking eyes with her father for a moment, Keira returned his stare with a frosty one of her own and then marched towards the bathroom.

Seb took a step forwards. 'I'm going to tell Keira we're leaving and that she must come with us.'

Shit. Birdie darted in front of him and put up a hand. He might be angry with Keira for disobeying him, but if he stormed over and Zara saw him, there was a chance she'd realise who he was and his involvement in the case. That would mean any chance they had of catching the burglars would be lost.

Despite how angry he was, the case had to come first.

'How about I have a chat with her?' Birdie expanded her chest trying to block his path. 'The last thing we need is you two getting into an argument. She'll come with me and then you can have it out properly back at the house.'

Seb opened his mouth, before closing it again, his nostrils flaring. 'Fine. You get Keira while I update the Castles and reassure them the police will be in place once they leave for London.'

'Seb, I know you're angry that Keira didn't listen to you but try not to be too hard on her. I'm sure she'll feel awful once she knows the truth,' Birdie said.

'Let's get this over and done with first,' Seb said, stalking away.

Birdie grimaced. She certainly didn't want to be stuck in the middle of them when they did finally confront each other. Sighing, she squeezed her way through to the bathroom and stepped inside. There was no sign of Keira or Zara, so she ignored the growing queue and stared at the four closed doors. But as they opened one by one, her stomach dropped.

Neither young woman was anywhere to be seen.

THIRTY

Monday, 6 July

Seb snatched up his phone at the sound of an incoming text message, but it was from Birdie telling him she was on her way. Sending a quick reply, he dropped the phone back on the kitchen table and resumed his pacing. Where the hell was Keira? The cold fury of seeing her at the high tea yesterday afternoon had morphed into worry by her continued absence.

He'd always assumed he was a reasonable father, which was probably what made him so unprepared for her blatant disregard of his wishes.

Fuelled by another wave of irritation, he marched back across the room and snatched up the phone to reread the text message Keira had sent him yesterday afternoon.

> I'm staying at Zara's and will be back tomorrow am for work. Sorry I disobeyed you. Please don't be mad. Love you K

There was also a line of emojis, which was a good thing, if Birdie's theory was correct. So why wasn't she answering any of his calls or texts? He'd sent enough of them, and although the first few might have been terse, the messages had changed in tone as his worry increased. Had she not been in touch because she was worried about how he'd react?

His pacing was cut off by the sound of the front door opening. Relief crashed through him, hitting like a tsunami. *Finally.* Bonnie darted to the door, but Seb was quicker and strode into the hallway only to see a mass of bright red curls.

Oh.

'I could take offence at how disappointed you look,' Birdie retorted, holding out a reusable coffee cup. 'But since you also look like you haven't slept a wink, I'll refrain from calling you out on it. I thought you might need some caffeine.'

'Your restraint is appreciated.' He took the coffee and forced himself to smile.

'Still no word?' Birdie sighed, while Bonnie danced at her feet. 'Maybe her battery went flat?'

'She could've borrowed a charger,' Seb said as they headed into the kitchen.

'Maybe she didn't realise until it was too late?' Birdie offered. 'Are you sure you didn't freak her out with the messages you sent? You did look pretty pissed off yesterday.'

He exhaled loudly. 'I might've done. I shouldn't have let my emotions get the better of me. Any word from Twiggy?'

'The Castles left for London half an hour ago and officers are watching all entrances to the property. If the burglars hit the place today, this'll be over.'

Seb nodded and rubbed his face. Usually when a case was coming to an end, there was a sense of satisfaction in knowing that their work had made a difference. But right now he didn't care if the whole Chelsea Porcelain Factory collection was stolen. His concern must have shown on his face because Birdie rested her hand on his arm.

'Try not to worry. Keira's a sensible girl. She's not totally naive. I'm sure she'll be fine.'

'I don't like us fighting,' he admitted. 'I'll feel better once she walks through the door. It's after nine and she did promise to be back in time for work.'

'Why don't we drive to Leicester and visit Zara? If Keira's still there, at least you'll stop wearing out the floor from all that pacing.'

Seb, who'd been tempted to make the trip several times already, agreed. He stopped only to leave a note for Keira, in case she returned home before they did.

The half-hour drive took place without incident and soon they were pulling up outside Zara's apartment block. There were four visitor parking spaces but no sign of Keira's silver car. The tightness in his neck increased.

'There's more parking at the back of the building,' Birdie said, clearly reading his mind. 'Let's see if Keira's car's there. Or Zara's. She drives a Merc.'

They skirted the building until reaching a second car park where Keira's small silver car was jammed between two large SUVs.

Seb's stomach tightened as relief and anger continued to battle it out in his chest. Why had Keira told him she'd be back for work this morning, if she'd planned on spending the morning with Zara? Hadn't she listened to any of his messages?

They got out of the car and headed towards the entrance, until Seb stopped dead in his tracks. He turned on his heel and returned to his car.

'Wait for me,' Birdie complained as she hurried after him. 'What are you doing?'

'I need something from the car,' he said, not breaking his stride as he pressed the fob and pulled open the door. He reached into the glove compartment and brought out the small lock-picking kit he kept there. Then he straightened. 'Let's go.'

Next to him, Birdie frowned as they walked towards the glass doors to the apartment block. 'Damn. I forgot there was a concierge. What if Zara won't let us up? Last time I was here, she couldn't really say "no thanks" to Twiggy and his police badge.'

A breeze had picked up and it blew her hair across her face.

Seb ignored the wind and peered inside to where a man dressed in a uniform was standing behind a reception desk. Birdie was right. If Zara had recognised either of them yesterday, she might not let them inside. Now he'd seen Keira's car, Seb had no intention of leaving without speaking to her.

Another gust of wind picked up as the glass doors slid open to let someone inside, and a swirl of leaves and litter blew in across the marble floor. The concierge had a brief conversation with the guest and waved them through before glaring at the mess.

The man muttered something under his breath before disappearing to a back room.

'Let's go,' Seb said, walking purposefully towards the door. Birdie immediately followed him as they slipped in through the unattended reception area and she led him to a fire door at the far side of the lifts. Even if Birdie hadn't hated lifts, he doubted they'd be able to use them without a swipe card.

'Zara's apartment's on the eighth floor,' she explained as they jogged up the stairs, a shared sense of urgency putting a halt to all conversation.

Birdie led him to a sleek black door and knocked in a rapid series of beats, before leaning forward to listen for movement. Seb could tell by her expression that she couldn't hear anything.

'Try one more time,' Seb instructed. When there was still no answer, he reached for his lock picks. He slipped on a pair of disposable gloves and stepped up to inspect the door. He was pleased to see that it had a regular barrel lock instead of an electronic one. Despite the expensive feel to the apartment block, the lock was cheap and not one that would prove a challenge.

'Bloody hell. You're not seriously going to break in, are you?' Birdie's eyes widened before lowering her voice. 'Twiggy won't be happy.'

'I am, and I don't care what Twiggy thinks.' He crouched, holding the small tension wrench and pick. 'Please make sure no one's coming.'

'Seb—' she started then broke off and stepped behind him,

effectively providing a shield. 'Fine. But to be clear, I'm no longer the impulsive one in this relationship.'

Seb didn't answer as he squeezed in some lubricant and inserted the wrench so he could test the binding pins. In a matter of minutes the lock disengaged and the door opened. He put away his tools and stood.

'I don't mind if you'd prefer to wait outside,' Seb said, pushing open the door and stepping into the apartment.

'No thanks. We're in this together,' Birdie said, following at his heels.

He gave his partner a quick nod and continued walking through the apartment. It appeared more like a show home than somewhere a person lived. The bookshelf only contained two pot plants and some decorative vases. There were also several large coffee-table books that looked like they were brand new.

It was all for show.

Birdie reappeared from one of the bedrooms. 'Both beds are made and the towels are dry. The bathroom around the sink is spotless, which makes me think they weren't here last night or this morning.'

'Did you notice an overnight bag?' Seb asked, trying to calm his rapidly pounding heart.

'I'm sorry, Seb.' Birdie shook her head. 'I don't think Keira's been here.'

He closed his eyes and tried to push back all the things forcing their way into his consciousness. His anger was long gone and replaced by fear, worry... and guilt.

Was she in danger? Had something happened? Was that why she hadn't responded to his messages last night?

Enough, he commanded to himself. Catastrophising wasn't going to help his daughter. Keira was smart, and whatever was happening, she'd be okay. He had to believe it.

He took a steadying breath. 'Call Twiggy and inform him we're coming to the station. I want them to locate her.'

'Just to be clear, you do realise that it might jeopardise the case if it becomes public knowledge that Keira's missing and Zara's involved in a burglary ring.'

'I do, and I don't care.'

'That's fine with me. I'll call him now.' Birdie pulled her phone from her pocket and made the call.

'Thanks.' Seb gave a sharp nod and marched out of the apartment.

The sooner they were back in Market Harborough, the sooner he'd find his daughter.

THIRTY-ONE

Monday, 6 July

Birdie twisted the silver ring that Melinda had bought for her birthday around her finger as she watched Seb clench and unclench his fists while towering over Twiggy, who was staring at the computer screen.

She'd never seen her partner so on edge before. Understandable, of course, but still. And where did the lock-picking kit come from? She was sure she hadn't seen it before. But now wasn't the time to ask. The main thing was that he calmed down because the tension radiating off him wasn't helping anyone.

Seb made a grunting noise and Twiggy's shoulders tightened in response.

This had been going on for the last hour, ever since they'd arrived at Market Harborough police station and had started going through CCTV footage from around Zara's apartment, hoping to see her Mercedes. But the more Seb acted out his frustration, the tenser Twiggy became. Birdie had the terrible feeling it would end in an argument. She needed to step in before things got worse.

Taking a deep breath, she turned to Seb. 'I need a word.'

'About?' he growled.

'It's private.' She tapped his arm, gesturing for him to follow her.

Seb joined her at the far end of the room but his stony gaze remained fixed on Twiggy. She had to defuse the situation but couldn't simply tell him not to worry and that they'd find Keira because he was too smart to be fobbed off with platitudes. That aside, she needed him to calm down and stay focused.

'I know you're worried, but right now your behaviour isn't helping Keira, is it?'

A muscle flickered in his jaw and for a long time he didn't speak. Then he let out a long breath and raked a hand across the stubble on his jaw. 'No.'

'So no more breathing down Twiggy's neck, okay? You know he's working as hard as he can.'

Seb nodded and squared his shoulders, as if trying to shake off his concerns. 'Thanks, Birdie. It's not often I let my emotions get the better of me.'

'That's why you're an excellent detective. *You're* our best chance of finding her. That super brain of yours doesn't often miss a trick, so keep focused. Okay?'

Some of the colour returned to Seb's face and he nodded. 'I promise not to lose it again.'

'Good,' Birdie said, relieved to see his usual calm air descend around him. 'We'll do our best to make sure she's okay,' she added, trying to ignore her own guilt and worry.

If she'd gone straight to Keira after spotting Zara planting the jamming device yesterday, they wouldn't be in this situation. But instead she'd stopped to text Twiggy and then tell Seb about it, so by the time she'd tried to find Keira it was too late. Which meant this was all—

No.

She cut off the thought. What was the point of lecturing Seb to hold it together if she didn't do the same. Taking a deep breath, she rejoined Twiggy at the computer.

'Found anything?' she said, trying to keep the worry out of her own voice.

'Not yet.' Twiggy shook his hair, making him look more unkempt than ever.

'What about CCTV from the motorway?' Seb demanded.

'There's so much, it's making it impossible to go through at speed.' Twiggy looked at Seb. 'Keira's phone's being tracked by the digital forensics unit and we should hear about that very soon.'

'I see.' Seb nodded.

'Has there been any activity at the Castles' property?' Birdie asked, aiming to distract Seb by diverting his attention – even if it was to a part of the investigation that was no longer their responsibility.

'Tiny sent a text ten minutes ago to say that it's all quiet, but we're keeping teams in place for the next twenty-four hours. If they strike, we'll catch them.'

'Has the jammer been disconnected?'

'Not for now. While police are there, we don't want to run the risk of blowing the operation. But if they don't show by tomorrow, we might have to disable it,' Twiggy said, as his phone rang. He glanced at the screen. 'It's digital forensics.'

'Answer it,' Seb commanded.

Birdie stiffened. However, Twiggy didn't seem remotely offended as he made a grab for his phone.

'What have you got?' Twiggy barked.

She held her breath as Twiggy scribbled down notes before finally finishing the call.

'Well?' Seb demanded.

'They've tracked Keira's phone from yesterday at the high tea onwards. It's pinged various satellites as she headed north from Great Bowden.'

Birdie's palms prickled as the colour drained from Seb's face. Why hadn't Keira responded to any of his messages? They'd hoped it was because her phone was flat but this proved it wasn't.

'Can you see where the phone was located last night?' Birdie asked, thinking of Zara's deserted apartment.

'It's been bouncing around Leicester,' Twiggy said then frowned. 'The last ping is from Dane Hills, Leicester. Here, I'll bring up a map.'

Birdie's heart pounded as Twiggy zoomed in on the area, which included the suburb of Glenfield. Why was that name so familiar? Next to her Seb stiffened, and his jaw flinched.

'What is it?' she demanded. 'What's there?'

'That's where Ewan Thomas's wine warehouse is located,' Seb responded, his voice devoid of emotion but his eyes flashing with fury.

'Damn.' Twiggy pushed back his chair and stood up. 'Sorry, mate,' he said, looking at Seb.

'Good work, Twig.' Birdie reached out and gave him a grateful squeeze on the arm.

'Just doing my job.' He gave her a gruff nod. 'Clifford, you want me to arrange for some backup to follow us over?'

Seb was already reaching for his car keys as he shook his head. 'Have them on standby but without sirens. I don't want Thomas alerted until I know that Keira's safe. Is that clear?'

'Crystal.' Twiggy reached for his coat. 'Come on. Let's rescue your daughter.'

THIRTY-TWO

Monday, 6 July

Seb pressed his foot down on the accelerator, slowing only as the motorway exit approached.

Next to him in the car, Birdie was glued to her phone, bringing up the floor plans of the wine warehouse, trying to work out the best way to enter it, while Twiggy sat in the back, having a muffled conversation with Sergeant Weston.

'Is there an update on Zara or Keira, Twig?' Birdie asked, as Twiggy finished the call, turning her head so she could see in the back.

'No,' Twiggy quickly replied but thanks to the rearview mirror, Seb could see the officer's worried expression.

It didn't improve his own mood.

'So why *was* he calling? I hope he wasn't trying to stop us because if that's the case I'll call him back and tell him what he can do with his idea,' Birdie barked.

'Save your breath, Birdie. He's as worried as we are. He wanted to give me an update on the Castles' house.'

'Which is?' Birdie hurried him along while Seb's grip tightened around the steering wheel.

'The operation was a success.'

'Were Thomas and Zara there?' Seb asked, his attention immediately caught.

'No. The only people there were Imogen Thomas and Tim Richards. They were caught red-handed in the house. The team watched them go inside, without the security system going off, and five minutes later they were outside, loading the ceramics into a Transit van. They're now at Market Harborough station waiting to be interviewed, which won't be for a while because they refused to speak without their solicitors present. Sarge will keep us posted.'

Seb swore under his breath, half tempted to turn around and interview them himself. But he knew it would be fruitless. If they wanted the case to stick, they'd need to follow due process. No matter how annoying it was.

Birdie twisted to face him. 'If Imogen and Richards are being held at the station, then Thomas and Zara won't be aware the burglary failed. This gives us an advantage.'

Seb grunted in agreement and turned left into Glenfield, following the road towards a collection of industrial units. If Thomas wasn't expecting them, it would be easier to confront him.

Feeling mollified, he continued driving until an old brick building came into view. Unlike the quaint wine store that was designed to create olde-worlde charm and even older world wealth, the warehouse was shabby and rundown. There was no signage apart from the street number to let him know it was the right place.

Seb drove down a service road and into the car park. Zara's Mercedes was parked next to a battered old Range Rover.

This was the place.

He parked as far away from the cars as possible.

From the back, Twiggy made a rustling noise as he unclipped his seatbelt. 'Backup's five minutes away, if we need them. Do you want me to join you in there?'

Seb's instincts were to storm the place and rip it apart until he found Keira, but Birdie had been right to take him aside earlier. He needed to stay calm and focused. He took a deep breath and considered the options.

If Twiggy went in showing his police badge it might cause Thomas to do something stupid. It was much safer to play ignorant and assess the situation before making his final decision.

'You stay outside the building until we give you the word.' He turned to Birdie, as he unclipped his seatbelt. 'Let's pick up from our conversation with Thomas the other day. We'll pretend to be there to talk about the wine order.'

'Got it.' Her eyes were bright and clear as she opened the car door. 'You do the talking, since he all but ignored me last time, and I'll see what I can discover.'

'Agreed.' Seb climbed out and they marched up to the building. Twiggy followed them part of the way before breaking off to stand in the shadow of the Range Rover. 'Give us ten minutes and if you don't hear anything, then come in.'

'Roger that,' Twiggy responded, giving a thumbs up.

They reached a loading bay at the rear of the building, with a single green door next to it. Birdie ignored the doorbell and instead turned the handle. It opened and she glanced at Seb.

'Ready?'

'Ready,' he confirmed.

They stepped inside and a security sensor picked up the movement, emitting a sharp alarm. Seb scanned the small reception area. No one was working there, and the layers of dust suggested the desk hadn't been used in a while. There was a door at the far end, which opened and Thomas appeared, glaring at them both.

The suit was gone and he was wearing a pair of jeans and navy, checked shirt with the sleeves rolled up. There was a layer of sweat on his brow and smudges of dirt. Had he been moving something?

His brow was puckered with annoyance, but on seeing Seb, he seemed to collect himself.

'Mr Clifford... this is a surprise. I don't usually allow people to visit the warehouse. How did you even find it?'

'It wasn't hard,' Birdie assured him, with a smile. 'You look flustered. Did we catch you at a bad time?'

'Not at all. I was surprised, that's all.'

'Do you have visitors?' Birdie asked.

'No. I'm all alone.'

Birdie frowned. 'That's strange because I saw two cars parked outside.'

'One belongs to my cleaner,' Thomas quickly replied. 'Sorry for the confusion; I'm delighted to see you both. Is there a reason you came here instead of my other premises?'

'I discussed your wine with my parents and they're considering ordering; however, they wished me to inspect the wine storage area, before committing,' Seb said, forcing a smile. 'My father's most particular.'

'I understand, but it's not possible for you to inspect the wine store at the moment because we're in a state of upheaval,' Thomas said, too late realising that Birdie had slipped past him and was now standing in the open door. 'Excuse me. You can't go in there.'

'Why not?' Birdie took a step through and Seb quickly joined her.

'Health and safety regulations.' Thomas hurried after them, his charming manner disappearing. 'Please will you leave.'

Seb ignored him and walked further into the space. There were rows of high shelves stacked with boxes of wine, and a large area for unloading on which several large packing cases could be seen from beneath blue tarpaulins.

But there was no sign of Keira.

Seb increased his stride, going further into the shelving units.

'I expected more than just boxes of wine.' Birdie frowned, jogging to keep up with him. 'What happened to wooden wine barrels and dusty bottles of wine lying on their sides? I'm almost disappointed.'

'This isn't the movies,' Thomas snapped, colour rising up his cheeks as he tried to step in front of them.

Seb shouldered his way past Thomas and turned down the next row. Still nothing. Panic pounded in his temples.

Where was Keira?

'Look... there's a door behind that shelving unit.' Birdie pointed. Seb pivoted abruptly and marched towards it.

'Stop. That's private. I'll call the police if you don't leave immediately.'

'No need, they'll be here any minute now,' Birdie retorted from somewhere behind Seb. The pretence they were interested in buying wine, dropped.

'What the hell are you talking about?' Thomas barked, his voice laced with panic. 'You must leave. I mean it this time. I haven't done anything wrong.'

'You don't sound like someone with nothing to hide,' Birdie countered.

Seb ignored them and increased his pace, his heart pounding with adrenaline, until he finally reached the door and twisted the handle.

'Don't open that,' Thomas warned.

Seb ignored him and wrenched it open in time to see two figures standing side by side. One had blonde hair but he barely noticed as his gaze locked on the six-foot girl with a willowy figure and dark hair.

Keira.

THIRTY-THREE

Monday, 6 July

Birdie watched Seb cross the room in four long strides to reach Keira's side. The tension in his shoulders had eased and relief was plastered across his face. Keira's expression, however, had morphed into confusion as her gaze travelled from her father to Birdie.

Birdie had expected to find Keira trapped in the room, her hands tied, but instead she seemed relaxed and calm. Didn't she believe that Thomas was involved? Or had she thought she was still trying to uncover clues for them? Either way, Birdie couldn't help being annoyed, since Keira's actions had not only put herself in danger but seriously jeopardised the case and caused Seb immense worry.

'Are you okay, Keira? Did he hurt you?' Seb demanded.

'Hurt me? Of course not. Why are you both here?'

'Why are *you* here?' Birdie responded, since Seb seemed incapable of speech.

Keira's gaze landed on Thomas. 'Zara told me she had a business meeting with Mr Thomas and I thought it would give me a chance to see what I could discover and report back to you.'

'Has something happened?' Birdie pushed.

'The only thing that's happened is you two are trespassing, and I won't stand for it,' Thomas complained, but no one paid him any attention.

Instead, Seb fixed his gaze directly on Zara. 'Imogen Thomas and Tim Richards have been arrested in an attempted burglary at the Castles' house.'

'Why should I care?' Zara snapped, glaring at Seb and Birdie. 'Why are you here, anyway?'

'Don't play dumb,' Birdie answered, shaking her head. 'We know you're involved in the burglaries. You go to the selected venue and place the jamming device, to make it safe for the thefts.'

'No way.' Keira gasped, a horrified expression marching across her face. She stared at Zara. 'Tell me they're wrong.'

Before Zara could answer, Thomas pivoted on his heels and ran through the warehouse. Birdie swore under her breath and turned to follow him but Seb was already on the move.

'I've got him. Make sure Zara doesn't leave,' he shouted over his shoulder before sprinting after the wine merchant.

'Don't worry, she's not going anywhere.' Birdie blocked the doorway as Zara tried to barge her way past and follow Thomas.

'Get out of the way. You can't keep me here; I haven't done anything,' the young woman said.

'We know you've been working with Thomas the entire time, so don't deny it.'

Keira stared at her friend, confusion in her eyes. 'You told me that Ewan Thomas asked you here to discuss a sponsorship opportunity. You lied.'

'It's Birdie who's lying, not me. She's trying to frame me for something I haven't done.'

'I took a video of you planting the jammer at the Castles' high tea,' Birdie said.

At the mention of the video, Zara's bravado fell away, and Keira's face crumpled in horror.

'You've no right to stop me.' Zara suddenly lunged towards Birdie.

'No, but I do.' Twiggy appeared in the doorway and forced Zara back to a nearby chair. 'Sit.'

Seb joined him a moment later, leading a panting Thomas back into the room. He shoved him down into the other chair and folded his arms.

'The game's over,' Twiggy informed them. 'You're both under arrest.' Thomas's face remained impassive as Twiggy gave the police caution, but Zara's expression was one of disbelief.

'I have a team of officers on the way, along with a search warrant.'

'You can't do that,' Thomas spluttered.

'I'm not sure you understand what *search warrant* means?' Twiggy retorted, sounding so much like his old self that Birdie wanted to throw her arms around him and give a tight squeeze. 'It will be a lot easier if you start talking.'

'I have nothing to say,' Thomas spat.

Twiggy shrugged. 'Then I suppose we should be pleased that your daughter and Tim Richards are both singing like canaries.'

At the mention of his daughter, Thomas paled. 'This isn't Imogen's fault. Please, I'll tell you everything you need to know, but don't prosecute my daughter.'

'What about me?' Zara demanded, fury burning in her eyes. 'Are you going to hang me out to dry?'

Thomas refused to look at her, instead giving Twiggy another pleading stare. 'My daughter's innocent. You must believe me.'

'It's not my decision,' Twiggy informed him. 'I suggest you start at the beginning.'

The fight faded from Thomas. 'I was sick of being broke. Setting this place up cost a bomb, and half of my clients don't think twice about not paying me, or wanting me to wait months and months for reimbursement. They always have excuses about why they can't afford it and it's not like I can take the wine back once it's been drunk.' His mouth twisted into a sulky line. 'While I'm struggling to keep going, they fill their houses with art and collectables worth millions.'

'So you decided to even things up. Did you look for ways to get around the security systems, and then approach Pip Range?' Birdie asked.

'How did you find out about that?' He sighed. 'I heard she was the one to approach. She said the devices would work across a range of security systems, so I ordered ten of them. Happy?'

'Delighted.' Twiggy made a gesturing motion with his hand for Thomas to continue. 'What next?'

'I met Richards and he talked about the huge black market for high-end art, because once it was stolen it was almost impossible to track. It would end up in someone's private collection and would never be heard of again. It sounded perfect and I convinced Richards to help.'

'I understand convincing Richards to join you, but why drag your daughter into this? Or Zara, for that matter?' Birdie demanded, trying to get her head around his reasoning. 'Did you have something on them?'

Thomas narrowed his eyes and refused to answer. Birdie opened her mouth to push him further, but before she could say anything, Keira, who'd been standing still, suddenly crossed over to Zara and stood in front of her.

'Why did you agree to do this?' she asked, a pleading note in her voice. As if willing Zara to deny it.

Zara scowled. 'It's complicated. Not that I expect you to understand.'

'Why? Because I haven't broken the law before?'

'No, because everything you've ever wanted has been handed to you on a plate,' Zara snapped.

'Really? Well it shows how much you know about what I've been through,' Keira responded, her voice hard. 'To think I thought you were my friend.'

Was Keira thinking back to her mother's death and her journey up to Leicestershire to meet the father who didn't even knew of her existence? It had been a risky move, that could've ended up so differently.

'You poor little princess,' Zara shot back, seeming to forget her own privileged upbringing.

'Is that why you invited me to the high tea, and here today?' Keira asked, two spots of colour forming on her cheeks.

'I thought I might need an alibi.' Zara shrugged, clearly not feeling any remorse in the decision.

'Are the stolen items under that tarp in the loading bay?' Birdie cut in, having noticed Seb's jaw tightening and not wanting him to lose his cool.

'Yes,' Thomas snapped in a belligerent tone. 'So, there is no need for the police to tear this place apart.'

'I'll be the judge of that,' Twiggy said, as his phone rang.

After a brief conversation he pocketed it.

Sirens could be heard in the distance.

'Are they here?' Birdie asked.

'Yes, I need to brief them first. In the meantime, I suggest you two don't do anything stupid,' Twiggy said, nodding at Thomas and Zara.

Thomas glared at Twiggy, before folding his arms and sinking further into the seat.

'Zara, I still don't understand why you got involved in all of this,' Keira said, looking close to tears. 'You must have known it wasn't right.'

Zara stubbornly poked the floor with the toe of her shoe before sighing. 'I didn't have a choice, okay. Thomas made me.'

'But how?' Keira persisted. 'Was he blackmailing you? There must be a reason why you'd risk blowing up your life like this.'

'It wasn't by choice.' Zara brushed a tear away from the corner of her eye. 'I wish I'd never met Thomas. Or become an influencer. I only did it because I thought I could make the world a better place, but then it all went wrong.' All the bravado had gone from the young woman and instead she looked scared.

'What happened?' Keira pushed.

Zara didn't look up as she spoke. 'I was approached by a group of ethical fashion designers. They were into sustainability and zero waste and wanted to work with me. I agreed to promote them. It was a no-brainer since I loved what they were doing and they paid me well. But... then I got the clothes and they were so fugly... I mean they made me look like I was huge. A potato sack would have looked better, so I didn't end up using them.'

Keira gasped as understanding hit her. 'But you still took their money?'

'Yes. Then I sold the outfits on a designer wardrobe app. At the time I needed the cash and some people actually like potato sack chic.' Her shoulders sagged. 'Unfortunately, one of the designers was Thomas's niece, and he threatened to expose me unless I helped him with a little problem. By that time my channel had really taken off and I could have lost everything if the truth came out.'

'So you went along with him rather than admitting what you'd done and returning the money?' Keira said, her voice filled with disappointment.

'It turns out she's not as ethical as she claims to be,' Thomas added as Twiggy came back into the room along with two police officers.

'Sorry to interrupt the party but we're ready to escort them to the station for interviewing,' Twiggy said as the two officers led Thomas and Zara away. 'I'll call you with an update once they've been questioned.'

'Thanks, Twig,' Birdie said as he left the room.

Once they were alone she glanced at Seb, hoping his mood had improved but instead his expression was icy.

'We'll discuss this in the car,' Seb said, marching off.

'On a scale of one to ten, how mad do you think he is?' Keira asked, her hands wrapped around her middle.

'What do you think?' Birdie responded, not wanting to upset her, but there was no point in sugarcoating it.

'I can't believe I was taken in by Zara. All she wanted to do was use me,' Keira said, not answering Birdie's question.

'You weren't to know. She was clearly very convincing, and

you were upset by Hamish going away and perhaps not thinking straight.'

'That's just an excuse. I've been working with you and Dad long enough for there to have been some warning bells. That is, if I was any good at my job. Which clearly I'm not or I wouldn't have missed something so important.'

'Don't say that. You're good at what you do, and we're lucky to have you working with us. That said, you shouldn't have gone against your dad. He may come across as being overprotective, but trust me, he knows what he's doing.'

'You're right. I'm really sorry.'

'Come on, let's get out of here. This place gives me the creeps.'

'My car's still at Zara's,' Keira said, as if suddenly remembering.

'Your dad can stop there on the way back and you can drive it home.'

Keira nodded, suddenly looking a lot younger than her twenty years. Feeling sorry for her, Birdie squeezed her hand. She knew Seb would eventually calm down but she suspected she'd have to mediate between them before he got to that state.

THIRTY-FOUR

Monday, 6 July

Seb's face was an impassive mask as he started the engine and reversed out of the car park and headed towards the motorway. It wasn't Birdie's place to intervene so instead she focused on the road ahead, waiting for the shit to hit the fan.

'What do you have to say for yourself?' Seb finally said, craning his neck and staring into the rearview mirror to where Keira was sitting, huddled up in the back seat.

'Dad, I'm so sorry for not listening to you and going to the high tea. But how was I meant to know that Zara was involved? No one told me.' She paused and let out a soft gasp. 'Wait... *when* did you know about it? Was it before the high tea? Is *that* why you didn't want me to go?'

'It came up as part of the investigation,' Seb said in a cool voice. 'I decided it was best not to inform you.'

'You lied to me. Why didn't you trust me? Did you think I'd blab to Zara?'

'No, but I thought you might accidently let something slip, because you haven't worked undercover before.'

'You're unbelievable. Why didn't you tell me, Birdie?' Keira asked, her voice getting dangerously high. She was obviously close to tears.

'It wasn't Birdie's decision to make, it was mine,' Seb cut in.

Birdie closed her eyes. What a mess. If they weren't in the car she'd force them to look at each other while they spoke. She'd tell Keira how worried Seb had been about her, how his mind had been working overtime thinking of the worst things that could possibly have happened. Instead, she was stuck in the middle, not able to do anything.

'You should have told me, Dad,' Keira said, a hint of defiance lacing her words. 'I'm not a child. You should treat me like an adult.'

'This *is* me treating you like an adult. As an adult, who's also employed by my company. I expect you to obey me when it comes to casework. Are we clear?'

Keira didn't answer and Birdie could no longer bear the tension. 'Keira, it wasn't just that you turned up at the high tea and put the investigation at risk, but you went AWOL. You didn't reply to any of your father's messages and you didn't turn up to work this morning. Imagine if one of us did that; how would you feel?'

Keira sucked in a sharp breath as she appeared to be considering Birdie's words. 'I didn't realise. I thought everything was fine.'

'Well, it wasn't,' Seb said, though the anger had left his voice.

It seemed to be the undoing of Keira, and from the backseat she burst into tears.

'I'm so sorry. I really didn't mean to mess up and promise it won't happen again. Please don't hate me.'

'Nobody hates you,' Seb assured her. 'But we – I was worried. I apologise for shouting but I hardly slept last night.'

'I had no idea. I feel awful. How dare Zara use me like that? I'm so stupid. I wish I'd never contacted her in the first place. I made everything worse. I'm so sorry.'

'Apology accepted, but don't be so hard on yourself. We all get deceived at some stage in our lives. It's how we learn,' Seb replied.

Birdie twisted around to face Keira. 'Why didn't you answer your dad's calls or texts?'

'What messages? I sent Dad a text saying I was staying at Zara's and would be back at work this morning. I didn't hear back.' Keira frowned and pulled out her phone from her bag. After a few seconds scrolling she glanced up at Birdie, appearing puzzled. 'I don't understand... it looks like our message history has been deleted and you've both been blocked.'

'Did Zara use your phone at all?' Birdie asked.

Keira let out a long groan. 'I don't believe it.'

'I take it that's a yes,' Birdie said.

'Yeah,' Keira agreed. 'Not long after I sent the text to Dad, she said her battery was going flat and could she borrow my phone. I was busy doing my makeup in the other room and never even heard any messages come in. But she didn't know you suspected her then, so why did she do it?'

'Covering her tracks, I suspect,' Birdie said. 'It explains why you didn't answer. Where were you? We know you weren't at Zara's last night.'

'We went to the pub with some of Zara's friends and crashed with one of them. I did plan to be at work first thing this morning but Zara was desperate to go to Thomas's warehouse. She said he had this new organic wine coming in and he was going to give her a massive sponsorship deal.'

'Surely you must have thought it was too much of a coincidence?' Seb said.

'I swear I didn't. Of course I freaked out when she mentioned his name, but figured it was the perfect opportunity to get some inside goss on him. That's the whole reason I originally started hanging out with Zara, remember? To help solve this case from the inside.'

'I also remember that I wasn't keen for you to do it,' Seb retorted.

Birdie hoped there wouldn't be another argument but, instead, Keira held up both hands.

'Yeah, okay. I walked straight into that one. No more undercover work for me.'

'Not until you've been trained,' Seb corrected before frowning. 'There's one more thing I'm not clear on. Did you meet Imogen Thomas when you were hanging out with Zara?'

'No, I didn't even know they were friends. I vaguely remember her from school but hadn't realised she was Ewan Thomas's daughter... Wait a minute... how do you know that we didn't sleep at Zara's apartment? There's no way the concierge would have told you.'

Birdie burst out laughing and looked at Seb. 'I'll leave you to tell your daughter about your lock-picking abilities.'

'What?' Keira blurted out, for the first time sounding more like her usual self. 'You're not seriously telling me that straightlaced Sebastian Clifford knows how to pick a lock?'

'Like I said, not my call,' Birdie reminded her, before reaching into the glove compartment and extracting the slim set of tools that Seb had used and holding them above her head so Keira could see them. 'But I can attest to the fact he owns these.'

'Dad?' Keira said in awe. 'I can't believe you broke the law.'

'It's not a story I would like circulated,' Seb said in a cool voice but there was a hint of a smile tugging at his mouth.

Birdie settled back into her seat. She didn't doubt that the pair of them would have more conversations about what happened, but at least now the tension had eased.

Her phone pinged and Twiggy's name flashed up on the screen, followed by a text message.

> We've got full confessions from them all, which means it's time to celebrate. Meet you at the pub. Sarge is buying.

THIRTY-FIVE

Monday, 6 July

'I feel bad that Keira's not coming out to celebrate, but there's no way I'm missing out on Sarge buying a round of drinks. I do believe it might be a first,' Birdie quipped as she stood beside Seb's car, waiting for him to lock it. 'How was she after I left?'

Birdie had gone back to her own apartment for the afternoon, and they'd arranged to meet outside the pub.

It had given him time to discuss the events of the day with Keira. It had been tense, but the heat from earlier was no longer present, and by the time they'd finished, a new agreement had been reached.

'She's getting over it, but it will take a little time.' Seb pocketed his keys and they headed towards the entrance.

'Poor thing. As wrong as she was, I can see it from her point of view,' Birdie admitted.

Seb reluctantly nodded. 'After listening to her reasoning, I understand her motivation. I don't agree with it, but we've made our peace.'

'I'm pleased,' Birdie said. 'Though I'm still not sure why she's not here?'

'She said she couldn't face going out. I think she's worn out from the emotional toil. I left her watching a film curled up on the couch with Bonnie and Elsa.'

'That girl knows how to hunker down. How are you feeling?'

Seb sighed. It was a good question. He prided himself on staying calm but there had been nothing calm about his reaction to Keira's disobedience. Maybe *he* needed to hunker down on the couch at some stage, too? Not that he'd ever admit that to his partner.

'I'm fine. We've cleared the air and had a good talk about what happened. It's hard for me to remember she was raised differently from me.'

'I'm pleased you're cutting her some slack. Keira grew up in a regular family where you didn't need to know who to bow and curtsey to.' Birdie paused. 'But... she shouldn't have gone behind our backs, and she knows that. I think she's learnt a valuable lesson.'

Seb did as well. That aside, Birdie was right. Keira's upbringing had been different from his and he needed to remember that.

'Who knows, one day we might even be able to laugh about it,' he said, already feeling lighter at having discussed it.

'Possibly by the time you have a housewarming party?' Birdie gave him a mischievous look.

'Is this your way of asking if I've decided whether to buy Rendall Hall?'

'Wow... nothing gets past you.' Birdie laughed. 'I figured that now the case is over, you'd have had time to flip a coin to decide.'

'It's like you can read my mind,' he responded, far too used to her teasing to fall for it. They entered the pub and he scanned the room. 'It looks like Sergeant Weston and Twiggy haven't yet arrived. We'll sit over there and wait for them.' He nodded towards a table in the courtyard.

'Well... come on... Don't keep me in suspense. Are we going office hunting?'

While Birdie might be wrong about the coin toss, she was right about him making his decision. Keira had been through a lot in her twenty years and needed some stability. Buying the hall would give her that.

'No, we're not. Before leaving this evening I agreed on a price with Sarah and have instructed my solicitor. I've decided to keep my London apartment, though. We can use it as a base if we're working close by, plus after university Keira might wish to locate to London and it will be there for her to use.'

'Congratulations.' Birdie beamed at him, before picking up a brewery coaster and tapping it on the table. 'I'm happy for you.'

'Thank you,' Seb said, before noticing the thin lines around her mouth. Her coaster tapping increased. 'How are you? Has Melinda heard about the job?'

Birdie pulled a face. 'They're doing reference checks, but I think it's a formality. We're going to try a long-distance relationship.'

'I hope you're successful, and remember there's always a place to stay in London whenever you need it.'

'Thanks, Seb,' she replied, sounding unusually serious. 'I appreciate the support. More than you know.'

'Well, in the words of someone wise: I've got your back.' He smiled and noticed she was distracted by something.

He turned to see Twiggy and Sergeant Weston heading in their direction holding a tray of drinks.

'Clifford. Birdie.' Sergeant Weston gave them both a gruff nod and thrust the tray at Twiggy. 'Make yourself useful and hand these out.'

'What did your last one die of?' Twiggy muttered as he passed Birdie a half of cider and Seb a pint of Guinness.

'Thank you.' Seb had no idea how they'd known their drinks order but he took it all the same.

'Thank *you*,' Sergeant Weston responded, holding up his own pint of beer. 'The top brass have finally stopped breathing down my neck. Couldn't have done it without you.'

'Twiggy, did you hear that? It sounds like Sarge is missing me.'

Birdie's eyes had lost the melancholy expression and were twinkling.

'Yeah... like a hole in the head,' Sergeant Weston retorted, holding up his glass to hide what Seb suspected was a grin.

'I'm sure he does deep down,' Twiggy added.

'I agree.' Birdie took a sip of her cider. 'I hope this means you'll be hiring us again.'

'Did I mention the hole in the head?' Sarge grumbled but his mouth was twitching with the start of a smile. 'Now, if you've finished hustling for work, do you want to hear what happened?'

'What do you think?' Birdie asked, rubbing her hands together in anticipation.

'A mastermind criminal, Thomas was not. Well... maybe up to a point,' Twiggy corrected.

'What Twiggy means is that Ewan Thomas didn't take much prodding to spill the beans,' Sergeant Weston added. 'He met Richards when he was visiting Imogen at university and they struck up a friendship. Thomas told Richards his plan and asked if he wanted to be a part of it. It was later that Imogen and Zara became involved.'

Birdie put down her drink. 'Why did Tim Richards agree? He has a good job and the way the Castles went on about him, he's a big deal in the ceramics world. Why throw it all away? I don't get it.'

'Because, like Thomas, he needed more money,' Twiggy explained. 'He owed his ex-wife a fortune in child maintenance, and there were other debts. Thomas had assured him they wouldn't get caught.'

'And like a fool, he believed him?' Birdie sighed. 'Did Imogen start dating Richards before or after he began working with her dad?'

'We think it was after, and she'd started spending more time with him,' Twiggy said with a shudder. 'Though who's to say if the relationship will last now this has happened.'

'What next?' Seb asked.

'Everything's been forwarded to the Crown Prosecution Service and we're waiting to hear from them regarding the charges,' Sergeant Weston replied.

'I'll drink to that.' Birdie held up her glass.

The talk turned to the cricket season as the late afternoon sun began to cast shadows over the pub. Another couple of rounds were bought but Seb swapped to sparkling water because he was driving. He was about to leave when his phone pinged with a text message from Keira.

His heart pounded as he stared at it, and a dull fog seemed to fill the room.

> Dad, come home now. Something's wrong with Elsa...

THIRTY-SIX

Tuesday, 7 July

Seb stared at the dark mound of soil. It was shaded by an oak tree and light danced across Larry llama and the old pair of Seb's slippers that Elsa had purloined years ago and made her own. In time a plaque would be made to mark the spot, but for now these items would suffice.

A lump formed in his throat.

The vet had been kind when she'd arrived the previous afternoon and had given them time to say their goodbyes to Elsa. It hadn't been an easy decision, but the last thing Seb wanted was for her to be in pain. Thanks to his decision to buy Rendall Hall, he could bury her somewhere where she'd always be close.

From behind him he heard Birdie and Keira talking in low voices while Bonnie hovered over one of Elsa's old sticks, as if unsure whether she was allowed to touch it or not. Seb hitched in a breath. It wouldn't be easy but life would go on, even without his companion of fourteen years.

Goodbye, girl.

Seb turned and walked over to Bonnie. She gave a startled bark as Seb picked up the stick and threw it across the garden. She stared at him, her eyes bright with uncertainty.

'Yes, you can have it,' Seb assured her.

With that Bonnie let out a second bark and zoomed after it.

'Are you okay, Dad?' Keira asked as he joined them. Her lashes were glistening with tears and her skin was blotchy from crying.

'I am,' he said, nodding. 'Are you? It's been a challenging week.'

Keira exhaled loudly. 'I'm not too bad, thanks. It's been hard for all of us having to deal with unexpected stuff.' She glanced at Birdie. 'But everything will work out with you and Melinda, you'll see.'

'Yeah... We'll make it work,' Birdie responded, the confidence in her words betrayed by the expression on her face. 'Anyway, you need to tell your dad.'

'It's not the right time.' Keira stared at the ground. 'I'm not even sure whether to do it.'

Seb glanced from Keira to Birdie, and back again. 'Will someone please explain?'

'Okay, I'll tell you,' Keira said. 'Hamish called first thing this morning. There's something going on right now with his work and he can't start for another month. He asked if we can still go on our trip. But considering everything that's happened, I'm not so sure it's right for me to go.'

The heaviness that had been pressing against Seb's chest eased and he managed to smile at his daughter. 'Go. You deserve to have a nice summer.'

'But what about you and Bonnie?' Keira studied him, indecision in her large eyes.

'I can manage to keep her fed, watered and amused,' he promised. 'I'll be fine. I'll be busy sorting out buying the hall so you don't need to worry about me.'

'We also have a business to run,' Birdie said. 'I'll make sure he's okay,' she added, giving Keira's hand a squeeze.

'I'm perfectly capable of taking care of myself,' Seb retorted.

'Now, unless we want Bonnie to dig up *all* the flower beds, I'd better check up on her.'

Keira launched herself into his arms. 'Thanks, Dad. You're the best.'

Seb returned the hug and relief coursed through him. Their relationship was back on an even keel.

Quietly his thoughts returned to Elsa. She was no longer in pain. He had incredible memories of their life together, and she would always hold a special place in his heart.

Across the garden, Bonnie was gleefully attacking a clump of lavender. Her silky red fur was streaked with soil, and her eyes bright with mischief.

An unexpected laugh broke free from his mouth. It surprised him how good it felt. Elsa would have approved. Perhaps she had known, even then, that this was what he needed. It was why she'd taken to Bonnie so readily.

He jogged across the grass, his steps lighter than they had been in a while.

'Come on, girl,' he said, ruffling her ears. 'Let's see where the path leads.'

A LETTER FROM THE AUTHOR

Dear reader,

Huge thanks for reading *Twist of Fate* – I hope you were hooked on Sebastian and Birdie's journey. If you want to join other readers in hearing all about my new releases and bonus content, you can sign up here:

www.stormpublishing.co/sally-rigby

If you enjoyed this book and could spare a few moments to leave a review that would be hugely appreciated. Even a short review can make all the difference in encouraging a reader to discover my books for the first time. Thank you so much.

Thanks again for being part of this amazing journey with me and I hope you'll stay in touch – I have so many more stories and ideas to entertain you with.

Sally Rigby

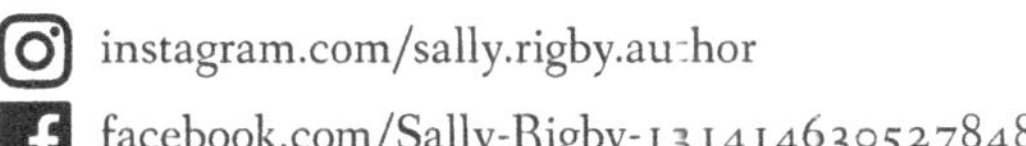

ACKNOWLEDGEMENTS

First and foremost, my thanks go to Amanda Ashby, whose brainstorming sessions proved invaluable in shaping this story. There's nothing quite like batting ideas back and forth with a good friend to untangle a tricky plotline.

I'm enormously grateful to Naomi Knox and Kathryn Taussig for their editorial expertise. Their thoughtful suggestions have made this a far better book than it would otherwise have been.

My sincere thanks also go to the wonderful team at Storm Publishing. From editing, to cover design, and marketing – all of which help readers discover Sebastian and Birdie. Their hard work behind the scenes makes all the difference.

Finally, as always, thanks to my family for their unwavering support.

www.ingramcontent.com/pod-product-compliance
Lightning Source LLC
LaVergne TN
LVHW031336150826
845673LV00012B/2920

* 9 7 8 1 8 0 5 0 8 9 2 2 3 *